UNDER CITY

BOOK ONE

N. FLORENCE

UNDER CITY

Cover Design by Seventhstar Art

Editing by Corbeaux Editorial Services

First Edition: November 2023

Content Warnings

Reader discretion is advised. This book contains material that may be triggering for some readers, including:

Bullying.

Alcohol use.

Sexually explicit scenes.

Possession-like events from main POV.

Forced marriage.

Kidnapping.

Colonialism, including systemic violence and implied eugenics.

Enslavement disguised as conscription.

Graphic violence.

Author's Note

As an Australian writer, I have a habit of putting *u*'s everywhere and replacing *zed*s with *s*'s—also known as writing in Australian English (it's quite close to British English). It's easier for me to write and publish in Australian English than it is to retrain myself to spell differently.

Also, I just really like the way *colour* looks compared to *color*.

If this is a deal-breaker, *Under City* might not be for you. If it's not, and you've gotten past the content warnings, you're going to have a lot of fun in this not-so-little world I've created.

Welcome to *Under City*.

I'm glad you're here.

For all the good girls
holding a broken shadow within themselves.
Let it out.

CHAPTER ONE

Annalise

I t was the day I melted the minds of two men.

Twigs and leaves rustled and snapped under my bare feet as I walked down the steep hill. Low branches reached towards my arms, my legs, catching the long shirt I used as a nightdress every now and then.

There was something in the morning's silence that spurred me along. A song that only I could hear demanded to be released from my chest.

It vibrated through the wisp of fog that led me down the hillside. Its low drone clung to the sweeping land and pulsed around my ankles. I heard my song mirrored in the dense rush of water that spilled over rocks and roots in a nearby brook, beating its syncopated rhythm towards the lake.

The water was calling to me. It sang of the winding of cord. The soft drop of something piercing the river's surface. The murmurs of a sleepy conversation gently stirring with excitement.

Someone was at my lake, and they weren't supposed to be.

The water sang to me of the intrusion, and I sang back.

It wasn't until I reached the lake's edge that I saw the effects of my work.

At the shoreline, a few feet from where I emerged from the thicket of trees, I saw it. Two bodies writhed in pain, a man and who looked to be his greying father. Their fishing gear and camping chairs were strewn among the rocks and pebbled sand as if an argument had erupted moments before. The old man screamed and clawed at his ears. Blood dripped down the sides of his face and over his fingertips. Terror etched in the young man's eyes as he struggled and failed to both secure his father's hands and protect his own ears from my melody.

I stopped singing, though the last notes had bubbled out of me and continued to ripple in the space between us.

The younger man caught sight of me and moved quickly to shield his father from my view. It went against all logic that this was my doing, that I inflicted such pain upon the two souls.

Yet, like the man, I knew.

A scream welled up inside me and released from my mouth before I could consider the hell it might unleash. The old man was the first to stop fighting, his body went limp the second that bone-chilling sound left my lips.

His son took longer to die. The body convulsed; eyes turned so far back in their sockets only the whites were visible. A sour stench filled the air and mixed with the scent of wet earth before the son stopped moving.

After a moment of stillness, I ran.

Up the hillside. Colliding with trees, tripping over branches and rocks in my haste. Away from the terror. Away from the song that followed me everywhere. Away from the dead, mangled men.

Gold light had reached the hilltop by the time I broke through the trees that hid my home. The house lit up in streams of yellow and white. It would usually be enough to steal my thoughts and take me to a place of joy.

Not this morning.

I halted.

The illuminated figure inside wrapped her thin fingers around a steaming mug of something hot. Likely Earl Grey. Her tangled white hair was bunched lazily into a bun above her head.

It was painful to look at my mother sometimes. We looked so alike, only my brown eyes and two dark bumps on my cheek stood in stark contrast to the pale features that belonged to her. They were reminders that I wasn't really like her at all. There was something deeply wrong with me.

How could I step foot in that house after what I'd done? What I kept doing?

I meant to take a step backwards, to turn and retreat into the safety of the harsh bushland behind me.

But my legs refused to move.

A coldness stiffened around them as two large hands gripped my shoulders.

The faint beginnings of a second scream escaped my lips before that same coldness squeezed at my throat, cutting off all sound. What managed to break through was so small and short, I didn't expect to see my mother's head to snap to the window. I didn't expect to see her eyes widen with fear and—

And—*knowing*?

A gravelly exhale of disappointment warmed my ear. "Too slow." The man said it to himself, but I couldn't ignore the low, commanding pull of his voice. Or maybe that pull was the physical grasp of his hands dragging me backwards into the thicket behind us.

Bang! The screen door clattered open.

"Stop! Stop!" my mother screamed as she barrelled after us. "I seek asylum for my daughter." Her words came out so fast, registering them took me a second. She stood a foot away. Fierceness shone in her eyes, but they were directed at the figure behind me.

I clearly noted the oddity of those words. *I seek asylum for my daughter.*

Not *Let go of my daughter*, or *Leave, you're trespassing.*

The figure behind me stilled. Skin pinched and burned as I twisted in his grasp. If I could just get a look at *who* she was talking to, but those large hands wouldn't budge.

Am I being arrested? Had someone been watching me, waiting for me to mess up again so they had an excuse to throw me in a cell?

I never really belonged in Lucknow. I was so relieved to finally leave this small town when I earned the opportunity to go to university in the city. If only I had managed to stay away for good.

I'd wanted to block out what had happened forever. My mother eventually pried the events out of me, but she hadn't done a very good job of convincing me of my innocence. In the past year her worries had steadily grown. She'd since taken to making sure I never had to leave the safety of the house or the lake.

I was thankful for that.

Images of what my song had done at the university and to those two men collided in my head. Someone had finally figured out the truth. A single thought passed through my mind, and I stopped resisting.

Maybe you deserve this, Annalise.

My mother spoke again. Slower and clearer this time. "I demand that the Kingdom of Dubnos offer the safety of its borders to my daughter, Annalise Elizabeth Rhine."

"We are not in Dubnos." The voice that responded was gravelly. It resonated with a low, earthy vibration and an accent.

"Prince Dariush, your royal duties appointed to you at birth supersede whatever tasks you've been given by the Tuath Dé. I am asking you to take her to Dubnos!" Her voice shook with an undercurrent of desperation, and an old forgotten accent of her own leached into the corners of her words. Then, she whispered, "Don't let them have her."

Don't let them have her.

Well, that was completely ominous. Were federal investigators readying themselves to secretly run tests on me in a padded cell somewhere in the middle of the desert?

"What are you talking—?" I started, shrugged off the stupid question and yelled to the man, "Get off me!"

Fear for my own safety replaced the unshakable guilt that had ruled me for over a year. I moved with intention.

I sank my nails into his one hand that wasn't gloved, strange he was wearing a glove at all, and twisted. My body broke free of his hold. Or maybe the stranger had loosened his grip on purpose.

There was the initial thought to push him farther away, to punch him in the face and run, but the moment I spun around all thought of retaliation was gone.

A spear of black skin cut through his left cheek, descended his neck and plunged beneath the collar of his dark grey linen shirt. That black spear was slightly furred. It matched his dark hair and made his pale blue eyes seem vibrant against his tanned skin.

The man was stunning, otherworldly, and something about his presence was calming, despite his stern glare. So why did my stomach knot and a lump form within my throat at the sight of him?

Something sharp in his gloved hand glinted under the early morning sun. A blink and it was no longer a glove.

Black fur covered his left arm, making way for claws at the ends of his fingertips. They were so polished they could have been made of stone.

I was looking at the arm of a beast.

I stumbled backwards, reaching for my mother who was quick to step between me and the intruder.

Nerves radiated off her, but instead of fighting she turned her back on the man and grasped my head in her hands.

"Ow, m—" My protests were cut short.

"You are not human." Her words sounded both far away and all too loud. Blurred, like a finely detailed painting that was left outside in the rain before the paint could fully dry.

"You are a siren. A rhinemaiden like me. Like our ancestors before us. But you are more."

I barely heard her.

Her face seemed foreign. This woman had raised me on myth and folklore from around the world. Most overlapped in some way. It made sense that pieces of it could be real, but what I had experienced, what I had done to those men—it all felt so out of my control. I couldn't justify such a monster's existence, and knowing I was that monster only added to the chaos building inside me.

The missing pieces in my story clicked together and pushed out other pieces with sudden force, lies that had been painted as reliable truths. It left more holes than before.

Anger swelled in my chest.

Why had she kept this from me? Why tell me I'm a monster only after I've tortured two people? Killed two people?

My mother didn't acknowledge my shaking. She dropped her hands and turned to the man. "Don't take her just yet. I need to give her something." Not waiting for him to agree, she ran into the house.

So, she's going to just let me be arrested? If anyone should be thrown in a cell, it should be . . .

An inky undercurrent of hatred stirred from the depths within me and took hold. My hands pulsed.

I opened my mouth. Turned to the backdoor my mother had disappeared through.

And—

Coldness pulled tightly at my throat for a second time. I tried to fill my lungs with air.

Nothing.

I tried again. Whatever darkness I'd been holding on to drained from my heart and was replaced with the primal desperation of survival. I heard the dry sucking sound of my fruitless attempts to breathe. My home upon the hill was the first to start swaying. Then the trees and golden rays of morning sun followed suit.

A white figure moved towards me. They were holding something, yelling something.

Are they calling my name?

My body dropped backwards into solid warmth.

Then my sun-kissed home on the hilltop was gone.

CHAPTER TWO

Zorya

Weapons swung in a blaze of fury and focus.

"Aoife! You're out!"

The girl wouldn't have been able to hear the teacher's final call over the cheers from the crowd above—and my recent blow to her head followed by the thwack of her own body weight on the ground. Her fighting had been exceptional up until that point. I was impressed, but my final roundhouse kick was swift and solid. There was no chance for Aoife to block that attack.

"Zorya!" Old Harvey barked.

What now? I won, didn't I? I thought, observing the groaning bodies of my classmates on the floor.

Harvey didn't look old by a long shot. He'd served in the White Guard for only ten years before being offered a teaching position. Despite a knee injury that gave him a slight limp, Harvey was in perfect health with barely a wrinkle on his face nor a strand of silver in his dark, well-kept hair. It was his eyes that looked like he'd been through hell more times than he'd care to count. His eyes looked like that of every other teacher at the college. Old, worn-down and thankful for the brief respite from service their teaching job provided before their return to the field. I couldn't understand why they would shy from their duties, especially when we were taught to fight through pain and injury.

Upholding Tuath Dé rule and protecting the fae from the many threats of the world was our purpose.

"You're lucky testing has been calculated. No teamwork is an automatic fail for team combat," Harvey barked.

"Don't worry so much, Harvey. I'll make sure my squad can keep up with me." My words breathed with arrogance, even I could hear that, but the applause of the Tuath Dé crowd above me let me know I had earned every ounce of it.

"How would you know if they've made you a squad leader?" he countered.

"Jaz, Nate, Dina, Ellie and Hendrik all have their ceremony at eleven. Same time as me." I paused to give the man time to figure out what had been obvious to me.

He didn't respond.

"Tell me, Harvey. Which one of us is more suited to lead?" I had barely gotten that last word out when a rogue stick weaved itself between my knees and pushed them in two very different directions with sudden force. My face hit the floor and laughter erupted from the face in front of me.

Jaz. He'd been there to keep my ego in check from the day we both entered the sorry halls of the fara school at age eight.

I picked up the stick tangled at my feet and aimed it at his stupid smug face.

"It wasn't me!" he yelled, shielding his head.

He didn't need to tell me who the culprit actually was. I knew as soon as two large arms wrapped around my thighs and hauled my body over a sizeable shoulder.

A shriek of laughter escaped me before I grabbed hold of a leg and angled my body weight to the floor. My attacker and I fell with a loud thud, both of us laughing, groaning and gasping for breath.

"Naranbaatar! Zorya! Jaz! GET UP!"

Uh oh. It took a lot to piss off Harvey, but roughhousing in front of Tuath Dé was definitely going to do it.

The man held a small piece of paper in his hand. Someone must have delivered a message while we were busy with team combat—or play-fighting.

"Change of plans, *squad leader*." He pressed the paper into my palm, face stern and still. "You three will be attending your ceremony at 0800. Get your asses to council now."

I read the note confirming what Harvey had just said. A pit opened in my stomach.

"Fifteen minutes? It takes fifteen minutes to get there!" I didn't say what else was on my mind. What about the others? I didn't have much of a relationship with the girls, but I felt a sense of responsibility to them. Like they were counting on me to treat them fairly. Being a woman in the Tuath Dé Empire's fara army wasn't an easy ride.

Then there was Hendrik. We'd been casually flirting ever since the graduation timetable came out. We wouldn't have been allowed to act on any feelings for at least a decade—not that there were any *real* feelings between us yet—but the chances of us being stuck with each other for the rest of our lives felt like enough of a free pass. Protection was contraband, but if we were paired together there were always ways to get it.

Gods. Will they pair me with Jaz? Nate? They were like brothers to me.

I couldn't bear to look in Hendrik's direction. This changed everything.

"Then you better get moving," Harvey barked.

I had two thoughts burning through my mind as I ran towards the changerooms.

The first was *What the fuck do the Tuath Dé think they're playing at?*

And the second, *I don't think they're going to make me a squad leader.*

***

The council's military court halls were in fact, ten minutes away. If we ran, the three of us could make it there in five.

Plenty of time to change my tank top into something more respectable. But it wasn't what I had imagined wearing on my graduation day. Then again, I supposed this was a marker for what was to come. A life of wearing combat-ready clothes and running by the Tuath Dé's elusive schedule.

If I were to chop and change where I was going to be every day, I'd have never made it through the fara college. I grimaced at the idea of what might have happened had I not graduated. Every fara heard the rumours. We all knew of someone who couldn't keep up and just didn't show up to class one day.

I threw my sweaty singlet top into a communal wash basket and slipped a clean, grey shirt over my head, the army's symbol of an embroidered black knotwork tree clearly visible over my heart. Nate and Jaz were at the door waiting for me to get my shit together before I even had a chance to straighten myself up. Boys. Of course they were waiting on me. They didn't need to fiddle with bra straps or tight, clinging fabric. Hell, Nate hadn't even worn a shirt that entire practice. All he had to do was slip on his uniform top.

I rolled my eyes.

We'd been dressing in the same changeroom for years now. The council had put in a one changeroom rule to free up space for beds and training equipment. We were all used to it, but both of them insisted on turning their backs whenever I got changed. Weirdos.

The three of us exited the changerooms in silence and rounded a long corridor leading to the heart of the building. As the corridor opened to the busy walkways, shops and units that made up the Glistening City, I suddenly felt self-conscious of my appearance.

I always felt that way around these people. The Tuath Dé were a tall, proud bunch. Their hair was always smooth and shiny. Their skin was flawless. And they never seemed to struggle with weight, no matter how often they sat down to eat and drink. They loved to dress as elegantly as the building they all resided in.

Gold railings lined a hundred or more balconies that all sat on top of each other. Even though the glass ceiling was miles above, the light still seemed to bounce off the marble flooring, the crystal chandeliers and the gold-plated public furniture.

Public furniture that fara weren't allowed to use.

Every inch of this place, save the fara quarters below, was a piece of artwork. There was a reason it was called the Glistening City.

Next to these people I looked dull.

My hair, a dark mahogany, was unruly no matter how many times I brushed it. My stature was short, and weight clung to my curves no matter how much exercise I did. But my skin was the biggest insult, to my life, to this place. My right cheek was marked with a black stain just below my eye. The mark was an odd shape, not quite triangular, not quite rectangular. It took up my entire cheek and curved slightly towards my chin, and it was hairy.

As far as fara marks went, mine was an eyesore. I looked to Nate as he hurried through the walkway, trying not to break into a run so as to not annoy the Tuath Dé around us.

Nate's mark was elegant. A faint sun of white sat on top of his forehead, barely visible against his pale skin. It caused a strip of white to split his coarse black hair at the top of his head and decorate the man bun he always rocked so well. Everything about him sang of the family he was taken from, his dark hair and almond eyes, right down to the meaning of his name. Naranbaatar, "sun hero." The Tuath Dé hated that.

Jaz on the other hand was even more blessed than the both of us. Being born to Tuath Dé parents on the day of Samhain meant he was fara in gift only. Like us, his purpose was to move between worlds, keep the peace and protect the fae. Unlike us, he was tall, flawless and completely free of markings. He could easily have fit in with the Tuath Dé. If only they hadn't discarded him to the pit that was the fara college.

A break in the crowd opened up, and the three of us quickened our pace. We were making good time. We just needed to get to the fara elevator and glide on up to the council court level.

My audible groan as I noted soldiers guarding our elevator startled an elderly Tuath Dé woman to my left. The tall woman looked as if she might chide me for daring to voice disappointment, but she simply walked up to the soldiers in front of us.

"Our elevator is broken. I can't possibly be expected to walk all the way to the next one." The woman spoke as if the soldiers might carry her wherever she wanted to go with a snap of her fingers.

"We're here to prioritise the Tuath Dé, since the main elevator is broken. You'll be able to use the lift when it arrives to ground floor, ma'am." The soldier's response was even.

"Good," the woman said in a shrill tone, making sure to look at me as she said it.

What a poor use of army resources. I don't mind being their soldier, but sometimes they are so arrogant.

Sometimes was an understatement. I had been forced to bend to the will of arrogant Tuath Dé my entire life. Thank fuck not all fae were like them.

Knowing full well that we wouldn't be able to ride with the woman—there was a reason we had separate elevators—I glanced at the boys.

And smiled wickedly.

"Oh no you—" Jaz began, but his protests came too slow. My will imposed itself on my image. I saw myself morph clearly in my mind, and it was done. To anyone who'd bother to look my way, they would see a tall, dark-haired figure in a simple black dress. No markings. No red eyes. Ears faintly pointed towards the heavens.

I glided towards the soldiers as the elevator doors opened. The woman was startled when I stepped in after her. I shoved aside the feeling she might have seen through my illusion. Glamour required confidence. You needed to believe you looked whatever way you decided you looked—only then would everyone else believe it too.

The woman smiled with relief. Her shoulders relaxed.

There were many different types of fara. It wasn't really a fae race itself, more like an umbrella term for fae that had evolved with the ability to move through the veil.

As far as I knew, glamour was common among daywalker upir. Very common. Like one hundred percent common.

Then again, the pool for such a survey wasn't huge. The daywalker population under Tuath Dé rule had recently dwindled to one. Me.

That part of my people's history was something I didn't like to think about. It made me empathise with rebels. They had gone silent in recent years. This was something the Tuath Dé had paraded as a victory. I saw it as an opportunity for them to plan an attack with threefold the force. At least, that was what I'd have done if I were a rebel.

I shook the thought away. Thinking of the rebels always made me feel like I had to choose between two things that were important to me: my responsibilities to the Tuath Dé and my heritage. And since I didn't have much in the way of family to teach me of the latter, there was no point throwing away my future with the Tuath Dé too. I had my survival to worry about.

As the elevator doors closed, I spotted Jaz and Nate, ran a hand through my hair and subtly flipped them off.

There was a stairwell behind the elevators which they'd have to start ascending if they wanted to get to the military courts on time. They had, what? seven minutes to run up thirty-two flights of stairs?

I couldn't scrub the wicked grin from my face.

Luckily for Jaz and Nate, that run was typical in a normal day of training, and at least they were warmed up.

CHAPTER THREE

Annalise

"Wake up." The gravelly voice vibrated through my hand and head, jostling me awake to a warm wall of grey.

I pushed the far-too-close prince away too soon and fell. Something stabbed me as I hit compacted earth. A small twig had embedded itself into my stark white thigh, and I winced. A few small beads of red rushed to the surface, and I pushed my nightshirt down, eager to cover it. The action did more to smear the blood down my leg, and I opted for just looking away.

"You're an idiot," the prince said, letting out a dry laugh. He threw a brown duffel bag at my stomach followed by a pair of my sneakers. Both hit their target with a thud.

Then he stepped over me. Stepped. Over. Me.

This guy is an arse.

"Get some clothes on. I'm not letting you into the Glistening City looking like that." The prince gave me the once-over, his jaw setting with disapproval. Then he proceeded to lean against a tree, waiting for me to move.

"I'm not changing with you looking," I said, helping myself up.

He waited a moment. I geared myself up to protest, and anger washed over me, then he turned.

I rummaged through the bag, pulling out pale blue jeans and the only long-sleeved black top I owned. The bag had my mother's packing written all over it. Filled mostly with wants, things she thought I might like to have on me just in case, followed by a few bare necessities shoved in as an afterthought. Beneath the two pieces of clothing were two paint brushes, a water paint palette and a book I hadn't seen in many years.

I glanced at the back of the prince's head and decided to keep the book in the bag. It was old, bound in wooden panels held together by waxy twine. I ran my fingers over the carvings. A bare-breasted woman leaned against a rock, waves fanned around her, and peeking out from the side of the rock was the large fork of a fish tail.

Big bold letters framed the woman like a border, *Tales of the Water Women*. I knew some of the stories within it by heart. It was a book my mother had read to me over and over again, but why would she think I'd want this now?

When you're a kid dreaming of mermaids that make deals with gods in the name of love, and fairies that sew dresses out of dew-dropped spiderwebs, you don't expect that the monster lurking in the shadows might one day look an awful lot like you.

I shoved the book deeper into the bag.

"Where's Mum?"

"Safe from you," the prince shot back.

Guilt flooded me. If I'd been ready with a retort, it would have died in my throat.

"I'm not dressed yet," I managed to say after a few long moments when he started to turn. He grumbled but kept his back to me, and I hurriedly threw the clothes on.

Part of me was still mad at my mother for keeping this all a secret. What if she had told me the truth from the start? Maybe I'd know how to control all of this. The two men wouldn't be dead. I wouldn't be a monster.

My thoughts wandered. No, I was a monster the day I was born. I felt the pull of that song. The look on that man's face as he watched his father writhe in pain, as he himself felt that same pain consume him.

I'd never be anything other than a monster.

I shoved the ripped, oversized shirt I'd been using as a nightgown into the duffel bag and rummaged for socks. I didn't know why I still held on to that shirt. It was speckled with holes, and the fabric was thinning from the years of wear and machine washing. I had a perfectly kept silk nightdress in my closet, one that I'd bought myself when I had a casual retail job in the city. For some reason, it didn't ever feel right to slip that beautiful pink, flowy fabric over my head.

Another thought struck me. What if I had hurt my mother? I'd rather die than make her feel that kind of pain. I'd never harm her willingly, but that song. The rage that bubbled just below the surface when she'd turned her back on me and walked into the house. It wasn't right. She was just trying to help.

She had forgotten to pack socks.

I breathed deeply and pulled my white sneakers over my bare feet. Even now I struggled to keep my emotions in check—over socks.

"Hey. My phone's not in here." I was sure Mum would have packed it. The way the prince turned and exhaled sharply told me he'd had this argument already. Somehow his jaw seemed more tensed than before.

No response.

"Fine. Who are you taking me to?" *If this man could find me so quickly after my attack at the lake, whoever he answered to must have had eyes on me long before it.*

"The Tuath Dé," he grunted.

"Huh?" *Did he just swear at me in another language?*

"The Tu-a-Dey" he said slower, then turned to face the tree he'd been leaning on, studying it like it had some interesting bit to add to our conversation. "And don't ask so many questions around them. They don't like it."

The prince knocked on the tree three times with his human hand, taking extra care to ensure the gold ring on his pointer touched the tree each time. It clanged, as if hitting metal instead of wood.

Odd.

"Who are they?" I began to ask, but my words caught in my mouth as gold liquid rippled out from the space the ring had touched. It widened to form a circular, mirrored surface as tall as the prince.

Is that a portal?

Not for the first time this morning, I was afraid of where the man planned to take me.

"*What* are they? Monsters like me?" The word slipped past my lips before I had time to catch it. What would it matter? He'd seen the truth of what I was capable of already. There was no shoving that part of me back into the shadows.

His head snapped in my direction; a crease formed on his brow. "You aren't a monster."

"Ha." The shell of a laugh fell out of my mouth. He obviously hadn't been paying attention. Was this normal for him? Was it normal for twenty-two-year-olds to leave fisherman writhing in pain in the early hours of the morning?

"You didn't choose to kill them."

His kindness startled me, and suddenly I was wrapped in more guilt. Had I chosen? The thing inside me, the song, it wanted out.

"When you attacked those men, you didn't know what you were doing. The outcome was beyond what you knew to be possible, but now that you know the truth you have two options." His voice was serious, yet soothing. Whatever direction this conversation was headed—I didn't want to hear it.

If I tried hard enough, I could imagine he wasn't talking to me at all. Like it was another girl who had committed a heinous crime. Another girl who had irrevocably wrecked her own life and dragged two men into the flames beneath her.

Except, the words could only have been meant for me.

The man looked me up and down once more in that judgey way, assessing me against some criteria I wasn't privy to. He seemed to conclude that I passed. Barely.

"You can wallow and hide and eventually suck more death and chaos into your little corner of the world, or you can take control of your gift and actually live. Your choice."

"And what if I don't want to leave my *little corner of the world?*" I kept my face still. If I waited for him to step through the portal first, I could make a run for it.

"Everyone leaves their comfort zone eventually, by force or choice." The man closed the space between us, only breaking eye contact as he bent down to pick up the duffel bag at my feet.

"Annalise." The man's voice became softer as he said my name, sugar on his lips.

"Yes," I responded, mirroring the softness in his voice as if I could lie in this gentle moment forever.

"If you pick option number one, I get to kill you." He shoved the bag into my hands with force. It took effort to keep my footing.

I couldn't keep the heat of embarrassment from rushing to my face. The man was toying with me. I should have thrown the bag at his head.

He turned for the portal and waited by the swirling mirror of gold, holding out his beastly arm as if to say, "After you."

I walked up to the mirror and stopped. What if this was a trap? What if it was just gold water in there, and he was planning on closing the portal after I stepped in? I could drown. "I kill people with my voice, but you get to make pretty light from rings. How is that fair?" I said, fixated on the molten ripples. They were so beautiful.

He pushed me in.

**

The air around me shifted. It became warmer, stale even, and slightly dusty. It didn't move around my face the way it did in the forest behind me. It was still. Until my head slammed into something solid.

I opened my eyes to see that I'd stepped into my new home. A dank, windowless cell lined with shelves of—*cleaning products*?

No. It was a supply closet, loosely illuminated by the golden circle behind me, and I'd fallen straight into a door.

"That happens when you walk with your eyes closed." The prince did little to hide his amusement.

"You expect me to walk through gold liquid with my eyes open?" I pointed to the portal accusingly as the ripples shrunk inwards and disappeared. I turned for the door. *Stick me in a cell and throw away the key, but don't mock me.*

"Wait." He grabbed my wrist before I could turn the doorknob. It should have been more of a shock to feel the warm fur of his left hand encase my wrist, but it wasn't. His claws tilted purposefully away as if the force of his grip was fine, but to nick my skin even a fraction would have been a sin.

With what little room the closet offered, the prince was unbearably close. Heat rose from his chest, swirling between us like a summer storm rolling into harbour. My heart quickened in response. There was probably all of a centimetre between us, and the prince was taking his time. Like he was weighing up what to tell me, how much to tell me.

"Just . . ." He started again, faltered, and released a breath. "These people have rules. They're very particular about them. Keep your eyes down, do exactly as you're told, don't stare. You'll let me do the talking."

"What are you now? My arresting officer *and* lawyer?" My tone was sardonic, mostly to brush off the closeness. I pulled my wrist out of his grip and rubbed the spot that had been left cold in the absence of touch. The air shifted, suddenly too much distance between us for my liking. What would happen once he turned me in? Would I ever see him again?

"The Tuath Dé don't do lawyers. If you want to live, don't speak." His hard demeanour returned, jaw setting like stone.

"What do you mean? I'm not going to get a fair trial?" My voice shook in a way I hadn't expected. I'd done something terrible. I deserved to rot in a cell for it, but wasn't there a process to these things? What world had I stepped into?

"There won't be any trial. They don't need to know." The prince kept his gaze on mine for a moment longer. It was easy to lose myself in his pale, blue-grey eyes. A dark ring surrounded that ghostly colour. It sucked me in, drew me closer to him, yet at the same time he seemed to be looking straight through me.

What he'd said took a heartbeat to register. He'd keep my secret.

Relief left me the second it arrived, replaced by confusion and distrust. What was the point in bringing me here if he wasn't going to tell anyone what I'd done? If that was his plan, he should have turned his back and let me live out my lonely, boring life in Lucknow. And wasn't it better to keep a monster locked up, away from everyone? What could have possibly convinced him that the right thing to do was to let me go?

He was going to spare me the fate of rotting alone in a dark cell, but what did he expect in return? Something told me this man didn't do anything for free.

Artificial light pushed its way into the closet as he opened the door, brushed past me and stepped into a white hallway.

I stepped into the hallway after him. Elevator doors opened to our right, and I forgot all about that *don't stare* rule.

A tall, elegant woman stepped out.

No. A woman had stepped out of the elevator, and I was sure she had looked tall and elegant at first glance, but as she stepped farther into the hallway, what had looked like a black dress was clearly a black-and-grey uniform. She'd lost a few inches in height in just a few steps. Brown eyes revealed a red stain, and I swore the mark on her face—something that I hadn't noticed at first—was growing darker.

The woman had a birthmark like me. Like the prince.

She blanched at the sight of him.

"Prince Dariush. I-I—" the woman stammered.

Dariush! That's his name. It occurred to me his name hadn't stuck in my mind. I'd been thinking of him as "the prince" this entire time.

"You'll never do that again in this place." Dariush glared at the woman.

She looked like she was about to say *sorry.* Then she saw me, the closet we had walked out of, and chose to hold his stare instead.

"I think our *overlords* will find your secrets are far more interesting than mine." She cocked an eyebrow.

I liked her.

"Really? Remind me what happened the last time a daywalker kept secrets from our—*overlords.*"

The woman looked as if she'd been slapped in the face. Her shoulders slumped slightly in defeat, and she looked away. Dariush was clearly the higher ranking of the two, but the woman had an air about her. Like she was on some sort of personal mission.

As Dariush turned down the hall, I thought to offer a smile, say hi maybe. I had broken one rule, why not one more? And someone who was willing to throw Dariush's attitude back at him might be worthy of friendship.

But the woman shot me that same judgey once-over that Dariush had, and in that moment, I chose to keep my kindness to myself.

Not a friend then.

CHAPTER FOUR

Zorya

Fuck.

How could I have been so careless? I had let someone see my glamour. Walked straight up to them as it dropped, and it was the Tuath Dé's fucking prince of all people.

I shifted in my hard seat in the waiting room and glanced at the man. He was leaning against the wall closest to the wooden doors separating us from the council's military courts within. A dark, brooding stain in an otherwise bright hall decked out with light wooden chairs. He seemed to be in a foul mood.

My doing, I bet. I smiled at the thought.

He couldn't be a real prince since the Tuath Dé had claimed the Kingdom of Dubnos, an undercity deep within the earth, as an occupied state well before he was born. Obviously letting him have a title at all had gone to his head.

No one at the college knew what Dariush was. His beast arm wasn't something I'd seen on any other fara, and there were only whisperings of what he could do.

The council would know. No one could keep a secret from them.

Well, except me.

The prince just needs to keep his mouth shut.

His gaze flicked to someone else in the waiting room. At first, it had been a struggle to keep my cool as I followed Dariush around the corner. Noticing her was like noticing a low, full moon on a cloudless night.

Geira looked how all valkyries looked to me. Scorned angel warriors plucked straight from the battlefields—minus the wings. She was tall, the same height as a Tuath Dé woman, with a muscular frame.

That frame was more noticeable now as she stood statuesque, facing the doors, arms behind her. Her golden hair braided against the length of her back.

She had the most beautiful fara mark I'd ever seen, a molten stain of pink, red and purple covering the right side of her face and neck. It brought attention to her slim and unsmiling mouth.

She was everything I had trained so hard to be.

Our teachers had told us the story of the battle that had lost Geira and Dariush their pairs, as well as the rest of their squad, in a rebel attack on a Tuath Dé village just outside Dubnos City. It happened a year ago. There had been a handful of Tuath Dé casualties. Elders unable to escape the flames of a burning building. Dariush's squad leader and another soldier had entered the fiery building in an effort to rescue them. Geira and Dariush, along with two other squad mates, were tasked with ensuring the safety of those who had escaped the fire. When a bomb decimated the building, those on the street were attacked by gun-wielding Red Knights, rebels hiding among the rooftops.

Cowards. What fae uses a human's weapon?

Dariush and Geira managed to survive and save many Tuath Dé lives.

The story made my heart swell every time I thought of it. Looking upon them now, I realised just how godly they had seemed to me. And just how completely Dariush had blown that vision up after he stepped out of the closet with that stranger.

I bet Geira did all the work that night and he just took credit for it.

The valkyrie's eyes turned to the side in their sockets and caught my gaze. I looked away immediately.

Anyone else. I could have been staring at anyone else.

My gaze shifted to the unknown woman sitting in the chair closest to Dariush.

There was an air of fragility and innocence that shrouded her. She was white all over, the kind that was reminiscent of ivory bone or powdered sugar, from the hair on her head to her pale, lanky fingers. Except for those fara marks, two black dots on her left cheek, and eyes so brown they could pass for black in the right lighting.

I crossed my arms and leaned back in my seat, making an audible huff as I did. It seemed unfair that some fara got small and neatly placed dots on their face, while others—me—were given a hairy black mark that stood out like a sore thumb.

I had never seen this woman in my life. Faras, like the rest of the fae, were few in number and we stuck together. Plus, we had a sacred duty to the TDE. Everyone knew everyone. So, why didn't I know her?

She couldn't have been older than me. If she was younger, she'd be in class or training in the fara quarters.

She was avoiding eye contact.

Why is she even here? I was eager to think of a reason why I might never have to see the girl again.

Bang! The sound of a door slamming open, followed by puffed groans, echoed down the hall.

"I could wring her neck—" Nate didn't finish his sentence as he rounded the corner, noticed just who he was in the presence of and sat in the chair closest to me.

Jaz didn't do anything so inconspicuous. "*What the fuck?*" he mouthed widely at me, nodding his head in the direction of the prince and Geira. Pointing at them would have been less obvious, but neither of them gave him their attention.

Once he found a seat, *next to the new girl*, he mouthed at me again, "*Who is she?*" this time he did point.

I shrugged.

The woman looked uncomfortable, her eyes glued to the floor as if by simply ignoring everyone they'd all go away. I could sense her heart beating erratically in her chest.

She probably didn't want anyone to talk to her, but Jaz had other ideas.

"Hey, I'm Jaz," he said with a smile. He wasn't being *overly* flirty, just his friendly self.

The woman sat up a little straighter and beamed at him. It looked like she might have responded when—

"No talking," Dariush barked from his place on the wall.

She rolled her eyes, leaned back, made a loud huff.

If you don't like the guy, what the hell were you doing with him in a supply closet?

I counted the figures in the room more deliberately now. On first arrival I'd assumed Geira and the prince required an impromptu meeting with the council.

But Jaz and Nate had been late. If anyone else was expected to be here for our pairing and graduation ceremony, they'd be here by now.

Dariush and Geira were due to be placed with new squad members and receive their new pairing.

If Nate, Jaz and I were to join their squad, the girl made number six.

That idea grated on me. I had never met her before, and she acted as if she'd never seen another fara before. The way her eyes had shifted to my mark and to the prince's when they stepped out of the closet. The way her heartbeat had jumped with excitement.

There was only one explanation for a fara of her age to be excited around others with fara marks.

My blood began to boil. I wanted to throw something. At the girl. At the council.

I had spent over a decade committing myself to becoming a squad leader. Putting myself through every obstacle the Tuath Dé placed in front of me. Taking on every opportunity. Making sure I met every requirement. I was so sure I had it in the bag when I found out my graduation was with five of my classmates. I knew their abilities and ambitions. I was the obvious choice.

Sitting here in front of this girl I realised not only was the leadership role I had worked my arse off for unlikely now, but I was being placed in a squad with someone who had never trained a day in her life and probably didn't even know the first thing about living with the Tuath Dé.

Screw Dariush. I'd tell them exactly what I'd seen.

My rising entanglement of nerves and anger snapped as the thick wooden door opened with every indication it had done so by itself.

Here we go.

CHAPTER FIVE

Annalise

The five soldiers beside me stood practiced and purposeful, their gazes focused forwards on nothing in particular as we waited to be addressed. In an effort to not stare at the lithe figures seated in front of us, I fixed my attention on the patterns in the tiled floor. They were interesting enough. Smooth knotwork of gold and white worked together to create the image of a tree every nine tiles.

Maybe I can entertain myself with them till all this is over.

I tried and failed. My ears pricked up as I caught snippets of the conversation being held in front of me, and while no one said my name, the topic of choice was clear.

"She is here now, Neeta. We may as well make use of her," an elderly man said calmly, his choice of words careful and slow, as if English were a second language.

A hot rush of anger flooded my senses. *How rude.* I was being talked about, not to, while I stood silently in a room full of—

A familiar coldness washed over me, gripping at my mind and throat, and I was reminded of Dariush's warning. I breathed in deep.

"Use for what!? She. Has. No. Training!" The second voice, which I assumed belonged to Neeta, was a croaky screech, each word echoed by the thwacking of wood on wood.

Despite her chaotic aura, the woman could have passed for a greying super model. Still, the image of a green-skinned witch dressed in judge's robes appeared in my head, and I slapped a hand to my mouth. It did nothing to suppress a small snort that resonated a little too loudly through the room.

"I'll train her." Dariush stood tall, arms behind his back, eyes cast forwards at nothing in particular.

Five faces darted to Dariush and gawked as if they'd just seen a thousand-year-old statue awake from stillness to make a speech. It didn't matter that a half second earlier I'd laughed at an elderly woman of some importance. I hoped the councillors hadn't heard it.

"You dare speak!" Neeta's bone-chilling shrills were piercing. She was about to throw her twisted-branch walking stick at Dariush before another interjected.

"Calm down, Neeta. We've kept the man waiting long enough." The slender, well-groomed man seated at the centre of the long table continued, "Prince Dariush of Dubnos, fara soldier and loyal servant of the Tuath Dé"—the man's voice, calm when addressing Neeta, now emanated a bright tone as if he was talking to an old friend. His smile was wide. It looked like he might be laughing despite the lack of warmth in his face—"You've been summoned to submit a squad for review to the council."

At this point I had completely forgotten Dariush's warnings about keeping my head down and began watching the two men converse, hopeful that someone was on our side. Whatever side that was.

Our side?

"Yes, Councilman Tierney." Dariush stared forward, keeping his tone neutral.

"This squad, being assembled by such a skilled warrior as yourself, is meant to reflect the finest our military college has to offer. Is it not?" Tierney, still smiling, leaned back in his chair and opened his arms widely.

"Yes, Councilman Tierney," Dariush responded again.

"Then what is this!? Are you mocking us!?" Tierney pointed an accusing finger at me, infuriating me less than the fact that he hadn't looked at me once this entire time. Almost every person in the room flinched as Tierney slammed his fists down onto the wooden table.

Dariush remained still.

"No, Councilman Tierney," he said as those cold invisible wisps wrapped around my arms and legs and mind again. *Don't intervene,* they said, but not even the bubbling fire within me or the humiliation of being completely ignored like this could force me to go up against a man throwing that kind of temper tantrum.

"Explain!" The man's temper was hot, though it seemed more controlled than Neeta's, which somehow made it more terrifying to witness.

Dariush paused momentarily and began his explanation, a dutiful soldier responding to a superior. "Councilman Tierney, members of the council. A recent investigation led me to an incident in Lucknow where a twenty-two-year-old female had recently fended off the attack of two humans. The damage was distinctly fara. I

discovered the woman living among humans with no knowledge
of her true nature. I felt that the council would consider it unwise
to allow an of-age fara with unknown potential to roam the human
world alone." Dariush paused slightly, making sure the details,
mostly lies, were sinking in.

Tierney, no longer red with rage, waved for Dariush to continue.

"As you've noted, the fara is untrained, but of graduating age.
If placed with a less-abled squad, her potential won't be reached.
Which will pose a burden on the council's resources. The soldiers I
have selected for this squad are the highest-achieving graduates and
will be able to share the burden of teaching such an individual."
Dariush went silent. There was no more to say.

"What are the fara's parents?" A porcelain-looking woman seated between Tierney and Neeta eyed me with suspicion.

My breath hitched.

"Unknown. Evidence suggests at least one parent was a valkyrie,
Councilwoman Haeva," Dariush responded.

Councilwoman Haeva raised her eyebrows and leaned back in
her chair, taking in that piece of information.

"A product of deserters, I assume?" It was the man with English
as his second language who spoke this time. More a statement than
a question, as if it were the only possible explanation.

"That is yet to be confirmed, Councilman Kāne," Dariush responded.

"Are we supposed to just assume these rebel parents are dead
or that this girl was their only offspring?" Neeta barked wildly,
completely ignoring Dariush's statement.

I tried to make sense of that, but I'd lost the trajectory of the
conversation.

"Ah, Neeta. Great point." Councilman Tierney was talking directly to Neeta. He was grinning again and even chuckled to himself. Neeta shifted in her seat, obviously uncomfortable with Tierney's attention. This was going over my head. It was all I could do to take in the keywords. Maybe Dariush would share the missing information if I pressed him.

After pausing for a moment, Tierney turned his attention again to Dariush. "You know we allow two fara children per paired soldiers to keep numbers consistent. The rules are vicious but clear."

A deathly silence filled the room. There were things being said in that silence that I couldn't make sense of. The man's words were purposeful, sinister in a way that I couldn't read.

Dariush must have known what Tierney was hinting at, for he went as still as the stale air that entombed us.

"Having a reasonable understanding of fara law, Dariush, you must have known that any third offspring would have no claim to a place in this world." A chuckle rose from Councilman Tierney again. "But, as my lucky prince would have it, I have faith in your instincts. So, I see no problem with allowing this charming fara to live and serve whilst we gather some *concrete* evidence."

There it was. My mind went blank as the pieces were spelled out. They were discussing the conditions of my right to *live*. More so, it was up for debate.

Tierney looked at three council members, encouraging their approval. Each obliged with nods. One council member wasn't asked to contribute to the decision. The woman sat at the end of the table next to Councilman Kāne, three wooden boxes displayed in front of her. A purple triangle-shaped mark rose from her right jawline and found its peak just above her eyebrow. Her eyes were full of fear and fixed on Dariush. She was there entirely for show.

Whatever the council was considering doing with my life, it was unanimous—at least between the council members who mattered.

"Lucky, lucky, lucky!" Tierney rose from his chair with excitement. Four councillors followed suit, but only three shared the man's enthusiasm. "The squad you have presented stands. Prince Dariush of Dubnos, you will be paired with—"

The man's eyes found mine. His smile turned smug, an eyebrow raised. He knew I'd been watching the entire council meeting. "Girl! What's your name?"

I stopped breathing.

I'd broken the first rule, and this terrifying man was goading me to break the second. The coldness brushed against my lips, confirming my suspicions. *Don't*, it said. My answer stayed in my mouth. There was no way I could answer anyway.

I looked to Dariush who interjected, "Annalise."

"You will be paired with Annalise—*the valkyrie*." Hints of scepticism edged the councilman's words before he scribbled the name on a piece of paper and continued to read out the names on his list. "Jaz, child of Samhain, you will be paired with Geira the valkyrie. Naranbaatar the mora, you will be paired with Zorya the daywalker. Councilwoman Haeva, please officiate the unions."

"Honoured fara." Councilwoman Haeva took over, sweetly reciting words she seemed to know by heart. "It is by the order of this council, the Blessed Tuath Dé Empire, and its Hidden Cities that you have been bestowed with this partnership. Your pairing is till death as is your service to this council. May you be loyal in every aspect of your service. Accept this honour with these gifts."

Dariush and the two boys moved to the silent councilwoman who opened the three wooden boxes in front of her, each revealed four silver bangles. I almost followed until a blonde-haired woman beside me grabbed my arm and shook her head.

Each came back with a set of four bangles and the group re-arranged themselves around me. Dariush silently waited for me to stop gawking at everyone else before he fastened a bangle to each of my wrists. The two pieces of jewellery consisted of thick silver and locked with a short wand of white crystal.

I looked at my wrists dumbfounded.

Weren't they just contemplating killing me? Why give me jew-ellery?

A purposeful cough brought my attention back to the man in front of me. He was holding two slightly larger bangles, one in the palm of each hand. It took a moment before I realised he wanted me to put the bangles on his wrists.

Why is my mind being so slow?

With far less grace than he had shown to me, I fastened one bangle onto his right wrist and turned to the left arm to repeat the process.

I stopped. The fur reminded me of the two black dots bellow my left eye. Two dots that had left me starved of friendship through most of my school years and clinging to toxic ones when they eventually came. I wondered what childhood must have been like for this man. Even surrounded by people, magical beings rather, with facial birthmarks of all shapes and colours, Dariush's arm stood out. It made him seem other in a world full of weirdness.

Shaking away my sympathy, I took the remaining bangle and held firmly onto the man's upper wrist. This time the bangle slid on with ease and locked in place with a delicate click.

Another cough, from someone behind me, brought me back into the room. Everyone else seemed to have returned their attention to the group of councillors in front of us.

"May the blessings of the Sacred Tree be ours," Haeva finished. The words landed with a sense of ownership, like *ours* wasn't meant to include those who stood before her.

"Prince Dariush, you and your squad will join the Samhain descent from Hag's Mouth tomorrow at sundown. Dismissed." Councilman Tierney waved his hand and turned his attention to a collection of papers Councilman Kāne had handed to him. Taking the head councillor's lead, Councilwoman Neeta waved her hand and the large wooden doors in the front of the room swung open.

Everyone, excluding me who had only just let go of Dariush's hand, let one knee touch the floor before rising and turning for the door.

"Oh, and Prince Dariush." The squad froze as Councilman Tierney continued, his attention split between giving orders and flipping through paperwork. "You won't be paired a third time."

I looked from the long table at the end of the room where the beautiful, bossy people resumed their discussions, over to the open doorway, and down to the piece of cold metal around my wrists. The bangles were thick and heavy. Each curved perfectly to the shape of my wrist. While they weren't uncomfortably tight, there was no fitting a finger underneath them. Now that I looked closer, the fastening latch seemed to have completely disappeared.

They looked like pretty handcuffs. My mind felt cold. Muffled. Like my thoughts on all this were behind some barrier. Like on some level I understood what was happening around me, and I'd know what to do if I could just break past that coldness.

A strong hand grasped my upper arm and pulled me out of the room.

CHAPTER SIX

Zorya

Geira was a glowing coal. Her eyes burned through Annalise as the heavy wooden doors slammed shut. Dariush almost dragged the pale woman as he headed for the elevator. Something about the way her dark brown eyes stared through me as Dariush pushed past had felt odd.

"Oh, don't brush this off, Dariush! *Our loyal servant!*" Geira bowed mockingly. "What happened? We had a plan! Who is she?"

This made Dariush stop. Without so much as looking over his shoulder, Dariush spoke with equal fierceness. "Plans change, Geira. She's none of your business." He moved down the white hallway and disappeared around a corner.

A shrill of frustration escaped Geira as she kicked a leg of the wooden chair I had been sitting in before the ceremony. The leg cracked where it met the seat of the chair but didn't break away.

Jaz and Nate watched dumbfounded as the valkyrie took a moment to calm herself.

I took the distraction as a chance to slip back into the council courtroom.

Getting into the best squad was what I'd worked hard for, but that dream included becoming a squad leader. If I didn't act now, I might never get another opportunity to take it.

My left knee had barely skimmed the ground before Tierney spoke.

"Speak."

I stood and faced the council, ready to tell them— Ready to tell them what? That they'd made a mistake? That would go down well. Tell them that I'd caught their precious prince in a supply closet with that strange fara woman, and then what? They'd give Dariush a chance to speak and he'd give them information I swore I'd never part with.

They'd end me.

"I request extra duties as a means to earn my entrance into the White Guard." I was so surprised by what had escaped my mouth that I almost forgot to finish my request with "Councilman Tierney."

Silence filled the room. All councillors, excluding Tierney, looked at me as if I'd just spoken an insult. They'd all heard the declaration of what I was. A daywalker. A dorka—a fara whose very essence was darkness.

It was called the *White* Guard for a reason. They only accepted solas fara into the White Guard. Valkyries, sylphs. Those born of light and definitely not a bloodsucking upir. Even though I was the only upir they had.

The terms had always felt arbitrary to me, just more lines the Tuath Dé drew for their own amusement. I didn't feel like the *big, scary beings of badness* they made us out to be. The other dorka, mostly mora and shifters, didn't feel bad to me either. From what I could tell, the only thing that separated us from solas was the fact that our orbs, the power that we could temporarily pull out of ourselves at will, were cold and dark where the solas' were bright and warm.

I sucked in a breath. Tried to look through Tierney as he lifted his head, face unsmiling.

"You may leave," he said before returning his attention to the papers in front of him. It took a moment for the others to return their attention to whatever agenda had been set before I made my stupid request.

I kneeled and left quickly.

***

Deep, scratchy growls emanated from the speakers. "Break what binds you." Geira smacked her hands on the dashboard in time to an impossibly fast beat, talking the lyrics that were hidden beneath the vocalist's screams.

Dariush had been the one to put the song on, but the most enthusiasm he'd shown for it were small taps of his fingers on the steering wheel as he kept his gaze focused on the road. A peace offering to a friend, maybe?

"Yeah! Who's this?" Nate leaned over the front seat to check the mobile phone sitting in a compartment under the AC dials.

"The lead singer's a woman," Geira said. She doubled down on her hand drumming, only stopping for the drop.

"This is a chick?" Nate's jaw dropped as a particularly impressive growl vibrated through the SUV. We were about an hour into a fourteen-hour trip from London to Hag's Mouth, and this was the first time I'd seen Geira do something other than silently burn with rage in her seat.

I was glad the music was helping someone because it did nothing to ease the queasy feeling in my stomach. I'd fucked up. If they weren't thinking of making me a squad leader before I opened my damn mouth, they definitely weren't thinking about making me one now.

A White Guard? Ugh, where had that even come from?

I should have just told them about the closet thing and denied whatever Dariush spilled about me.

No. I was loyal to the Tuath Dé, even if they were mostly a bunch of shits, but what Dariush could use against me was too big a secret to let slip into their hands.

A melodic chorus broke the song's heavy beats for a second time, and Annalise hummed along from the back of the car. A sharp pain erupted through the back of my head.

"Ah! What the fuck?"

The complaining didn't come from me. Jaz and Nate rubbed the backs of their necks, the three of us all seemed to share the same pain.

"Did you feel that?" I asked.

"Yeah, it was like someone shoved a knife into my neck," Jaz said.

I rolled my eyes because Jaz exaggerated everything, especially pain.

"Weird" was all Nate had to say about it. The front seats stayed noticeably quiet, though Geira shot Dariush a questioning look.

We stopped every four hours for breaks, including to catch a ferry. Dariush drove most of the way, only letting Geira take the wheel for the final stretch.

It was some time after midnight when we arrived at Hag's Mouth, a campsite that sat just inside a cave carved into a rocky mountainside somewhere in the southwestern part of Ireland. We slept in sleeping bags on the ground next to the SUV and got up early to prepare for the hours-long procession into the earth.

The Tuath Dé we were charged with escorting beyond the veil and into the undercity deep below our feet took their sweet-arse time getting ready for the day. Almost every family had spent the night in tents large enough, and well equipped enough, to be considered a fully functioning home. Of course, my new squad, and all fara soldiers assigned to the descent, were called on to help with the dismantling of the structures.

Because who would go camping without their own personal army to save them from physical labour?

Our descent began shortly after midday. There wasn't any point in starting earlier. Should a Tuath Dé, or any other fae, try to cross the veil before sundown on Samhain eve, when the veil thinned away to nothing for three months, they would turn to ash. It was one of those things that kept us fara so useful to the Tuath Dé. We could pass through the veil unharmed all year round.

As the path became increasingly steep and the walls crowded around us, a hole opened up in the side of the cave revealing an assortment of intricate pulley systems and a sheer drop.

A shipping container about three metres high, two wide and six long was being attached to a system of pulleys, a second and third waited to be attached behind it. I wanted to stop and watch the workers, mostly non-Tuath Dé fae, lower the containers into the hole, but the procession kept moving, and I was swept through a smaller tunnel and down a set of stone stairs. I could hear the

echoes of their commands and grunts behind me as I walked farther into the earth.

The descent was disappointing. After we'd walked a good five
hours, by which point I'd become deaf to a young Tuath Dé man's
incessant complaining, the air lifted around me and hummed. The
energy signalled that we'd walked through the space where the veil
would have stood strong and near solid less than an hour ago.

Shortly after, Dariush used hand signals to communicate to the
squad that he'd sighted a sluagh—a beast that lived in the depths
of the earth and the main reason we were called to guard Tuath
Dé on their pilgrimage. It didn't take me long to find its shrunken
shadowy form that had morphed to fit the cracks in the stone walls.
It watched as our charges walked the protected path and passed
through the wards into Dubnos's first town, completely unaware
of the faceless form that assessed them. The thing only vanished
when it seemed to become uninterested in our movements.

Fáilte wasn't much of a town. The narrow tunnel we'd been
travelling through opened up to a pocket in the earth. If you focused on the rows of warehouses and the open spaces used to house
the large shipping containers while they were sorted, you could
pretend the town wasn't entombed in stone. Little shopfronts
attached to the warehouses tried to distract from the swathes of
stalactites that clumped together in areas and made the cave ceiling
feel lower than it was.

We should have kept walking with the other fara soldiers, guiding Tuath Dé towards the end of the underground town where
open tram carriages waited on tracks to ferry them through another tunnel to their next destination. Instead, Dariush led the squad

towards a woman who stood in the centre of a large open stretch of road.

Her grey-streaked red hair fizzled outward, adding to the frantic scene before us. It seemed that everyone wanted to speak with her, ask for her opinion or direction. I watched as each of the busy underdwellers, a mix of fae and a few humans, took their turn to ask the woman their questions.

"Dariush!" the woman said loudly with a smile, cutting off a desperate human-looking underdweller who'd barely gotten their question out.

"Aunt Hestia," Dariush responded with a bear hug.

My mind raced. I hadn't even known the queen had a sister. Maybe this was his father's sister? I shrugged the questions away. It wasn't like I was going to ask.

Then the woman turned to Geira and greeted her with the same warm hug.

"I missed you." Geira smiled to the red-haired woman.

"You must be the rest of the squad. He said he was being assigned a new one." The woman's voice became soft, like she realised too late that she'd said something insensitive.

Dariush brushed it off. "This is Hestia. She's the keeper of Fáilte and the commander of resources."

I didn't know the Tuath Dé had a commander of resources.

"For my mother," he added.

"I'm the one responsible for making sure Dubnos has enough clothes to wear and food to eat," Hestia said in simpler terms. A woman of a similar height to Hestia, wearing blue overalls and a black headscarf, placed a hand on her shoulder. With a turn of her head, pointed ears peeked from Hestia's frazzled mane of reddish locks. A physical feature that signalled her out as a Tuath Dé despite her important role within the Dubnos Kingdom. Strange choice for the queen to put a Tuath Dé in charge of resources. Dubnos may have been a colony of the TDE, but the kingdom and the empire had a strained relationship.

The woman who'd interrupted didn't need to say anything. There were plenty of impatient stares from the people behind Hestia, all desperate for her guidance.

"I'm sorry, Dariush. I'm terribly busy. I've set you up in the house, make yourselves comfortable." She began to turn away, only to turn on her heel again as if she'd remembered something ultra-important. "Oh, Geira, dear. There are new jumpsuits for you to try on. Just send back the ones you don't like. I'll pick out a few things for the rest of you and send them up. Let me know if I need to make any adjustments to the fit." She stressed that last point.

"You really didn't give me enough time to organise all this." She shot Dariush a playful *tsk* before returning to the growing chaos behind her.

Within moments the woman was arguing with a man half her size about plates.

Dariush and Geira led the way to the back wall of the town's pocket in the earth. Lights danced between the stalactites above us like little stars, throwing a soft cool glow across the town similar to that of late dusk.

As we neared the wall of the cave, scattered windows became visible, and lines of ornate doors welcomed us at its base.

Dariush opened a dark green door and ushered us in, looking back at a handful of Tuath Dé loading themselves into an open tram carriage just shy of one hundred metres away.

Are we not allowed to be here?

The constant need to stuff down my doubts about this man and his methods was wearing on me. In the span of two days, he'd proven to be a leader who hated doing anything by the book. While I had no restraints about bending the rules on occasion, when warranted, Dariush seemed to ignore them outright.

Hestia's home was far more vibrant than the stony setting of the town. Decorating the rounded stone walls were woven squares depicting colourful scenes of battle and ancient myths. All the furniture was made of dark wood, softened by emerald velvet cushions and white knitted throws.

On the third floor, above what I could only assume to be Hestia's private space, Dariush split off with Jaz and Nate. I followed Geira into a room on the southern half of the floor. It was small for one that held three beds, but it had its own bathroom and a large wardrobe. At one end of the room was a stained-glass window and streaming onto the floor was a patchwork of colour.

I walked over to the window, curious to see outside as I knew the lights from the city of Fáilte were behind me. My breath hitched as I peered out, or rather, in. I was looking into the next city. And by the look of a large castle that sparkled under its own sky of starlight, I was looking at Dubnos City.

"Is that?" I started, making an effort to ignore Annalise's sulking as she entered the room and dropped her duffel bag on the middle bed.

"Dubnos City? Yeah, the trams will take the Tuath Dé on a bit of a wild goose chase to make them think the city is farther away than it actually is," Geira said in amusement.

I frowned. "Isn't that a bit deceptive?"

"If Queen Dubh wants to share that information with the council that's up to her." A little bit of joy had left Geira's tone. But whatever I had said to sour her mood was quickly forgotten as she spotted two piles of black and grey clothing neatly stacked on the middle bed.

She picked up the first pile and headed for the empty wardrobe, which was large enough to act as a changeroom.

"Get your bag off my bed, Annalise" was all she said as the door closed behind her.

"This one's mine," I said dryly, pointing to the bed closest to the window. A sliver of rainbow light was covering the foot of my bed. I tried to hold back a smile. I'd moved between a number of living spaces during my time at the college and never had more space to myself than a single bed and a few shelves for clothing and toiletries. Personal possessions that couldn't be hidden in clothing were either nicked by other students or confiscated by teachers.

Looking down at my double bed, I had never felt so lucky in my entire life. And to top it off I had access to an oversized wardrobe and a bathroom only steps from my bed. Even if I had to share this space with two other people, I was still living a luxury I'd never even let myself dream of.

I sat down at the end of my bed and breathed a deep and even breath, before letting my body fall into the softness of the sheets.

CHAPTER SEVEN

Annalise

M y new room might have been slightly bigger than the one I left behind in Lucknow, but that old room didn't come with roommates. I'd spent most of my free hour fighting the claustrophobia brought on by the descent, and again by the uncertainty of what I could and couldn't touch since Geira and Zorya seemed to be so particular about what was theirs.

Neither had shown me much kindness, but hospitality wasn't exactly what I was expecting when I walked through that portal.

I was counting my blessings I wasn't in a cell.

Geira spent most of the hour playing dress-up with her new jumpsuits, and only stopped when Hestia's assistant arrived with more outfits, a pile each for Zorya and me as well.

Every item in my pile was either black, grey, or blue so deep it might as well have been black anyway, and I mourned the collection of cute pastels and florals in my wardrobe at home.

Zorya seemed cautious of the pile of clothing the woman handed her, as if touching clothes other than the uniform she wore would turn her into a smoking pile of ash.

God, she's so uptight.

After twenty minutes, Geira emerged from her game of dress-up in the bathroom in an all-black jumpsuit with a dark grey floral pattern blending into the collar. Her sleeves rolled up to her elbows to reveal a matching pattern, and she'd paired the ensemble with the only black boots I'd seen her wear so far but had switched her frayed, black laces out for grey ones.

"You two should get changed. Once I've done my hair I want to be out of here," Geira said. "Newbie, what are you wearing?"

The question startled me.

"Um, I didn't know we were going out." I looked to the cuffs at my wrist. I'd figured this was it. That I was under house arrest until someone told me I could leave. Getting dressed up to go out shouldn't be on the cards, right?

"OK, show me what you've got," Geira said before opening my designated drawer and pulling out anything blackish. There wasn't anything neat about her actions, and I regretted having refolded each item before packing them away.

"Apparently Hestia doesn't think you'll be much of a fighter either," Geira assessed, holding up a navy-blue dress.

I blanched at the idea of fighting but pushed away my questions. *One thing at a time, Annalise. Find out why we're not in a cell first and work from there.*

I could have just asked Geira that question, but if Dariush hadn't shared what I'd done with the council he'd probably kept my secret from everyone else too.

That meant I'd actually have to confront that man at some point. He was so tricky.

There was a total of two dresses and three skirt-and-top ensembles in the pile Hestia had given me, and apart from the light blue jeans I had been wearing for over twenty-four hours, I didn't have any pants.

"Well, I guess we lean into it." Geira huffed and threw the dark blue dress at me. Catching it, I realised its molten pattern was actually varying shades created by the velvet fabric.

Forgetting thank yous, I moved to the bathroom beyond the walk-in wardrobe and began to peel my clothes off.

Ugh. I'm gross. "Do I have time to shower?" I yelled to Geira.

"The quickest shower of your life, Newbie," Geira yelled back with obvious disapproval. The tone was enough to make me re-consider, but I turned the gold-and-silver taps, wrapped my hair in a bun on top of my head and stepped into the steaming shower.

As I washed, taking in the savoury scents of salt and seaweed from the soap, my eyes drifted over the tiles. It took me a moment to realise none of them matched. Yet, each one felt like it belonged to the one next to it. Whoever designed this bathroom had an incredibly resourceful eye.

There were little pictures on every second one. Rowboats that drifted on clouds, the fishermen's nets cast out to collect stars. A moon with a castle built into its face. A bridge with a town of little people working busily beneath it.

I wondered how the stories might have been told, who'd painted them. Who'd decided that they should be put in a bathroom in-stead of a museum.

"I said *quickest*, Newbie!" Geira slammed her fist against the door twice, and I about jumped out of my skin.

Moving fast, I rinsed my body and cut the water before the suds had time to fully make it past the drain.

The dress was as comfortable as it looked. It clung in all the right places, flowing from the waist and brushing my thighs a few inches above the knees. A square neckline and structured, jutting shoulders made the piece look fierce, yet elegant. Like maybe Hestia was hoping to fool people into thinking I had some sort of mean streak in me. Looking at my reflection, I believed the image and hated the dress instantly.

I pulled my hair from its now sagging and slightly damp bun and made my way to the bedroom.

Geira's hair was done, along with her makeup. Thick lines of black surrounded her eyes and covered her eyelids, smoking out just beyond the crease. Her hair was braided in three places atop her head and pulled into a high ponytail. That combined with her all-black getup, she was the image of death.

Zorya had given in to whatever urge to dress-up had been hiding behind her scowl. Her thick mahogany hair was braided. The length of it kept swept over her shoulder. She still wore black on black though, a fitted long-sleeve top with a high neckline tucked into high-waisted jeans. It did nothing to hide her muscular frame.

When she turned her back to me, more interested in looking out the colourful window than acknowledge my presence, I noticed the plunging back of her top. A red pendant brushed across her spine from what seemed like a backwards necklace.

She looked almost as deadly as Geira, except maybe with a little less eyeliner.

"Chuck these on and get your hair out of your face," Geira barked and threw a pair of shoes at me that I had never seen before.

"Where did these come from?" The shoes were more like heeled boots. They laced up to just above my ankles and pointed at the toes. Small swirls and shapes decorated the toe and shoelace eyelets, and like my dress, they too were the darkest blue.

"Hestia brought them up just before," she snapped.

I had the shoes on in no time and decided a quick, neat bun was the only way I'd be able to "get my hair out of my face" without attempting some complicated hairdo.

Geira handed me a makeup bag, presumably from Hestia. I placed some delicate wings and mascara in record time, and then proceeded to apply the deepest red lipstick I could find in my small collection.

"Here, chuck this on too." Geira threw a wide strip of black leather at me from across the room. The weight of it stung my palms as I caught it. It was a vest of some sort. I wove my arms through two thin straps. The piece buckled in three places and covered my ribcage and chest, save for a bit of cleavage that I didn't know I had until this moment.

I must have looked nothing like that girl in the forest, because when I walked down the stairs to the main entryway Dariush couldn't keep his eyes off me.

Much like the rest of the group, he was dressed in mostly black combat attire. It wasn't much different to what I had seen him in all day. Except now, draped across his chest and shoulders, was a shawl.

Black fabric, pinned with a silver brooch at the space over his heart, swept over his left shoulder and fell to meet the back of his knees. The brooch caught my attention. Its twisted circle of silver surrounded small, white and red stones and more silver that took the shape of a crown.

His jaw clenched as he noticed my staring.

For some reason I felt my cheeks heat up and instantly fumbled with the cuffs on my wrists.

Dammit. Why am I the one embarrassed when he started it?

I didn't look at him again till we left the house.

***

The city was more like a dome encased in rock. Buildings, made almost exclusively from stone, reached two or three stories high before plateauing at the top. I imagined decked-out balcony spaces decorating every roof from all the noise and glistening light that erupted from those building tops.

It must have been night. Or some version of it.

Neon stars of every colour somehow littered the dome's ceiling, dancing around large stalactites that dangled dangerously from the darkness.

I took in a sharp breath, suddenly very aware of our lack of escape routes should one of those stalactites decide to disconnect from the nothingness above.

Vast pillars, mirroring the stalactites, rose sporadically between the mass of buildings. They seemed out of place among the stone buildings. Each pillar glistened, speckled with little windows and balconies along their sides. Their presence became more and more common as we neared the centre of the city.

It wasn't the castle that stole my attention. In front of the clustered mass of glistening pillars was the longest table I'd ever seen.

The table stretched on for the length of the road. Food stands lined the sides of the street, and people moved between them and the table, adding large dishes overflowing with food and taking back empty ones. Multicoloured, neon lights bobbed overhead, and musicians and performers danced down the street, all performing in unison.

Despite their acoustic instruments, the music reminded me of something I might have found at a rave. Techno-like metallic chimes pushed forwards by the resonant heartbeat of drums, all of it woven together by a melody of strings and ethereal voices. It reminded me—

I pushed back against that memory.

Every second or third person had paired a terrifying a mask with some sort of Gothic ensemble. Those not wearing masks wore vibrant colours.

At the head of the table sat a woman in black. Black hair. Black suit pants. Black crown of smoke and flickering lights upon her head.

I goggled at what I was seeing. I must have looked dumb because one of the boys, I hadn't memorised which one was Nate and which one was Jaz, nudged my arm to grab my attention.

"That's the queen of Dubnos," he whispered. "Surrounding her are the royal guard. She only accepts women to guard her personally."

I looked closer at the figures. Etchings on their grey-blue skin pulsed with a light glow. What I'd first thought to be crowns upon their heads, were horns. The four peaks protruded backwards from their temples and kept their long, free flowing hair off their faces.

They were dressed in a similar uniform to the soldiers I'd been walking with all day, except two light blue lines had been embroidered in a cross over their chests.

Dariush spoke with the queen, I heard nothing over the roaring of the festivities, but I imagined one of their topics of choice was me because the queen glanced my way, tilted her head as if assessing something and then nodded to Dariush.

Ugh. I felt a strange mix of being glad that she seemed to approve of me and being pissed off that she was given the opportunity to form an opinion of me in the first place.

Dariush eventually waved his hand, gesturing that we were free to enjoy the festival.

The five of us walked in silence as minutes ticked on. The boy who'd been the one to try and talk to me in that waiting room, Jaz maybe, picked up two pastries from the long table and handed me one. I hesitated. We'd been eating nothing but plain chicken-and-salad sandwiches over the past two days, and even though I was starving for something sweet, I'd come to assume that anything with flavour was against the rules.

"It's fine if we keep fit. They just prefer us to not eat junk all the time," Jaz said.

"But we can just take it?" I asked. While the mood was jovial, everyone seemed to be contributing to the festival in some way, and there were plenty of people working hard to get more food on the table.

I imagined they wouldn't have been pleased to see us taking their food, especially when we were doing nothing but walking around.

Jaz laughed nervously. "You don't know anything do you?"

Finally, someone who understood. I stared blankly at him.

"We're the Tuath Dé's soldiers. The underdwellers have to feed us because we keep them safe."

"Underdwellers?" I took the pastry and bit into it. It was sweet like I expected, but sprinkled through the middle was cinnamon and walnuts. I practically drooled.

"Oh, the humans and fae who live here," Jaz elaborated.

I shook my head and spoke, my mouth full of flaky pastry. "But they have a royal guard here."

"The queen rules over the kingdom, but it's a state occupied by the Tuath Dé."

I was straining to hear everything Jaz was saying. It must have been a contentious topic because he lowered his voice, and I had to lean in closer to hear him.

"The Tuath Dé have ultimate authority, and if they say the people of Dubnos are to feed us while we're here, then they'll do it."

I swallowed my oversized bite of pastry, and the creeping sensation of guilt nearly choked me. I looked down at the half I had left. I'd lost my appetite.

We kept walking, and Jaz filled me in on little titbits about the city in between passing me cups of wine. I tried to refuse at first, but the sweet smell made me curious, and it wasn't long before I'd downed my first cup. I followed it with a shot of clear liquid that Jaz assured me was *just like vodka*. It was nothing like vodka, and the harsh aftertaste made me appreciate the wine even more.

According to Jaz, there were quite a few Tuath Dé and other fae who'd made Dubnos their home. About twenty percent of the population were fomóire—the original race of the kingdom. They were the ones with pale blue skin and crown-like horns.

Those who'd chosen to wear dark masks for the festival were humans. Most had been living down here for centuries unable to pass back through the veil after they'd been lured here by old creatures. Apparently, that was illegal now thanks to some treaty between the queen and the Tuath Dé.

I kept my questions about humans living for centuries to myself. The details were starting to blur together with every new glass of wine Jaz handed to me.

He was so lively as we walked and talked. It was like he had all this information trapped in his mind that just needed to escape.

"I'm so glad I met you," I said, stumbling a little as I spoke as if the ability to do both at once had up and left me. "I'm going to be sticking to you like glue from now on. I have absolutely no idea what I'm doing, and I'm terrified of pissing someone off."

Jaz looked pleased with himself, then stopped walking, and I nearly stepped into the man who'd startled him.

"It's easy to piss my brother off. He doesn't know what fun is," the stranger said.

I gave him a once-over. He looked a little like Dariush, older and without the beastly arm. There was a glow to his skin, but unlike Dariush's golden warmth, his was an icy hue that reminded me of the queen's guard.

There was a devilish smile etched on his face, and I was suddenly aware of how close he was.

He bridged the little space between us and leaned down to whisper in my ear, "I'll show you what it means to have fun."

A shiver ran through me, but I stayed entirely still. How could I move? It felt wrong to just let his words and sudden closeness slide, but I was frozen. I had no idea what the rules were here.

I pushed a foot back, readying myself to back away once I figured out how to respond, but he grabbed my waist.

As quickly as he did, coldness exploded between us, and the man released his grip. Yelping and stumbling backward.

For a split second I thought I'd been the one to push him away, but in front of me a giant dog formed from shadows. It snapped and growled savagely at the stranger.

"Obsidian, heel." At his owner's command the dog sat, his seated height nearing mine standing, and stopped barking. He never once took his eyes off his target.

Dariush's brother shook slightly, his pale skin blanching even more.

"Don't touch what's mine, Aed." It was unmistakable whose voice vibrated from behind me. I felt his tall frame step closer. His anger heated my back.

It took everything within me to not lean back into him and steady myself. The city was beginning to sway.

Wait. What was his? He couldn't have meant me.

"Just testing her loyalty, brother." A sardonic smile laced the stranger's face, and I shivered at the slimy feeling that prickled over my skin.

I did lean back into Dariush then, and his hands curved around my shoulders protectively.

"You'd first have to understand what that word means. Fuck off," Dariush snarled and ushered me in the opposite direction.

Aed said something back to Dariush, which seemed to hit a nerve because a growl escaped his tight jaw, but I couldn't hear it over the noise of the festival.

As we walked back towards the queen's seat at the head of the impossibly long communal table, Jaz, Geira, Nate and Zorya lagged behind. I was flanked by Obsidian, the dog made of shadows, and Dariush who kept one hand on my shoulder the entire walk.

When his silence became too much for me, I stopped.

Obsidian and Dariush turned in unison.

"What do these cuffs mean?" I held out my wrists to him, shaking them with my demand. "Why did you say I was yours? What does it mean to be paired?" The words escaped my lips, calm at first but descending into a harsh, frazzled frenzy.

He didn't say anything.

He didn't need to.

"This is a marriage thing, isn't it?" I stared him down. "What? My mother made you feel guilty for arresting me, so you thought you'd keep me locked up by *marrying me*!?"

I'd done what he said, mostly. I didn't fuss or fight him. I hadn't been demanding once, and he thought it was OK to marry me without my consent. Without even asking. It could have been the very thing that had kept me alive through that meeting, but he didn't even give me a choice. He hadn't mentioned it once.

I pulled furiously at those cuffs. I'd break my wrists if I had to.

Dariush stepped towards me in an instant, snatching my arms in his hands. I ripped them away.

He stared at me for a moment longer, then spoke, but not to me. To a figure that had stepped in close to me once I'd started yelling at Dariush.

"Geira. I think we're done for the night." He turned on his heel and stormed off.

CHAPTER EIGHT

Zorya

G eira leaned into the kitchen bench, stony faced but attentive. She'd chosen to spend the early morning running through basic drills and warm-ups, ignoring us all. A brooding, blonde-haired Viking goddess with eyes that raged with the infernal heat of a weapon forge. It was intimidating. I only hoped that I could one day exude that kind of deadly aura.

I sat at the dining table in the centre of the room, facing a standing Dariush. The round table was a warm, pale yellow, far nicer than the stainless steel benches of the college cafeteria.

Nate and Jaz were on the side of the kitchen farthest from Geira. They busied themselves with making coffee and tea, a one-man job and an obvious attempt at avoiding the chaotic energy that had multiplied once Annalise had entered the open kitchen and opted to sit right next to me.

I huffed to make it obvious I wasn't pleased with her seating choice, but she didn't move.

It had been hard to watch Jaz and Nate get so comfortable around her so quickly. Of course, that was Jaz all over. He had to be friends with everyone, but he'd been my friend first. Shouldn't I get a say in who gets accepted into our group? I knew I was just holding on to jealousy, but the three of us had been best friends forever, and we'd won the jackpot. We were in a squad together. Why did we have to rock the boat now?

One by one, Jaz handed everyone a steaming mug of coffee. And one tea for Annalise.

She accepted the mug and breathed in its scent deeply.

"Earl Grey, how did you know?" she asked him, her face beaming. Jaz paled slightly at her thought that he'd gone out of his way to find out and flicked his eyes to Dariush.

Annalise seemed to get his message: Not my doing, his. The sour look returned to her face.

That brought a smile to mine.

Nate was the one to bring Geira her coffee. The boys obviously thought her mood had something to do with being paired with Jaz because they were making an effort to not get too close to her.

My idiots.

I noted Jaz had forgotten to make a cup for himself and felt pity for the awkward situation he was in.

Nate and I were lucky. We'd known each other forever. Even if we didn't feel anything other than friendship right now, it was still something. Jaz and Geira? Well, I knew she'd never be his type even if they did eventually become friends after ten years of service. I had no idea what her type was, but it didn't seem like it'd be Jaz.

Dariush and Annalise had something going on. She seemed to be insulted by everything he did. He pretended to be all business, but I could sense it in their blood, in their heartbeats. Nothing could hide the way their heart rates spiked when they were near each other. Or the way he looked at her when she was fixated on something. It was like she was some mystery he needed to uncover, like she was his only hope.

Absolutely revolting.

Nate sat himself next to Annalise at the table, leaving Jaz to brood by the kitchen bench a good two metres from Geira.

"Your teachers put that ceremony on a pedestal. Dangled it in front of your faces so you'd get off your arses." Dariush wasn't wasting time. There was a volume to his voice that made us all sit a little straighter.

I'd seen this kind of pep talk before. Old Harvey was fond of using it to crack the whip, so to speak. It always left me feeling a little unsure of myself despite whatever sprinkle of positivity he threw my way. I couldn't help but go into the next fight practice, the next gym session, the next strategy class with a burning determination to be better than I was.

"It worked. You three are the best your year had to offer. It's why I chose you. And, yes, I did choose you." He emphasised his last point, looking each of us, the ones who actually went to the college, in the eye.

"It might not have been as *romantic* as you dreamed it would be."

And there it was. A belittling tone drenched his words. It was that swift kick to the jaw that I'd come to expect after being told I'd done a good job.

"But you knew what to expect. You've had time to come to know your duty. Annalise hasn't received that luxury."

Oh, because being brought up away from this shit show was such torture.

I didn't bother hiding a huff of annoyance, and Nate shifted nervously in his seat beside me.

Dariush shot me a scowl before sharing a look with Geira that I couldn't decipher. When his attention returned to the table, his face was cold and impassive.

"She's spent her entire life believing she was human," he continued. "Believing nothing extended beyond the human world. Her training and education are our first priority as a squad."

The prince shifted on his feet, clutching the back of a chair in front of him before continuing. He was nervous about his next point. "These." Dariush lifted both hands to show the cuffs at his wrist. "Left is a symbol of your commitment to your partner. I don't have to remind you of the laws behind pairing."

It was Annalise's turn to huff in frustration this time. Dariush ignored her.

"Right is a symbol of your service to the council and your sacred duty. The TDE doesn't fuck around. They've been imbued with a compulsion magic."

Everyone in the room straightened a little, except Geira. This was news to us. Annalise, mouth open, fixed her gaze on the offending cuff. She looked as dumb as a goldfish.

"The TDE's been doing it forever, so don't get pissy about it. Bottom line: do as you're told, or you'll be made to." He didn't need to put on the *try me* act. None of us were going to fight him over it, except maybe Annalise. I knew he wasn't lying. It pained me to admit it, but I knew it wasn't his fault either. Of course, the Tuath Dé had something like this up their sleeve. They were completely incapable of trust.

Jaz, the least fazed by this information, took Dariush's silence as an OK for question time.

"We know what we are. I have no clue what she is," Jaz said quickly, pointing to the dumbstruck girl. "But what are you?"

Jaz, you idiot.

Dariush seemed uncomfortable with this new kind of attention but obliged anyway. He reached out with his clawed hand, placed it in the centre of the table and faced his palm up. Black wisps of smoke grew and morphed into a ball.

Annalise's already opened mouth dropped a little farther, her eyes wide. Coldness vibrated out from the dark orb. It seemed to draw the girl in. She stood in her chair and leaned in for a better look.

"I control shadows." He didn't elaborate.

I must have been drawn in by it too because when a flame came to life in my periphery, I found myself already standing. The white-hot light hovered in Geira's hand and bobbed over to a space on the table. Warmth tried to fill the space in front of me. A battle for control of the temperature created little sparks of static that danced on the air.

Nate and I produced our lights next. While it was somewhat rude to push another fara to show their light like Jaz had done, it was more of a slight to refuse to produce one if another had offered theirs up first.

Black sand swirled furiously in Nate's hand like a tiny sandstorm; flashes of lightning danced within it. It was a striking contrast to my pulsing, liquid orb of glowing, blood red. Each was a little glimpse at what made us special. No two orbs were the same, not even in the same species, but like Dariush's ours were as cold as a winter frost.

Any warmth Geira's light offered the room was smothered by a haunting chill. Fara were said to be either touched by darkness or light. They were dorka, or they were solas. No one had a good explanation as to how or why, but that distinction showed in our orbs.

It was then that I realised Geira was probably the only solas in the group. Jaz, having been born a Tuath Dé, would never produce an orb.

Despite the council believing Dariush's intel, there was no way Annalise was a valkyrie. There was something about her that felt far too familiar, and I was willing to bet the darkness that made every dorka what they were had something to do with it.

Dariush closed his palm into a fist, vanquishing the orb in a puff of black smoke, and the rest of us followed suit.

Annalise was still standing. All eyes turned to her as she blurted, "I can't do that."

Dariush focused on the girl. "Not yet, but soon you'll be able to do that and turn it into a weapon."

Her? Fighting? Oh, this'll be hilarious.

I choked back a snort of laughter. The girl looked like she was going into panic mode just at the thought of it, and I wasn't the only one who noticed.

"This is why it is our job to build you up as a soldier. You've never been taught about your abilities before." Dariush spoke to her with an edge of kindness that had been lacking in his speech directed at the rest of us. Annalise clearly didn't notice. "You don't even know what you're truly capable of."

Dariush waved his hand to Geira who, with an eyeroll, handed each of us a paper folder from the bench behind her.

I studied the contents. The first page had a recent photo of Annalise next to a detailed description of who she was and the details of her previous displays of power. Causing deafness in a female human two years ago, inciting mass headaches and aggression experienced by at least twenty-seven humans over a period of three months shortly after that.

Annalise, who hadn't received a folder and was looking over Nate's shoulder, looked like she might blow up over the intrusion when her eyes caught sight of something in the file. My eyes tried to zero in on what had caught her attention, but I couldn't make it out.

"What's a valkyrie?" The words fell out of her mouth. It was like she was incapable of thinking before speaking.

Gods, this girl's voice is annoying. I rolled my eyes so hard I thought they might get stuck in the back of my head.

"That's a joke, right?" I said to Dariush. "Valkyrie"—I looked Annalise dead in the eye and pointed to Geira, layering the condescension on thick—"are warriors. Think of a weapon and they're naturally skilled with it."

I returned my attention to the folder. My eyes caught details from the most recent incident, and I felt the blood drain from my face.

She'd caused irreparable mental injuries that resulted in the deaths of two human males two days ago. Moments before she would have been taken to the council. I wondered what caused the near-year-and-a-half break in activity.

"Are you offering up another suggestion, Zorya?" Dariush barked. It was clear his question was rhetorical, but I offered an answer anyway.

"These aren't battle wounds. These are—*demonic*." I pointed to the place in the file that had caught my attention. "And what about the way humans react around her? What about that girl who was left bleeding from her ears? Unless you want to tell me she cut them off with an axe—"

"STOP IT!" a shrill erupted from Annalise, igniting a sharp pain in the base of my skull. "Don't talk about her!" The others around the table winced.

The room's temperature dropped another degree, but my blood was boiling. I hated everything about this girl. Someone needed to knock her down a few pegs.

"Well, if you didn't fuck her up, we wouldn't have to talk about her." My words hit hard and true. Her face crumpled and reddened.

Oh, gods. Is she really going to cry?

"I hope you all made leaflets of yourselves that you're willing to share with me because I am *so* not OK with this invasion of privacy!" Annalise choked back tears. Her eyes darted between each of us and landed on Dariush before she kicked back her chair. She snatched the paper folder from my hands as the chair tilted over its back legs and smacked the floor.

She walked out, not bothering to fix the mess she'd made.

Dariush walked around the table and stood the chair back on its feet. His scowl was aimed at the door Annalise had disappeared through, but when he spoke it was a warning to us.

"I find any of you pushing her, there'll be hell to pay." Then Dariush's fists clenched the back of Annalise's chair and he leaned towards me, his face uncomfortably close to mine. "You have problems with her being here? Keep it to yourself."

CHAPTER NINE

Annalise

It was disorienting to witness daytime deep inside a cave. Small white lights bobbed high above and blanketed the town of Fáilte in a soft white hue akin to an overcast day. Rows of warehouses built out of a mix of old stone bricks, modern cement blocks, and the kind of ageing red bricks that had formed foundations for most of the houses in Lucknow, hid any view of the single-file tunnel entry we'd walked through the day before. Those boxy, mostly grey exteriors made the town feel uninviting. A flaw that vanished once lights were turned on in the warehouses and the colourful windows peppered a naturally marbled rock floor with a sea of rainbow.

The exterior of Hestia's home, a sliver of the giant cave wall, was hard against my back. My butt had gone numb against the cold floor a while ago, but I couldn't bring myself to stand and walk back into that house. Not after the complete tantum I'd thrown. Not after seeing the way Dariush had looked at me.

I'd felt those cold tendrils brush the back of my neck and wrists. They'd been respectful this time, refusing to break the barrier of my will as if they hoped they could quell the rising storm within me by touch alone. I wished he'd done more. He should have stopped me. Saved me from humiliating myself like that.

The file stared at me from its discarded place at my feet. I couldn't bear to open it again.

It was all just words on paper, things I knew already. Had lived through. So what was with my outburst? Wasn't it better for them to know what they were dealing with than end up as another of my song's victims?

A dull ache pulsed in my head, making my thoughts fuzzy and muted. It hadn't helped that a hangover had well and truly hit me by the time I'd made it to breakfast, but that wasn't a good enough excuse.

Zorya was a lost cause. She'd sensed something was off about me the second she laid eyes on me, but Jaz and Nate? They had been nice, and I was starting to feel like I had people in my corner. I'd stuffed that up.

"Got room for two more?" Nate's calming voice sounded from a crack in the front door. He pushed it open, revealing two glasses with little more than a splash of clear liquid in each.

I used cold hands to wipe tears from my cheeks that I'd so far ignored and moved to stand up. "It's not a very comfortable spot." The temperature of the cave town sat a degree or two below temperate. The chill was easy enough to ignore since there was no wind, but sitting on cold hard stone made it worse.

Nate shook his head and passed me a glass, choosing to sit beside me before I could fully stand. Jaz followed suit with his own glass and flanked my left.

"Bottoms up," Nate said as he offered his glass up for a cheers. The glasses clinked and the two boys downed their drinks with ease. I hesitated as the harsh smell wafted in my face. Something malty and—*nail varnish*?

"Ugh. It's way too early for this. I don't think I want to touch alcohol for another week after last night," I whined, scrunching my face.

"Oh, that's exactly why you want it. Chase away the hangover," Jaz said, tapping his head to indicate either that he'd thought it through or that he was getting rid of a headache.

"I don't think that's how it works," I said before surprising even myself and downing the shot anyway.

Vodka maybe, or something like it. I decided it was probably the same stuff as the shots we'd had the night before and regretted my decision instantly. The liquid burned down my throat, and I choked through the next few breaths. My "thanks" came out as a hoarse mumble.

Neither said anything for a long moment, and I was content to sit in the silence, taking in the lulling echoes of distant chatter and people walking through the town.

"You're right, this floor sucks. How long have you been sitting out here for? Couldn't you have moped in the lounge room? We have a fireplace!" Jaz squirmed.

"Jaz! Do you have to be so blunt?" Nate groaned.

"What? I think a stone is sticking into my arse." Jaz lifted himself off the floor long enough to brush down the space where he sat.

"Serves you right," Nate muttered.

A snort escaped me. "I thought you wouldn't want to talk to me after. . ." I let the words trail off.

"Pfft. That was nothing. You should see the arguments we get into with Zori," Jaz responded.

"You mean the arguments *you* get into with Zori," Nate shot back.

"Sorry," Jaz singsonged. "I'm not about that pacifist life."

"What do you mean? You're a pacifist?" I shot Nate a puzzled look. "But you're a soldier."

"I try to be." Nate shrugged and looked away. It seemed to be an uncomfortable topic for him. "Most of my weapons are nonlethal."

"Yeah, but they'll give you a right shock." Jaz obviously thought he was hilarious, and I was left to imagine what was so special about Nate's weapons while the joker of the two laughed himself stupid.

I couldn't help but smile. Jaz's laughter could have been magic, or maybe it was my lack of reaction, because tension visibly released from Nate's shoulders.

"You didn't hear that by the way," Nate added. "We're not supposed to alter our weapons." He picked up the file that lay discarded next to me, a hint of seriousness in his otherwise kind face. "Don't think about all this. It's in the past. I know it feels like an insult to them to look forward, but you can't live in that pain forever. What you do now matters."

He said it quietly, just before Jaz pulled himself together. I knew who he meant by "them." The victims. The two dead men. The girl who'd fallen in love with music and would never hear it again because of me. For a moment, I wondered if the pacifist soldier was pulling from some removed fragment of lived experience.

It didn't matter. That kind of thinking wasn't going to work for me. Letting myself forget, as if I even could, was the first loose thread that would unravel the hold I had on myself.

"Remember when Leah walked in on you and Rachael doing freaky stuff with those electroshock thingys?"

"Fuck, Jaz." Nate covered his face in his hands.

I was about as stunned by the sudden turn in topic as he was, but endlessly grateful for it. I'd assumed Jaz was too busy laughing at his own jokes to listen in on the conversation between Nate and me. How much of his joker act was just well-timed mood breaking?

"And *I* had to go on a date with her so she wouldn't snitch," Jaz teased.

"You never let me forget it," Nate mumbled as Jaz fell to his side, unable to contain his renewed bout of infectious laughter.

I let myself laugh with him.

**

Nate handed me a schedule at dinner which I promptly ignored in favour of a plate of pork, beans and a double serving of mashed potato. The second I'd taken my seat Zorya huffed, picked up her full plate and left the dinner table in a grand show that she'd be eating somewhere I wasn't.

I tried not to be bristled by it, but the fact that Dariush and Geira were also absent made everything sting a little more, and no amount of mashed potato could stop my thoughts from spiralling downward.

Had they decided to avoid me altogether? Had Dariush realised his mistake and gone to some supervisor to tell them what I'd done, what I was really capable of?

A more likely explanation for the squad leader and his second-in-command's absence, that they were preparing for the big week ahead, came to my attention when I read the schedule before going to sleep. Five a.m. wake-up call, morning workout between 5:15 and 6:15, shower, breakfast, out the door for patrols by 7:00.

Or back into the gym for training if you weren't already a super soldier.

There was a roster for who would train me too. Dariush was listed first and that was when I decided I could do with a sleep-in.

When I woke up, it was to Geira barking at me to get out of bed. She pulled the blankets off me when I didn't move.

I sat on my bed, holding back my anger, and waited till she got fed up with me and left, a sour-faced Zorya followed behind her. Pulling the blankets back over me didn't do much. It was shortly after five and I was already very much awake. I decided that since I couldn't go on my early morning walk to the lake, I'd spend my morning painting and singing instead.

There was no one around to hear me anyway.

After allowing myself to take the longest shower, I picked out a dark blue sundress with puffy shoulders and took my paints to the little library I'd spotted on the main floor.

I felt bad for a second.

A second.

And then I reminded myself that no one here cared about me enough to ask what I wanted. So why should I ask?

Besides, I'll be adding to the reader experience.

There were so many books. So many different genres and topics. I would have liked to rummage for the perfect fantasy, something with castles and dragons and romance, but this trove was full of a different kind of fantasy. Books that promised to tell truths on things that shouldn't exist. I found myself compelled to find another book that might elaborate on the one hidden in my duffel bag upstairs.

I'd flicked through *Tales of the Water Women* once since arriving in Fáilte. It was wholly disappointing. A bunch of nursery rhymes and poems too dark for any mother to want to read to their child, though I knew my mother had read this book to me before. It was also too nonsensical for me to pull any useful information from, and I was left feeling that Mum had wasted space in the duffel bag on something that was only sentimental to her.

My fingers stopped on a gorgeous gold-flecked spine.

The Sacred Tree: The Ultimate Guide to Tuath Dé Blessings was etched in the dark brown leather of the book's face, a border of gold swirls delicately camouflaged the letters. Something so beautifully bound had to be important.

As I pulled the book from the shelf, a black puff of smoke erupted by my side and— *Was it nuzzling into my leg?*

I jumped away and held the book over my head, fully prepared to bring it down on the dark shadow, before two reflective eyes peeked from its darkness. The round mass grew and morphed into the form of a giant, black Newfoundland.

Dariush's shadow dog sat tall in front of me, eyes in line with mine. The thing was huge.

"Obsidian," I breathed, hoping I got its name right.

I stretched my hand towards its snout slowly, and the shadow dog leaned in closer, sniffed once, then wrapped its head up my arm so I'd be forced to scratch behind its ears. A laugh escaped me.

"Thank you for saving me from the bad man." My words came out in a baby voice, but how else were you supposed to talk to a giant dog?

Obsidian barked once in response, which I took as both a "you're welcome" and confirmation that I'd gotten his name right.

I found a comfy spot on a green velvet couch and pulled a side table close to me, taking care to not spill the cup of water that sat next to my palette and brushes.

Obsidian took my move as an opportunity to snuggle. He lay down by the foot of the couch, his head resting on my outstretched legs like a blanket.

The book started with a contents page. Chapter titles were named after trees, flowers, fruits and nuts, and following each was a string of numbers which, on further inspection, seemed to be dates.

I flipped through the pages trying to decipher the connection. Apparently, the author thought any context worth mentioning in a preface was common knowledge. Most trees appeared twice, one labelled dark and the other labelled light.

A black silk bookmark attached to the spine was wedged tightly between pages at the chapter on Elm.

The chapter read: *Those born under Elm are gifted with crafting spaces of beauty, a gift that has been ridiculed as trivial compared to Hackberry's mastery of manifesting goals, which have seen many successes in war among military leaders born under the branch. However, both branches gift those Tuath Dé born under them with powerful skills in visualisation. It is only by taking the pilgrimage to touch the Sacred Tree that these branches depart in similarity. Elm-born Tuath Dé, whose gifts have been amplified by completing the pilgrimage, can force the form of a thing to change.*

It was a birth calendar.

The pieces of information began knitting themselves together, and the image formed clearly in my mind. All that was left for me to do was give it physical form.

I found a blank page in the front of the book and started mapping out the image. Before long, I'd brought the calendar to life in the form of a wheel. It was a complex system, and I wondered if there was actually any legitimacy in it. Four dates hadn't been assigned a plant, one of them being Halloween, except it was called Samhain in the book. The same word everyone kept throwing around at the festival.

The task of flipping back through pages to gather the right information, then painting that information onto the wheel in the form of images, kept my mind occupied and I found myself humming a made-up tune.

At first, I panicked. I looked to Obsidian to see if he had reacted badly to my voice. The shadow dog was fast asleep on my legs, as if my song were a lullaby.

At least someone likes my singing.

I continued. The music thrummed through my chest, each brushstroke keeping time to the rhythm. I could have been sitting there for hours, or days, and be none the wiser. Time didn't exist in the space between the pages and my imagination.

"Why weren't you in the gym this morning? That timetable wasn't a suggest—" Dariush's words pushed me out of my blissful state, but he didn't continue to berate me.

He was standing right behind the couch's arm. His eyes moved from me to Obsidian to the book. He leaned forwards and grabbed it before I could protest.

"Don't close it! It needs to dry!"

He stared at the painting for a long moment, then spotted my paint palette. I snatched it and my brushes to my chest, not caring that I'd just gotten water paint all over my dress.

"This is one of Hestia's favourite books," Dariush said flatly. "It's an heirloom passed down from her mother."

A pit opened in my stomach and swallowed me whole. I'd been so focused on having the kind of morning I wanted that I hadn't actually stopped to think about whose book I was painting in. It was a truly selfish move. I couldn't even plead ignorance really. I'd wanted to ruin something, bonus points if it belonged to Dariush, but of course this was Hestia's heirloom book. Everything in this house was Hestia's, and all of it was beautifully curated to fill the space. It was all important to her. Dariush spent so much time stomping around like he owned the world, and I'd just assumed whatever I was destroying was his.

A low chuckle sounded from the other side of the room. I snapped out of my spiral to find Dariush smirking to himself by the bookshelf. Hestia's book was balanced open in one hand while he pulled two more books from the shelf and held them between his beastly fingers.

"What?" I frowned at him.

"You're very beautiful. Moreso when you're feeling guilty."

Heat rose in my cheeks before the backhanded compliment fully found its mark. *Guilty.* Was I that readable, or had he been paying more attention to me than I first thought?

Thud.

A book hit the coffee table.

"You'll read chapter twenty-nine of this one today," Dariush said before dropping another book on top of it. "Then start working through this one." His playful taunting from seconds ago had vanished.

"Why?" I forced myself to sound stern even though my flushed face hadn't fully cooled, and the memory of his chest against my back was creeping into my mind again.

"Why what?"

"Why these books? What do you want me to know?" *Or not know.* There was so much I still didn't understand about myself or this world, and I didn't trust that he had my best intentions at heart. "You don't just demand that I study these books without giving me the subject matter, Dariush." It was the first time I'd spoken his name. The syllables felt odd on my tongue. I wanted to say it again.

He sucked in a short breath, like I'd poked him with a hot iron. His body went entirely still, eyes fixed on my lips. It had apparently occurred to him too that this was the first time I'd called him by his name. I couldn't tell if he liked it.

"You," he forced out after he'd regained composure.

"Huh?"

He picked up the book at the bottom of the stack, flipped the pages and stabbed the place he was looking for with a finger. "This chapter will tell you about sirens. Not half sirens, but it's a start." He shoved the open book my way, and I took it with both hands.

"Why not half sirens?"

"Just read the chapter." He glowered impatiently before pointing to the second book that stared up at us from the coffee table. "That one covers all known fara types. You can paint in them so long as you're taking everything, *and I mean everything*, in. And don't paint over the words," he snapped and picked up *The Sacred Tree* again.

"I'll be showing this to Hestia, but lucky for you, I think she might actually like it." His words came out softer as he looked over my wheel painted in muted hues of every colour. There was a tone of appreciation in his voice.

He moved to the door abruptly and disappeared through it. When he returned ten minutes later it was to give me an oversized bowl of porridge and berries and a mug of Earl Grey tea.

Earl Grey had a distinct floral flavour that people either hated or loved, and this wasn't the first time he'd served it to me. How had he known it was my favourite? I doubted my mother would have slipped that in while she made demands for my safety.

Dariush's every action was double-sided, like a flipped coin that had landed standing up. Neither heads nor tails.

He'd called me beautiful and guilty in the same breath. He'd threatened to kill me, then done all he could to spare me from execution. He acted as if what I wanted didn't matter, then did things like this that proved he was paying attention.

"Eat it now or eat it cold. You'll make up the missed gym session after lunch, no excuses." Dariush didn't wait for me to protest. He left the room.

I wiggled my legs and Obsidian opened a lazy eye.

"Can you save me from him too, please?"

A strangely worried expression flashed across the dog's face. Then he closed his eyes, conveniently avoiding my question entirely.

It became clear to me a few pages into the chapter why Dariush hadn't elaborated on the subject matter.

Sirens, according to the book, were only ever born with female reproductive organs and could only reproduce under very specific circumstances—by luring human men into a body of water and drowning them.

Once I'd gotten past the horror of thinking my mother might have done such a thing, it dawned on me the impossibility of it all. If it was only humans that sirens could reproduce with, then I, a siren and something else, was either the only exception to the rule in all of history . . . or I wasn't a siren at all.

I shovelled spoonfuls of lukewarm porridge into my mouth while flicking through the pages of the second book, desperate to find answers to my piling questions.

I mostly skimmed the book, flicking past chapters with strange names like mora, dorka and solas, and sylph. There was no record of a siren fara, nor was there much in the way of any kind of fara like me. At least not ones with gifts akin to a demonic songbird.

Feeling frustrated, I put the book aside and promised myself I'd study the contents in more detail over the coming days.

As I scoured Hestia's library for more books on siren genealogy and creatures of song, doubt crept into my mind.

Whether I was my mother's daughter or not, a single truth rang in my head. According to the laws of nature, even magical ones, I shouldn't exist.

CHAPTER TEN

Zorya

Thoughts of this day had stolen all the free space in my brain for the past year. My first official patrol.

Of course, I had imagined leading the patrol. Meeting with other squad leaders as our sections crossed over. Being the one to organise my team into groups of two, ensuring each soldier complemented the other's skills. If I had been given my own team, the one I was *supposed* to have, I would've teamed up with . The shifter and I often butted heads when it came to decision-making, but fighting? We were like a pair of twin blades. Nate with Jaz was an obvious choice, those two worked together flawlessly. Sometimes it was like they could read each other's minds. Which would've left Hendrik, a valkyrie, with Ellie, a sylph. Ellie was physically the weakest, but her eyes picked up everything and she was crazy fast. Teamed with Hendrik's brute size, they'd be unstoppable.

My mind drifted to the time and day that should have been *my* graduation ceremony, and I wondered if the council saw what I had in the two of them. Even though I had hoped to be officially paired with Hendrik, the thought of him with Ellie now didn't sting as much as it probably should have.

No part of our lives was truly our own. There was no point crying about it.

Dariush had put me with Geira today. So, not only was I not the leader of the squad, but her experience meant I wasn't even the highest ranking in the patrol pair.

"Wait here," she said as we neared a section crossover and spotted a neighbouring patrol.

Fighting back the sass that crept into my mouth, I folded my arms and stayed put. Geira's face soured as she walked towards the young squad leader across the road. Dylan was a familiar face from the college, as were the two who followed closely behind him. Aoife, the girl I had flawlessly roundhouse kicked in the face in the Glistening Arena, stood close to Hendrik. *Speak of the devil.* It seemed Dylan had split their squad into two groups of three.

I tried to think of any instance where such a grouping would make sense and came up short. Sticking together as a larger group against threats like the sluagh was always the ideal option, but we were patrolling a relatively peaceful part of a heavily warded city. Busy shops and cafés lined the streets. Between the Tuath Dé leisurely exploring the city and the underdwellers going about their busy days, there was a buzz in the air that made this area feel like the place to be. Our only purpose was to keep that peace and report any evidence of rebellion against the Tuath Dé Empire. Today's patrol was set to be mostly uneventful.

Hendrik waltzed over to me, tight blond curls and that pale patch under his right eye sat stark against his dark brown skin. He flashed me a toothy grin. I shoved down that giddy feeling that took over my stomach whenever he was around.

Geira gave him a stern look as she passed him on her way to Dylan, who was stubbornly standing at the corner of *his* section. Making Geira walk over to him was a slight, especially since she was the more experienced soldier. Maybe he thought it beneath him to start conversations with another squad's second. Dylan was always a dick.

Hendrik took his time crossing the road, making me wait for whatever he had to say to me. He was handsome, charming, but it was the kind of charm that was accompanied by a boastfulness.

His presence commanded the looks of a few women crossing the street in the opposite direction. One had turned around completely, walking backwards a few steps just to get a better look at his arse. I was half expecting her to stick two fingers in her mouth and give him a wolf whistle. He walked like he knew they were looking.

"What do you want, Hendrik?" I said, feigning boredom.

"Only the stars and the sun." He held a hand over his chest as if reciting some romantic piece of poetry.

I made a playful tutting noise. "Always wanting what's out of your reach." It was fun to turn on the charm every now and then, but images of Nate flooded my mind out of nowhere and I suddenly felt guilty. I knew I shouldn't have cared. I wasn't doing anything wrong, and Nate and I weren't required to have kids for another ten years. But what did pairing us so early mean to the council?

My parent's own pairing had meant something to them. Meant something to my father, at least. So much that once my mother had been caught out in her quest to overthrow the Tuath Dé, my father stood by her side. Choosing not to carry out the orders of those he had honourably served for decades.

My thoughts were disrupted as Hendrik stepped up onto the sidewalk and shoved a piece of paper into my palm.

"What's this?" I asked.

"Your extracurricular." He leaned into me, whispering in my ear as he said it.

I went to open the folded paper, my stomach knotting slightly. I liked flirting with the guy, but I hoped this wasn't a love letter.

"Not here," he said, zeroing in on the back of Geira's head.

What doesn't he want her to know?

"For your eyes only. It's from Tierney's White Guard."

My eyes widened. I stuffed the paper into the back pocket of my pants and checked to see if Geira had noticed our exchange. She was still talking to Dylan.

This was the council's response to my request for extra duties. *Why wasn't this information filtered through Dariush?*

I didn't have time to ponder that question. Aoife had left her side of the street and was walking over to me. She'd barely gotten halfway across the road when she shouted, "Can't help yourself can you, whore?"

Maybe Hendrik hadn't been paired with Ellie after all.

Geira's head whipped towards the woman at the sound of her comment. Then she returned her attention to Dylan. He shrugged at something she said before Geira turned on her heel, her face red with rage.

Aoife had reached the sidewalk where I stood, but Geira was a breath behind her. In one quick movement, she grabbed Aoife's wrists and pulled her into a lock, forcing the girl to bow awkwardly before me.

"You can apologise to Zorya now," Geira said in a completely calm tone. There was no mercy in her face, but it seemed the valkyrie felt better now that she had Aoife where she wanted her.

It was unnerving.

"Ahh! Get off me!" Aoife tried to push back, but Geira's hold kept the girl's arm at what I knew to be a painful angle.

"I'm growing impatient." Geira's words were only half heard as Aoife yelped in pain. She'd added a twisting motion to the lock, threatening to bend one arm to the breaking point.

"Fine! Fine! I'm sorry, Zorya!" Aoife let out and failed to fight back a whimper. Geira pushed the girl slightly as she let go. It was enough force that Aoife fell to the hard ground.

"Fuck off," Geira spat at the girl before glaring at Hendrik, the same threat simmering in her eyes. He didn't baulk. The air crackled with tension, neither valkyrie wanting to let the other win in some strange, unspoken battle for dominance. Without breaking eye contact, Geira pulled a long baton from its secured place at her back and flicked a switch. Two sharp blades extended outwards at the head to reveal an axe.

Well, that wasn't standard issue.

Hendrik paled instantly and quickly followed Aoife to the safety of their section, the three of them running along like scared children.

We walked a block in complete silence, and I wasn't sure if she was giving me the silent treatment or she just needed time to cool down. Either way, I left her to her thoughts.

Mine were enough of a distraction. If the TDE had sent me secret orders through Hendrik, Dariush mustn't be privy to that information. What could the prince have done to lose their favour? What do they not want him to know? That piece of paper was burning a hole in my back pocket. I was desperate to read it for so many reasons now.

"I need coffee," Geira grumbled as she turned abruptly and veered into a café we'd just passed. I followed her inside. The space was cluttered with mismatching tables and chairs, their only connecting features were their black and white surfaces, all of which had been purposefully graffitied with bright blue tags.

Geira wasn't the only one who'd decided now was the best time to grab a coffee.

"Double flat white," Geira said once we reached the front of the line. "Want anything?" she asked, turning to me.

"Same, thanks," I said to the human cashier, noticing how her blue-streaked hair and grungy outfit matched the decor. It felt wrong walking into a café knowing I wouldn't be handing over money for the goods I ordered. *How do food businesses survive down here?* On the surface there were allowances for small luxuries like coffee, but access to that money was filtered through squad leaders and teachers. Whenever I'd asked Harvey or another teacher for money, there'd always been some arbitrary task attached to my access to it.

"I know it's a bit early, but we've been playing around with a new syrup recipe for our Yule coffee special." The woman was trying, and failing, to hold back the excitement in her voice. "It's honey and cinnamon. Did you want to try it out for us?"

If coffee was a rare treat for me, syrup in coffee was on a whole other unattainable level. An enthusiastic yes began to sound from my mouth, but Geira's harsh rejection cut it off.

Of course she was a coffee snob.

The human cashier looked from me to Geira, unsure how to end the awkward moment. I was about to change my answer when

Geira chimed in again, "No syrup for me, thank you. But put an extra pump in Zorya's."

The cashier beamed and relayed the order to a coworker behind her. Geira and I stepped aside and watched a fomóire man work. He turned dials connected to thin taps to steam jugs of milk and pulled espresso shots from skeletal machines using heavy levers.

I'd seen coffee machines in cafés above the surface. They were clunky and looked nothing like the system of pipes and levers in front of me. Without electricity, anyone wanting to run a café in Dubnos would have to find alternative methods of pulling coffee shots and steaming milk.

When the cashier handed over our order I took a thoughtful sip, letting the milky liquid swish over my tongue. There was a natural sweetness to it that didn't overpower the coffee or the delicate hints of warm spice.

"This is heaven," I said before taking in another gulp.

The cashier beamed before turning to her coworker and declaring, "I told you honey works better than sugar!"

I left the café with Geira, the sense that I'd earned my coffee driving away all thoughts of the incident with Aoife.

"Are you all right?" Geira said as she shook her takeaway cup. She peered into the small hole in the lid before throwing back her head to consume the remaining liquid. I opened my mouth to say something automatic like "of course, why not?" And then it dawned on me what she was talking about.

"I feel like I should be asking you that. What was that?"

A pathetic drop landed on Geira's tongue. She scowled at the coffee cup as if it offended her by being empty. For a moment I thought she wasn't going to respond.

"She called you a whore. Doesn't that bother you?" she said finally, barely glancing at me as she spoke. She crushed the empty cup in one hand as we walked.

There was a focus in her gaze, a crease in her brow, as if rebels were lurking in the alleyways. As if she were still trying to distract herself from what had happened with Aoife.

How did this woman manage to look beautiful and furious at the same time?

I blinked. She'd threatened a fellow soldier for *me*. Aoife could easily go to Dariush and demand some sort of retribution.

"Aoife's been calling me a whore since we were fifteen. It's nothing new." I tried to throw in a laugh to lighten her mood. It came out strained. For some reason seeing her in this hardened state bothered me.

"I can't stand women who do that," she responded through gritted teeth.

"I'm used to it," I said, regretting my words instantly.

The valkyrie spoke her next words so low I thought I might have imagined them. "Don't be."

CHAPTER ELEVEN

Annalise

I had barely heard a word from Zorya since the meeting around that kitchen table after Samhain. Her face distorted in pure disgust anytime I dared share her space.

Maybe she just has a very unflattering resting face, I thought before considering one night when she'd left the living room mid-sentence during a conversation with Jaz because I had walked in.

No. Zorya didn't like me. It was even clearer that Zorya was not a fan of the rotating schedule Dariush had put together to dictate who would be teaching me, or rather babysitting me, and when.

If I was being honest, I wasn't a fan of the schedule either.

I had spent the last three days inside with Obsidian, learning from whichever squad member was required to teach me. In spite of their efforts, the walls were starting to press in on me. All I wanted to do was breathe fresh air.

Apart from my usual pastime of painting in Hestia's books, something she was surprisingly OK with, lessons had become my favourite part of the day. It was something to take my mind off my worries and break up my time completing mindless chores. Jaz centred his teachings around the Tuath Dé, their birth chart system, and the lore surrounding their yearly pilgrimage to what was called the Sacred Tree.

Nate talked in depth about the different types of fara and finished his lessons by guiding me through a simple meditation that I was supposed to practice every day. I didn't.

Geira's lessons were a bit more practical. My leg muscles and upper arms still ached from the basic fighting drills she'd run me through the day before.

Dariush told me he'd help me practice producing an orb tomorrow, and even Hestia had books she thought were noteworthy sent to my bedroom.

I would have gladly taken lessons from any of them, but today was Zorya's turn.

The disgruntled woman might have thought she was discreet about it, but the squad's living quarters were tight. Zorya had taken almost every measure to palm me off to someone else when her time came. She had pleaded with Nate and Jaz to take her place. Bribing them with chore-free weeks or taking their patrol shifts with Geira. I tried to not let their refusal sting, knowing that their stance had more to do with their wavering connection with Zorja than me.

It did anyway.

Even Geira was approached as a last resort, but the valkyrie told her to suck it up.

I had every expectation that Zorya would find somewhere else to be and leave me to enjoy the day by myself. So, when she entered the kitchen after breakfast and announced a well-deserved study break to Dubnos City, I knew her plan had changed—and that likely didn't bode well for me.

"Uh, no. You don't get to pull that on me." There was no way I was going to fall for this. I moved from the round, pastel yellow table in Hestia's kitchen with a dirty mug and placed it in the sink, laser focused on the first chore of the day: dishwashing.

"What do you mean?" Zorya said quickly to the back of my head. There was an ounce of sincere confusion hiding in the woman's defensive tone.

"You expect me to believe you genuinely want to hang out? This is the first time you've spoken to me in, let's see. . . ever." I continued scrubbing away at dirty dishes. My hands moved violently through the motions as I stopped paying attention to the quality of my cleaning. "I heard your offer to the boys. You obviously hate the idea of spending a whole day with me. So what is it, Zorya?" My fierceness felt wrong. Anger was building up in me again, just like it had with my mother.

A long silence filled the space between us as I focused on moving slower, breathing slower.

For a moment I thought Zorya had left. A cool wisp of velvet nuzzled against my waist, and I looked down to see Obsidian. The vitriol in my voice must have stirred him from his morning nap by the fireplace.

Sorry, Sidi.

I ran wet fingers through his smoke-like fur, scratching behind a half-raised ear. It was like touching something soft and solid, that at the same time wasn't there. My fingers dipped into the darkness of his fur, and I was reminded of Dariush's black arm.

I'd come to know the shadowy beast well during my stay and decided that, while he was twice the size of a large dog, Obsidian was every bit a house cat.

"I just—" Zorya faltered. "I just don't know if I can trust you. I'm trying, but you're a fara who's never had to face the responsibility of actually being one. We're different from Tuath Dé, and I don't know if I have the—"

Zorya sucked air into her lungs, and I took a moment from my scrubbing to turn and study her face. She looked to be sorting through a thousand drifting thoughts—deciphering the best military move with every rotation of her mental cogs.

I readied myself to say something reactive. A phrase like *you haven't even given me a chance* or *no one wants to explain anything to me* sat on the tip of my tongue, but that silent ticking from Zorya stopped me. From what Nate had told me about the military college during our lessons, it didn't sound like a place of sunshine and roses. Figuring she hadn't had much practice with making her concerns known through open conversation, I gave her space to form her words.

Zorya shot Obsidian a sour look, before picking up a chequered yellow towel and moving to the dish rack beside me. Seeming to sense the hostility between the two of us had evaporated, Obsidian left. Likely, to resume his sleeping in front of the fireplace.

Zorya dried and packed away two mugs before she spoke again, and when she did, her tone was softer. "When you were playing human, I was learning how to endure torture. How to kill shape-shifting monsters made of shadow. My mind was being filled with the rituals, names, titles, family trees of Tuath Dé that refuse to acknowledge my people. I'm a daywalker, an upir—not just fara," Zorya said passionately.

I let her continue, making a mental note to ask one of the boys later what those words meant to her.

"They don't care that my people had rituals, beliefs of their own. They don't care that my parents weren't alive long enough to teach me them. It doesn't seem fair that I have to teach you their ways now too."

I was starting to see her side of the story. "I was taken from my home, put into this strange system." I held my wrists out of the sink long enough for her to see the cuffs covered in soap suds. "I'm told the world isn't what I've always known it to be. Told that I'm not actually human, I'm a . . . valkyrie," I had almost said siren. I hated the feeling of the lie in my mouth, especially so now that she'd shared so much with me. "I don't think I can survive down here without help."

Zorya breathed in. "Well, you're definitely not a valkyrie," she said, picking up another mug to dry as she spoke.

"Really?" I asked, wary of where she was going with that statement. "Dariush seems so sure."

"He might be fooling everyone else, but he knows fully well that valkyrie can't—" Zorya paused as I sucked air into my lungs.

The thought that she might go on another rant about my displays of power shook me. The contorted faces of those two men still inhabited my nightmares, despite Nate's attempts to render my sleep dreamless.

Zorya must have noticed my apprehension because she landed on "can't do what you did."

So, there was some compassion under that hard shell.

"Then what do you think I am?" I said, trying to hide my hope. Maybe if she could guess then I could stop lying to her. To everyone.

"No clue."

And my hope deflated.

"But we're not going to find out in this dingy hole-in-the-wall." Zorya tossed her tea towel onto the drying rack and turning on her heel for the door.

"Does that mean you actually want to help me?" I said with a little too much excitement, dropping something metallic into the sink.

"*Want* isn't the right word. But it works for now," she said coolly over her shoulder. "Coming?"

I couldn't help but smile to myself. *Maybe Zorya doesn't hate me after all. Maybe she just needed a bit of honesty.*

Glancing at a lone teaspoon covered in shallow, bubbly dishwater, I pulled the plug and walked away from the gurgling sink.

Dubnos City in the light was a labyrinth of stone buildings, rising to meet plunging stalactites strewn across a peaked cave ceiling. The cave in which the city stood was church-like. The buildings its ornate pews and pillars.

Focusing on the path ahead was a hard task. The city was illuminated by lights that shone in different hues, flickering and moving in waves around the very peaks of the stalactites. White light speckled with green, red and light blue cast a refraction of moving colour on the cave floor. The opposite of a cloud's shadow on the earth below. It was unlike any sky I'd seen before.

With my attention completely on the ceiling, nothing warned me of the small pothole that snagged my foot and threatened to body slam me into the corner of the nearest building.

A hand grabbed the back of my t-shirt and yanked before bone and cartilage could crumble under the impact.

Fingers brushed the back of my neck.

CHAPTER TWELVE

B lackness.

A glimpse of ourself was all we were given.

CHAPTER THIRTEEN

Zorya

I let go of Annalise's shirt and blinked away darkness, keeping still as the world became visible again.

What the hell was that?

One moment I was saving Annalise from face-planting into the side of a building. The next, the world had gone dark save for flashes of a face. Two of them, pale and menacing. They might as well have been death personified.

I pushed the image from my mind, blaming it on a trick of the light thanks to mischievous will-o'-the-wisps.

Of course, I'd gotten caught up in their prank on Annalise. They just loved to taunt anyone they hadn't seen before.

I recalled my first encounter with the living lights at eighteen, just after initiation into the military college, the final four years of education I'd ever have to suffer through. I'd looked a little too closely at one of them. Its spherical frame bobbled in the air and became misshapen as it moved. Tiny hands pushed against a flexible membrane, as if a thumb-sized person were stuck inside it.

Those shimmering marbles had led me to the edges of the city wards to stare into the eyes of a sluagh on the other side. It was like they were trying to say "Think we're terrifying? We'll show you something worse." I was in no real danger with the wards up, and I never forgot the coldness in the sluagh's eyes, but I wasn't convinced.

I watched as Annalise blinked to regain her vision and slowed her gasps for air after being half choked by my rescue. It took her a second to regain her bearings. She ran her hands over her face, checking her nose and forehead for injury.

"You're welcome," I was unable to hide the uncomfortable mix of confusion and resentment in my tone. I straightened and turned on my heel before Annalise could catch the wariness that must have been plastered on my face. "Don't pay too much attention to the will-o'-the-wisps," I yelled over my shoulder with a little more conviction as I moved through the street. "They might not lead you astray. But they will get a kick out of distracting you into a broken nose."

"Those are living things?" From the tone of awe in her voice I could tell she was looking back at the sky.

I rolled my eyes, making a mental note to let her hit the wall next time.

"You mean like bugs? Fireflies?" she said, as her footsteps quickened behind me.

What, by the Sacred Tree, are fireflies?

Images of will-o'-the-wisps on fire burning everything they touched sprang to mind. That was more terrifying.

Not wanting to be the one to ask a stupid question, I responded, "If fireflies have a narcissistic personality and a constant will to harm, sure."

Annalise said nothing.

I sighed as guilt swept through me. It wasn't really her fault that she didn't know anything about this world, and here I was doing nothing to help her attempts to learn more. And I was about to do much worse. The least I could do was tell her about the will-o'-the-wisps.

"They have an agreement with Queen Dubh, so they can't *really* hurt you. They control night and day here. When they're low on the peaks, like now, it's late morning or early afternoon." I pointed to a group of green stars swirling around the nearest stalactite. "Covering the peaks, it's midday. On the roof of the city and it's midnight. If you don't see many up there at night, it's because they're hunting. It happens once a month. We call it a hunting night."

Like a new moon. I thought to add, in case she didn't understand the basics of the sun and the moon, but held my tongue.

"What do they hunt?" she asked from behind me.

"Animals. They used to hunt humans, bring them down to feed on with the sluagh when the last king was in power. But the treaty forbids that now, and all humans in Dubnos are protected by Dubh anyway."

My answer seemed good enough for her, and we continued on our walk through the city in silence, Annalise always one step behind me. Our pace slowed as we passed colourful stands filled with hot foods that smelled salty and sweet. I ignored a tightening in my stomach as I hurried Annalise along. Any patience I had developed for the girl during our short discussion had vanished by the time we neared our destination.

"Where are we going, Zorya?" she whined in protest. I had snuck a glimpse at the will-o'-the-wisps to check my timing, thinking that she wouldn't notice.

Great. I was going to be late, and Annalise was becoming suspicious.

"It's just around this corner, I think you'll like it," I said, turning to give her a wide smile as she tried to keep my pace. I hoped it seemed genuine, even though she had every reason to doubt me. I'd taken a gamble she'd fall for the story of a poor orphan soldier denied her heritage by the mean Tuath Dé, and it paid off. It wasn't by any means a lie, but I'd come to terms with my fate a long time ago.

The Tuath Dé may have some backwards rules, but there was opportunity with them. I had gladly given up trivial freedoms for a life of honour. For legacy.

As we rounded a street corner, I spotted the sign. In front of a shop sat a small piano with large letters spelling Open on the wing. Hunger gnawed at my stomach, or maybe it was guilt. Jaz had wanted to show Annalise this place after learning of her love for old instruments, and I was stealing that opportunity from him.

For a greater cause, Jaz.

Offering Annalise another smile, I walked into the store.

The large space was stuffy, cluttered with instruments of every shape and size, some piled on top of each other in large bookshelf-like structures. A young, ginger-haired shop attendant approached Annalise, sheepishly avoiding looking in my direction. My uniform and holstered knives did that to some people. He left quickly when she politely refused his help.

I was strategic with my next move. Even made sure to take my time in the store. I talked to her about the ones she played. Anything woodwind, she'd said, whatever that meant, but singing was her chosen instrument.

She talked in depth about the mechanics of a few items and marvelled at others that she'd only read about in books.

Only after ten minutes of looking, talking and refusing the shop attendant's insistence that she could try out the instruments, did I realise she was actively avoiding touching them.

I wanted to pry. Was this a clue as to what she really was? Did she avoid playing instruments for the same reason she'd locked herself away in a desperately small country town for a year and a half?

Grilling her about it was tempting, but I was running out of time. If I didn't leave now, I wasn't going to make it to the other side of town in time.

"So," I started, hoping the words would fall out smoothly and she wouldn't prod at my excuses too severely. "I'm going to leave you with the instruments for a little bit."

There it was. Annalise's face sank. She'd been expecting this.

"How long?" Her words were abnormally cold as her eyes drifted over what she had identified as an eighteenth century hummel.

"About two hours," I said quickly. "Feel free to look through the other stores on the street, there's a really cute café not far from here, but don't venture too far. I'll meet you back here before we head home."

Nothing. The girl said nothing.

"Annalise?" I said, waving a hand in front of her to try and at least get a reaction.

Annalise turned from the instrument she had shown excitement towards only a few moments ago. With her back facing me, she muttered a low "Fine" and stalked to something at the back of the store.

"Fine," I repeated, too stunned by her sudden turn of attitude to do anything more than walk out onto the street.

I moved through the city, my mind fixed on how quickly she'd gone from nerdy music ramblings to completely giving me the cold shoulder. I would have thought she'd be grateful for a day of freedom, even if I wasn't there to enjoy it with her.

Besides, Dubnos might be a dangerous place, but I picked a safe area on the other side of town for a reason. If I didn't care about her, I'd have let her come with me.

The girl was spoiled, but as I moved closer to my destination, my mind drifted to what I had seen in the music store. Her reaction to the instruments, it was like she was scared of them, or scared of what might happen if she touched them.

Guilt ate at me, and I stopped to looked up to the will-o'-the-wisps. It was too late to turn back, and I couldn't give up now. Especially not for someone I had met less than a week ago.

By the Sacred Tree, please don't let her get into trouble, I thought with an audible sigh. My pathetic prayer weighed on me as I continued on, away from Annalise.

CHAPTER FOURTEEN

Annalise

Two hours, Zorya had said.

I couldn't wait here for two hours.

I had no interest in spending the good part of my day in a music store waiting for someone else to retrieve me. Not when humming a single note could kill every human and torture every fae in this place.

Realising that distinction had made me feel a little calmer about being held captive in this strange city. The squad didn't react to my singing the same way those men at the lake had. Still, I had to be careful.

How would Zorya have reacted if she knew I was lying to her? If she knew she had put a monster whose weapon was song in a music store?

I should have told her the truth.

Guilt swept over me and amplified with every second I remained in the store. It was like all the air had been sucked out of the building, and staying put meant certain death, for myself and everyone around me. I'd lasted all of five minutes in the so-called safety of the music store after Zorya had gone on her errand.

I took note of my surroundings as I stepped into the street and breathed in the city's stale air. The streets were a blur of colour.

Colour that sloshed around in the city's "sky" and refracted onto the ground. Colour from the mismatched clothing of the city's dwellers, rushing around to get their day's chores done before dusk, or whatever makeshift form of dusk this place experienced.

Throughout the city I could see Hestia's handiwork, or that of her helpers. Cafés were strewn with random pieces of furniture that all seemed to fit the space. I passed shops with shelves and clothing racks that held no two of the same item, yet the collections in each seemed thought through. There were open galleries on every corner, and like the shops, those colourful places of sanctuary were carefully curated.

Everything had her mark on it. Ornate and matching. Well, as much as it could be considering everything brought into this place was secondhand. Apparently discarded by us humans and repurposed by the underdwellers.

Us humans?

There was nothing human about me. As I moved through the city, I took in the underdwellers and their home carved in the earth. A tram carriage that was pulled along tracks by nothing more than a set of crystals attached to its front made a stop in the middle of the street. Humans and fae jumped on and off the open structure with haste. Most moved around the Tuath Dé, who seemed to be oblivious to the rush.

A fomóire man in a leather jacket barged onto the tram a millisecond before it began to move again, effectively cutting off a young, pointed-eared man with a sweater hanging over his shoulders from getting off at his stop. There was muffled bickering followed by a booming "Would you like me to throw you off,

Ya Majesty?" from the carriage's open frame as the tram took off down the street.

Where the Tuath Dé were lithe and impossibly beautiful, the fomóire were horned and brutish. Side by side they were like ice and fire, water and oil, angels and demons. I couldn't tell which were worse.

Humans and the other fae were far more difficult to distinguish, and I began to make a game of figuring out who was what as I walked. Besides the marks on their faces and the uniforms, fara looked mostly human. Every now and then I'd spot someone who looked human at first, only to notice flames dancing in their hair or a strange tint to their skin.

A black-haired woman in an 80s band T-shirt walked in my direction. She was short, there were no fara marks on her face and I locked her in as "human" before shifting my attention to someone else. It was only as she passed me that I realised her irises were the same dark red as Zorya's.

Great. So, there are fara vampires and regular vampires.

I didn't need this to be more complicated. Every time I thought I was getting closer to understanding this world, something else revealed itself and shook the foundations of what I knew. It was hard to keep up.

As I walked the streets, a warming scent of cinnamon and honey filled my nose. My gurgling stomach propelled me further through the city streets and away from the music store.

It had to be past lunch time. I tipped my head back and looked upward, not sure what to expect. Wispy things, whatever Zorya had called them, were somewhere near the tips of the stalactites.

Annoyance flooded me as I realised I had no way of telling if it was just before midday, or a little after.

I stood still for a moment, rounded my shoulders and breathed in the decadent scent. Remembering what Jaz said about the people of Dubnos providing fara soldiers with what they needed, I set out to locate whatever kitchen or café was responsible with a little more haste.

Round a corner, down a set of stairs, through a tight alleyway, and a diagonal cut across a tram intersection and I arrived at a little storefront that was nothing more than a door made of blue glass and a hole in the wall to cater to those in a rush. A blue-grey arm extended from the window and handed a takeaway mug and a brown paper bag to a human woman sitting on her bike, white sneakers on both pedals, one hand resting on the windowsill to keep her balance. With one quick movement, the woman dropped an assortment of coins on the windowsill and placed the paper bag in a basket attached to the back of her bike. "Thanks, Ethlyn!" the woman shouted as she rode off, holding the cup in one hand and steering with the other.

A bell sounded above me as I stepped into the darkly decorated café. Scents more delicate than the sweet cinnamon and coffee on the air enveloped my nose. Savoury meats, fennel, thyme and something that I could only describe as stewed fruit. Pastries covered in berries, apples and an orange-coloured paste filled the glass cabinets in front of me.

"Hey, can I help you?" a woman, I assumed Ethlyn, was offloading a tray of steaming pastries into a round display cabinet. Up this close, her skin wasn't just blue-grey. It was decorated with faint, jagged etchings of white that ducked beneath her casual black T-shirt and apron. Her dark hair was braided away from her face, the length of it left to flow freely behind her, and haloing her hairline were two sets of black horns and a third set made of silver embedded into her head.

She might have passed for an eccentric, blue human if it wasn't for her horns. And those murky white eyes.

My stomach gurgled again at the sight of the pastries. It was loud enough for the woman to hear.

"I was told—" *What was I told? Can I just ask for food like this?* "I don't have any money because—well—I'm a fara soldier. Sort of." The words felt stupid in my mouth. I was dressed casually in a T-shirt, my old light blue jeans, and flats.

Nothing about my image screamed *soldier*.

The woman had barely glanced at my wrists before she turned to grab two paper bags and stuffed a hot, savoury-looking pastry into one. Handing the bag in my direction she said, "Pick another, I'd choose something sweet."

I blinked. I was a good two steps away from the counter but looking at that icy skin, sharp nails delicately avoiding ripping the paper bag, I felt like I wasn't far enough away. This woman looked like the queen's guard, and while I hadn't felt so scared around them on the night of Samhain, they hadn't paid attention to me the way she did.

The woman sensed my hesitation. "I won't bite," she said, shaking the bag.

Her words shook me out of my stillness. I willed my feet to move forwards and took the bag from Ethlyn.

"I thought fomóire women guarded the queen?" I didn't know what possessed me to say anything. I felt rude as soon as the words escaped my mouth.

The woman only chuckled, the sound clanging in my head like an alarm bell. Only the warning warred against something else. Something trusting. Familiar. The etchings on her skin flared with a dull blue hue, and I felt instantly drawn to her.

"I'm sort of a last resort. There are enough of us that we don't all have to be watching her all the time, and I'm useless with weapons," the woman admitted, chuckling to herself.

She wandered over to a large oven and held out her hand. A white flame sprang to life within it and something inside ignited. I took a single step forward, unable to tear my eyes away from the flame.

"I thought only the fara could do that?" I said, thinking back to the display of lights the squad had produced around the kitchen table.

"You think a lot." A crease formed between her brows, then a lighthearted smile took over. "There are plenty of fae who can produce a light. Especially those down here who need it. The world isn't all fara and Tuath Dé, you know."

I nodded, despite very much not knowing. I took a peek at the pastry inside the bag. It was something meaty, wrapped in flaky bread and covered with herbs. One bite told me the meat was likely lamb and the herbs a mixture of fennel and thyme. I almost groaned at how good it tasted.

Ethlyn chuckled again. "And what about you?" she said casually as she placed raw pastries into the oven.

I knew what she meant. If she were Zorya or Nate or anyone on the council, I'd lie and say I was a valkyrie. Only, this woman wasn't Tuath Dé. She wasn't even one of their soldiers. There wasn't any harm in telling one person, right? Besides, I was tired of lying. I needed a bit of truth telling.

"I'm a siren" I said, rounding my shoulders back and pushing down the familiar urge to avoid eye contact. "And something else. . . I don't know."

As I steeled myself, I caught a glimpse of curiosity in the woman's eyes before she shifted, making herself look busy and uninterested.

Shit, I said too much.

"That something else must be pretty important. They don't conscript sirens into the fara army." Her feigned boredom was palpable as she focused her attention back onto her pastry cabinet, rearranging a pile of almond-topped croissants. I shrugged it off as her trying to be polite.

"You must have one terrible squad if they've left you to patrol by yourself." Her tone lifted. It took me a moment to remember that patrols were a core part of a fara soldier's tasks.

"Oh, they don't let me patrol," I said quickly, hoping she didn't think I was here to snoop.

The woman stopped. Her eyes lightened as she considered something. "I want you to meet someone." She dropped an empty tray on the counter, moved towards the back of the store and vanished through a threshold.

I stood there for a few moments, unsure as to whether she was bringing someone out or I was supposed to be following her in. When it was obvious she wasn't coming back I moved around the counter, past the empty tray, the warm oven and a rack of cooling pastries, and slipped through the same doorway.

A short hallway led into another room. It could have been mistaken for a small library. At a table sat two people bickering over a map, half-buried under stacks of papers and books.

"My siren friend, meet Resh and Mabel," Ethlyn said. Her words brought the bickering to an end as their attention snapped to me. To the two dots on my face. To the cuffs around my wrists.

They knew exactly who I was, and they weren't happy I had invaded their space.

I gulped involuntary and looked around the room, taking in the bookshelves, the scattered desks, the neatly stacked piles of mechanical parts sitting by the door I had entered through. Anywhere but their faces.

"What the hell are you doing bringing one of them in here, Ethlyn?" said the woman. She fussed with her blue-streaked fringe in an attempt to hide the strawberry birthmark on her forehead. It was the only thing that signalled her out as nonhuman.

The girl looked no older than eighteen and didn't have cuffs on her wrists. For a moment I thought that maybe she was too young to be given the cuffs, but then I noticed her clothing. A lacy, white top and a red leather jacket. It wasn't the fara soldier uniform the others seemed to live in.

The way she looked at me was off-putting. Like I was a heartbeat away from changing her entire world for the worst.

What does she have to fear from me?

An image of the two men writhing in pain on a lake's edge flashed through my mind. I pushed it back.

"I thought you'd like to meet a fara soldier who's also a siren," Ethlyn said, emphasising her words as if to share some hidden message not meant for me.

"Fuck," the man whispered so low that if it wasn't for my keen hearing, I would have missed it. Unlike Mabel, he couldn't pass for human. His skin was a paler blue than Ethlyn's, but he was twice her size and the third set of horns that framed his hairline were natural—unlike Ethlyn's metal ones. Their blackened tips gave him a dangerous aura which was only emphasised by the multitude of decorative scars that covered his skin and the bridge piercing that sat between his eyes.

"Um, my name is Annalise," I said, trying to shrug off the overwhelming wave of discomfort that was rising in my gut. "What are you reading?" I'd meant to shake up a light conversation. To break some of the tension that had built from my intrusion. Since the old leather-bound books were the most interesting things in front of me, I'd chosen the obvious question.

It was the wrong question.

Mabel stood and walked over to me from behind the desk. Her bare toes peeked under faded blue jeans. "Why do you want to know?" she breathed, half a foot from my face.

"Uh, nothing important," I responded, my brain working quickly to find something else to say. These people obviously had no connections to the Tuath Dé. They certainly didn't like fara soldiers.

Maybe they can tell me what Dariush won't. Maybe they can help me find what I need to take away my curse. "I'm looking for someone who can help me." It felt wrong as soon as I said it.

"And what would *you* need help with?" she said flatly.

"I'm only half siren." My heart pounded. "The other half of me, whatever that is, has made life difficult. I'm looking for a way to go back to normal, to how it was before everything went . . . well, went to shit really."

The woman went still, frowned. A fire in her eyes was ready to erupt. She sucked in a breath and looked like she'd like to chew me out, but the man behind her interjected.

"That's a simple ask. I think I have something." He walked over to a bookshelf on the other side of the room and picked out a red leather-bound book scattered with jagged symbols.

I looked back at the woman who seemed to be placated by a bout of confusion. Resh was obviously in charge in some way, and she looked torn between going along with him and wanting to tell him off too.

"I'm not surprised you've had to go out on your own to find this information. It's much easier for them to benefit from your gifts if you're reliant on them." The man flicked through the pages as he spoke. "I assume they know what your other half is, and they've chosen to keep that information from you too." His accusations didn't seem unlikely.

The man paused on one page. "There we go," he said casually, moving again to another corner of the room where a cabinet stood tucked between more cluttered bookshelves.

Out of the corner of my eye, I spotted Ethlyn and Mabel looking at each other. A silent conversation spoken between the two of them. Their shared look evaporated the moment they noticed my eyes on them.

"Mabel, clear the table." Resh spoke and Mabel moved.

No please? I decided that I didn't really like Resh, even if he could help me.

Returning to the now-cleared table in the centre of the room, the man began arranging crystals around an open jar.

"OK, I'll make you a deal. I read out the chant while you use this to put a drop of your blood into the jar." He took a knife from a drawer in the desk and handed it to me hilt first. "Then I'll seal the jar and your gifts will no longer haunt you. It'll be like you're human."

"Would I ever be able to leave this place?" I asked too quickly.

The man laughed, followed by a snort from Mabel. "It'll *almost* be like you're human. Nothing can actually make you human."

So, I can leave.

My heart quickened. My thoughts solely on getting out of this cave, on seeing my mother again. No one would care to stop me because I wouldn't be a threat anymore.

"OK, I'll do it," I said, hope truly filling my heart for the first time since I had stepped through Dariush's portal.

"Please." The man motioned me to the table. His knife weighed heavy in my right hand as I lifted it over the jar, ready to prick my left middle finger.

My whole body buzzed.

It would finally be over. I could go home.

Resh began his chant. The lines and crosses etched in his arms and neck illuminated with a neon blue hue that stole my attention. That light bounced off something else, something shiny I hadn't noticed before.

A gun sat in its holster, peeking out from underneath a black leather jacket draped over the chair Resh had been sitting in.

"Wait," I said, dropping the knife to the table. It fell with a thud. "What do you get out of this?"

It was a good question. One I should have asked before agreeing to whatever ritual this was. I knew nothing about magic. Nothing about these people. Nothing about what really hid within me.

"I get to keep your gifts." The man smiled cunningly. "As payment of course."

Knowing I wouldn't like the answer, I asked the question anyway. "And what will you do with them?"

The man chuckled again. This time, his murky white eyes illuminated. His smile revealed sharp teeth. "Have you heard of the Red Knights?"

My world stopped.

Nate had spoken of the Red Knights. They were the rebel gang Dariush and Geira had fought against. They'd slaughtered countless Tuath Dé and fara soldiers alike.

I tried to think of what to say to that. Maybe I could tell him I had changed my mind and they'd let me leave, but Resh lunged for the dagger before I could string two words together, and two sets of hands grabbed my upper arms as I jumped backward.

"We made a deal, siren," Resh said, twisting the knife in his hand as he inched closer. "I think you should uphold your end of the bargain."

My body went rigid.

"No," I whispered, desperately willing myself to fight against the grasp of the two women.

The knife felt cold as it hit the notch at the bottom of my neck, a trickle of warm liquid moved down my chest. I only felt the sting as the man lifted the knife from my skin, a deep red streak coated the edge.

Seeing my own blood was enough to awaken the fight within me, the only way I knew how. As the man turned towards the jar, resuming his chant, I sang.

It was a made-up harmony, similar to the one I'd sung at the lake. It took a second to kick in, but when it did, a body to my left dropped to the floor.

Mabel scratched at her ears, trying to pull the melodic torture from her mind. Resh, seemingly unaffected, moved to her side in an instant, dropping the bloodied knife as he did. There was a vibrant glow of blue, and the two figures disappeared.

Ethlyn, who was half bent over and covering her ears, had been left behind.

I stopped singing and wasted no time taking back the knife that held my blood. My melody still echoed through the room as I turned for the door but moving for the knife had given Ethlyn enough time to recover.

With a growl, the woman lunged for me. I screamed, raising my arms to protect myself. She fell to the floor, a torrent of spasms running through her, but not before a deep pain sliced through my arm.

I ran from the room, through the café and into the busy street. The looks that followed me, a panicked and bloodied, knife-wielding woman, stopped me long enough to throw the knife down a dark alleyway.

Then I let my feet direct me home. I didn't dare look back.

CHAPTER FIFTEEN

Zorya

I pushed down the feeling of guilt as I rounded a corner and quickened my pace down a side street. If Geira could see what I was up to she'd be furious, and the fact I had left Annalise to wander the streets of Dubnos alone? Well, I didn't want to think of how she'd react to that.

Leaving Annalise behind wasn't my first choice. There were plenty of obstacles in the under cities that even skilled fara soldiers struggled to navigate.

I breathed deeply and pulled my shoulders back.

No. Annalise was fine on her own.

I recalled the contents of the letter I'd received from Hendrik. The one that was now a pile of ash in Hestia's living room fireplace.

I was to make my way through an alleyway and find a door disguised as a staff entrance to a pub named The Armoury. Finding the pub proved to be the more difficult task. It was nothing more than a sad door, a small window that looked like it had never been cleaned and a faded red A that dangled crookedly over the entrance. It could have easily passed as abandoned, but movement and light on the other side of the window's grime told me otherwise.

I moved onward, not bothering to look around as I slipped down the alleyway and through the staff door. If anyone had evaded my keen skill to tell when someone was following me, they probably deserved to find the entrance.

Being able to hear heartbeats across distances had its perks.

The small hallway behind the door was dark, but faint light and a familiar heartbeat in the room over told me I was in the right place. I greeted the man sourly before I saw him.

"What am I doing here, Hendrik?" My bored tone echoed off the walls. I made a note to adjust my volume as multiple faces turned in my direction. Their disdainful expressions lit up by flaming torches attached to the walls.

It was strange that they'd chosen to use such a medieval form of lightning instead of calling in will-o'-the-wisps or installing crystal lights.

"Always on your own schedule, Zorya." Hendrik offered a playful smile for a moment before remembering where he was. Eight fara soldiers in their usual black flanked the room as if some invisible force occupied the centre. On the opposite side of the room, a wide opening in the rock wall was guarded by two of the council's White Guard dressed head to toe in white combat gear. Gold embroidery in the shape of a tree decorated the space over their hearts.

A pang of envy shot through me for a moment, before I reminded myself as to why I was in the room in the first place.

Do this, whatever this is, and you'll have a uniform like that one day.

The room itself was nowhere near as wide as it was tall. In fact, the roof sloped upwards towards a gaping hole of endless black in its centre. A wheel attached to the rock wall turned slowly, pushing and pulling rope through the blackness. It was like feeding a water bucket into a deep well, only upward. The sight was disorienting.

"Do you know why we're here?" I repeated, making sure to keep my voice low.

"Yes," Hendrik responded, not bothering to hide his gloating. It irked me how much he liked being in the know when I wasn't.

"And?" I didn't hide my frustration.

Hendrik looked to me then. His heartbeat raced with nerves for a moment before he steadied himself with a deep breath. "Just keep an eye on the roof and draw weapons when the solas tell us to." He pointed to the soldiers in white. Despite Hendrik being a solas himself, he, like everyone else, only ever referred to the council's White Guard as solas.

I shrugged off the implication, that dorka like me didn't rise to become members of the White Guard.

"Why draw weapons at all? We're still within Dubnos's wards." I was aware of how close we stood to the city's edge. Regardless, we'd only ever need to draw weapons when travelling between towns where the wards were thinnest or when keeping the peace within them. There was no threat of sluagh here, and I doubted Red Knight rebels would be falling from the black pit in the ceiling.

The room grew colder in an instant.

Hendrik said nothing as a third member of the personal guard made their way into the room and stood beside his guard-mates.

"Weapons out," the guard said, and we all did as instructed. I had equipped myself that morning with tactical knives sheathed to each thigh, choosing to leave my throwing knives at home. Unlike most fara soldiers, I found the twin blades allowed for freedom of movement. With them, fighting became liquid. Like dancing. Just about everyone else in black, including Hendrik, produced long swords.

I steadied my stance and kept my attention focused on the pit above, not sure what to expect. The whirring of rope from a spot on the wall next to the white-clad guards became more erratic before it stopped completely.

A thunderous crash followed by a scraping of metal on rock barrelled towards us from the black pit above. We braced ourselves for impact, covering our faces as dust billowed outwards and entombed us. A final thump of something solid hit the ground in the centre of the room. Vibration shook through my legs, and as the dust settled, I saw what had fallen through that gaping hole in the ceiling.

"Ready!" a White Guard yelled.

A bellowing screech followed, and a creature of wings and shadow entered through the ceiling and landed on the giant metal shipping container in front of me. It bared its teeth in my direction, snapping as claws and talons dug into the metal beneath it. The creature looked desperate to retrieve the contents within. To gorge on it.

Hendrik moved first. The glistening steel of the sword cutting into flesh made of smoke. The beast howled as the injured paw morphed into a single spiked talon. I was looking at a one-legged eagle made of smoke. Tail feathers turned into three more talons, and a clefted beak housed multiple rows of sharp teeth.

The talon that was once a foot shot towards Hendrik, but my twin blades caught it mere inches from his face and sliced the shadowy weapon in two like scissors.

The beast howled and snapped as each fara soldier slashed into its smoke-like body.

Only as the howls became more desperate, its attacks less precise, did the White Guard start to move. They attached a crystal and two metal rods to the front of the container. The metal container hovered slightly before following the third White Guard down the large hallway.

The beast wavered uneasily on top of the container, too weak to either jump off or balance itself. As the container made its way through the threshold, an invisible force worked upon the sluagh and with one last painful shriek, the beast turned to ash.

The ward. They've altered the city's wards to move shipping containers into this room. What the hell was so special about the contents of this container if they had to move it into Dubnos in secret?

My eyes went wide, but there was no time to contemplate why we were doing this or where the White Guards were taking the container.

The whirring of rope started again. This time bringing a shipping container to a complete stop. Two soldiers in black managed to detach the rope from loops on top of the container before another howl echoed through the pit above, closely followed by a second, deeper growl.

We were still fighting both sluagh when the White Guard returned with the crystal, barely glancing at the beasts as he hauled the container into the city's wards. Both turned to ash as we slashed and manoeuvred them into the ward mere minutes before a third container was before us, along with another sluagh trying to disembowel the metal container.

The pattern continued on for hours. Shipping containers descended through the pit and sluagh followed. We slashed and prodded them, taunting them closer to the ward and only returning our attention to the ceiling as smoke became ash.

We had retrieved six containers before the White Guards announced the wards had been restored and we were dismissed.

"What the hell was that!?" I said to Hendrik as we made our way back through the disguised door and into the alleyway. We were both panting, but my right leg had developed some kind of cramp.

"No idea what you're talking about." His expression grew serious before evaporating into his favourite playful smirk. "You should really stop getting into bar fights, Zori. They just lead to you getting hurt." His eyes flicked towards my leg.

I looked down. A gash spanning the near length of my thigh, becoming deeper just before my knee, had bloodied the right side of my pants. One of my dagger holsters, now missing, had taken the brunt of the sizeable attack. A sluagh had made a hit and I hadn't even noticed.

Another fara soldier clapped his arm around Hendrik and began singing a pub song loudly, hiccuping midword for effect.

Hendrik grinned widely as the soldier stumbled along down the alleyway, collecting a chorus of voices feigning drunkenness.

The "drunk" soldiers sang to a tune I'd never heard before. Hiccups peppered the incomplete song, and mumbled words smashed into the next.

Hendrik and I watched as they rounded the corner and carried on down the street, as if they had actually been kicked out of a pub because of a bar fight and were on to their next conquest. As

if they hadn't spent their afternoon butchering countless sluagh
and moving containers at the secret request of the council.

"You should probably get that cleaned up," Hendrik said.

"Any idea how I can do that right now? I'm in the middle of
the city, and my squad thinks I'm off babysitting the new girl." I
winced as I tried to shift my weight onto the injured leg, testing to
see if I could walk by myself.

"You really got yourself in a jam there, huh?" Hendrik observed
mockingly. "I have a place just up the road from here. Small. Off
the books." He leaned in to whisper the words into my ear. "I could
get you fixed up there, then maybe you could repay the favour."
His heartbeat quickened to a distractingly off-kilter rhythm.

"That's dangerous."

"Not if you use protection." He pulled out a crinkly slip of pills
from one of his many pants pockets. I wondered how he'd gotten
his hands on them. "Rubbers aren't the easiest thing to smuggle
down here. Pills are easier to hide. I have, all different kinds at my
place."

Plan B.

I had used the emergency pill once or twice at the college, and it
had completely rocked me for the next two days. That stuff sucked,
but it was far more effective at preventing pregnancy in fae than
humans. Sex was completely against the rules, but the teachers
turned a blind eye, so long as no one got knocked up. I imagined
the rules hadn't changed much for graduates.

I decided after everything I'd been through today, I could use
some fun to take the edge off. More than that, I needed help right
now. Even if Hendrik's came with strings, I'd take it.

At least I know we'll be even afterward.

"Sure, if that stuff even works," I said, trying to come off like I wasn't familiar with the pills.

Hendrik gave me a wicked smile. "Of course they work, sweetheart." He pocketed the pills. "Lean on me. I'll help you walk."

Hendrik looped my arm over his shoulder, grasping my hip. I leaned into him, allowing him to carry the brunt of my weight as we hobbled along towards wherever his private room was.

We rounded the corner, heading in the opposite direction to the drunken crowd, and got about ten metres down the road before my mouth dried and the world spun.

I need blood, was all I could think before I collapsed onto Hendrik and the world went black.

Shaking woke me. I was on the ground and a very blurry Hendrik pushed his wrist to my lips.

"You need blood," he said, echoing my thoughts from seconds ago.

My mouth throbbed as incisors extended to pierce the flesh before me. Blood sprayed across my tongue, and I allowed myself to drink deeply as I was pulled into thoughts and memories hiding within the liquid.

Aoife was in front of me. Leading me towards a four-poster bed wearing nothing but a set of lacy pink lingerie. No, she wasn't leading *me*, she was leading me as Hendrik. The memory flickered, and in Aoife's place stood another woman, one I knew to have graduated the year before me. Her image flickered to other women I knew from the college, each guiding me as Hendrik to a bed. Their bodies pressed into mine. The room changed to a bedroom at the college. Each woman did the same thing. Kissed my neck, my chest, downward. My hands tangled in their hair. Guiding them. Instructing them on exactly how I liked it.

Then I flipped them over, pumping into them hard and fast. Finding my own release with no care as to whether they found theirs.

At the start I let them think they were special. Truth was, I didn't give a fuck what they thought. They assumed this was some hot passionate display of something more and that I'd worship their body in return, or at least cuddle afterward. Why were they all obsessed with lingering?

My interest faded the instant my release came. I'd thoroughly debased them, taken what I needed, and now they were just an annoyance.

They all reacted the same too. Each face crumpled as they were told to leave. On occasion one would refuse. Those few were forced out of the bed, out of the room, sometimes before they could fully dress themselves.

I pulled back from Hendrik's arm, forcing my mind back into the street where I had fainted. A foul taste filled my mouth, sour and overpoweringly floral. Like I'd just licked the sweat off my own skin and chased it with a bottle of perfume.

A face flashed in my mind, and I was thankful hers hadn't been among the collection.

Hendrik gave me a moment to wipe the blood from my mouth before raising my arm over his shoulder again and lifting.

"I-I can't sleep with you," I stammered. My timing might have been poor.

Hendrik chose that moment to let go of my arm and drop me to the floor. I landed on my backside and yelped as a sharp pain stretched through my injured leg.

"What the fuck was that for?" I started to say, but my words were interrupted by Hendrik's sudden change in character.

"Why the fuck not? I gave you blood!" he said, running his hands through his hair, taking two steps backward.

I thought to call him out on his dickishness, but I held back. Hendrik had become someone I'd never seen before. Agitated. Reactive.

"I-I can't do this. I just fainted—" I tried to explain myself, but my words went unheard as Hendrik spoke over me again.

"Aoife was right," Hendrik boomed, throwing his arms in the air. "You're a fucking tease, Zorya! Find your own fucking way home!" He turned in the opposite direction, and I watched as he jogged up to the gritty pub, smashed his fist angrily into the dangling red A sign and continued towards wherever his friends had stumbled off to.

I looked down at my leg and breathed deeply, tears threatened to spill onto my cheeks.

I deserve this. Maybe not Hendrik's reaction, but to be left injured in a dirty street to hobble home by myself? That I deserved.

Turning onto the side of my good leg, I crawled out of the gutter and over to the wall of the building behind me. Holding onto a short ledge in the wall, I lifted myself up, thankful that the sluagh hadn't slashed my arms too. I allowed myself a second to catch my breath before moving again. The first step onto my injured leg was agony, but at least the bleeding had stopped. The wound was still very much open. I'd need to drink more blood, and soon, before my body could start the healing process.

This is what I had left Annalise for, and to top it off, I had burned my only bridge to working with the White Guard.

There was no way I'd be able to find Annalise and make it back home before my leg completely gave out or before I needed more blood. If she was even where I had left her.

I looked up to see the will-o'-the-wisps had inched closer to the base of the peaks and the light of dusk had blanketed the city streets. I moved in the direction of Hestia's hole-in-the-wall.

My thoughts darkened with every, shattering step.

CHAPTER SIXTEEN

Dariush

A ll Zorya had to do was give her a fucking book and keep her safe in the house. Instead, she'd taken Annalise into the city and left her there, all to follow up on some stupid errand for the council. Geira told me the solas boy had handed Zorya a note during their first patrol. We were both very familiar with the secret duties the White Guard liked to give newly graduated soldiers.

They'd never let a dorka rise to their ranks, but that never stopped the solas recruits from shovelling down unfavourable work to an ambitious dorka.

I'd had a mind to force Zorya to put out the flames, to show me the piece of paper she'd been burning in the fireplace that night. I was standing by the doorway at the time. It would have taken a lot more energy with her than with Annalise, but the shadows within her wouldn't refuse me. Still, I'd promised myself not to use my control over darker souls for trivial things.

My mind flickered to the day I stopped Annalise from snapping at her mother, and again to that moment in front of the council. They hadn't been trivial matters.

And neither had this turned out to be.

I'd been wrong about Zorya. With exceptional grades and a rebellious reputation, I thought I'd stumbled upon a rare freethinker. I thought she might have been like her parents, sympathetic to their cause maybe. Instead, she'd become more like the other fara soldiers, obediently following the masters that raised them with no consideration for the family they were stolen from.

I wouldn't put my faith in her again.

Annalise had proven she couldn't be left anywhere by herself. I arrived home from patrol with Geira to find her gone. I was about to rip the entire city apart to find her when she stumbled through the backdoor, her arm sliced open.

She was too delicate, too sheltered for the world I'd pulled her into. Fate was playing some sick game with both of us.

The day I met her, I thought I'd made a mistake, or that the Nine Daughters' prophecy had sent me to the wrong place. Her voice was too beautiful. She was too much light, too much goodness. How could I ever deserve someone like her?

I still felt that way, even when I saw the shadow within her take over, death consuming life, anger stealing joy. Even as those two writhing bodies screamed themselves to a hellish end.

Had the shadow within her appeared so violently that day as a way to call out to my own? I thought about that a lot. The deaths she blamed herself for might have been prevented if I just hadn't sought her out.

If I hadn't been a selfish cunt.

She'd clearly been in a fight today, but I hadn't pushed her to talk about it yet. As I took in her fragile state, shrinking in a leather armchair, knitted blanket around her shoulders, I wondered what happened to the other guy.

Fuck.

The other guy. There was no way she ran away from an attack without using her song. And if her attacker survived it, they'd have seen the change the song made in her. I could only hope whoever that was, they were either dead, stupid or not inclined to tell the council.

One of the queen's healers worked on her arm. The underdweller, a Tuath Dé who'd found a new home in Dubnos, possessed gifts that could mend living bodies. She'd managed to stop the bleeding and, judging by Annalise's pained expression, looked to be in the process of fusing veins, nerves and muscle back together. It would take a few days to a week for the fingers and wrist to regain full motion.

Had Annalise been human, her recovery would take a month with the help of the healer. If the healing had been performed by a human doctor, that time would have stretched past six months.

It always amazed me what humans could do despite how fragile they were and with what little time they had in the world. Human technology didn't work beyond the veil, but I often found myself wondering about the ways it could benefit this kingdom. I even shared that information with my mother once.

Since the queen had never left her kingdom for the entirety of her reign, there was no way to prove to her just how remarkable the human version of magic was.

She'd brushed me off and told me that I could find a way to make it happen when I was king. I thought she was taunting me, or that she'd forgotten which son she was talking to again, like she did from time to time. Aed was next in line for the throne, but then she grabbed my arm desperately. Her usual cunning and sharpness vanished to reveal fearful eyes flickering wildly with colour and a voice as faceted as a fractured geode.

"I'll never let the Red King take the throne again. He's just like him," she'd repeated over and over. I knew I should have left it alone when she'd snapped back to herself and rattled off about Hestia's Samhain plans like nothing happened. I couldn't.

We'd had a long chat after that.

It was the queen's vulnerable state of unknowing that came to mind as I watched Annalise from my perch in the doorway.

Annalise winced again from her seat. I'd given the healer plenty of time to sew the foundations of her work. It was time to get answers.

"You're mostly done. Talk." I felt a look of disapproval from the healer and ignored it. My focus was on Annalise, whose dark eyes were wide, framed by a very pale face.

Tread softly, Dariush.

I kept my gaze level. The healer must have realised that I wasn't interested in her being there, nor was I about to back down, because she stood, mumbled something about advising Hestia and left the room.

"Where did Zorya leave you?" I asked firmly as I walked over to her. My bravado was an act. Her scent of bergamot and dried lavender filled my nose as I stepped closer. It made me want to fall to my knees and hold her tightly in my arms. This hold she had over me had to be supernatural, but I couldn't let her see it. It would make the betrayal that much worse when she found out why she was really here. I settled for crouching close to her beside the armchair.

Her eyes never left me, and for a moment, it looked as if she had forgotten how to speak.

"Uh—a—music store," she spluttered.

I picked up a clean, damp cloth that had been placed next to the healer's supplies on a short stand by the chair and held her wrist carefully in mine. Her cold fingers brushed my forearm, knuckles kissing my skin like drops of morning frost. I needed to warm her up.

Slowly, I wiped dried blood off her skin. The quicker I got information out of her, the sooner I could get her warm, but I couldn't rush her either.

She was going to have to be more specific than that. There were a lot of music stores scattered around the city. "What was the name?"

"I-I don't remember." Something in her deflated slightly, and I knew she wasn't lying. She wanted to answer me.

Good.

"But there was a café a few streets over. A woman—she was a fomóire." Her mouth fumbled around the foreign word. "She gave me a pastry. I was hungry."

My fingers on her wrist caught her pulse quickening. *Panic.* She sucked in a breath. *Did she feel guilty for what happened to her?*

The blood was almost all cleaned up, but I continued brushing the cloth over her skin in long, slow strokes. Annalise didn't take her arm away.

"Is that where this happened?" I kept my voice even.

She nodded.

"I started talking to the woman. Ethlyn, I think was her name." Annalise frowned as if trying to make sense of the memory. "She took me to see her friends in the back of the store. I said too much and—and—" Her voice quickened, and I slowed the rhythmic movements of my hand. "There was a man. He . . ."

Her pause stretched on too long. So, I stopped.

It was almost painful to do it, but I forced myself to let go of her wrist and pulled back. I placed the bloodied cloth back on the stand and waited for her heavy breathing to slow down.

She leaned in slightly, not liking the distance either. Not moving her arm from the place I'd held it. She wanted that skin-to-skin contact again. That rhythmic sensation to distract her from the world.

I waited.

"He tried to take my . . . song." A pause and another frown. "I *wanted* him to take my song," she corrected herself, tears threatened to spill forward, filling the corners of her telluric eyes. They were almost as dark as the two marks on her left cheek.

I took hold of her wrist again because she'd continued like I'd wanted her to and told me more than I expected, but also because I couldn't hold back my need to comfort her much longer.

I laid a hand on the space beside the partially healed gash in her arm, my thumb softly moving in circles. Tension left her shoulders and she continued.

"They seemed to be interested in what I was. And—and I asked him if he knew how I could get rid of the siren song."

It took everything within me to keep my movements even in spite of an old conversation racing through my head.

Annalise had called herself a monster the first day we met. I knew she held herself responsible for the death of those men, but to think she'd pull herself apart, risk so much, to remove that part of herself. I should have seen it.

"He said he could do it, but I changed my mind at the last minute." *And he attacked me* were the words I knew she'd left out.

Annalise was looking away now, her face pale. I could only imagine she was reliving the attack as we spoke.

Rage washed over me. I wanted to break something. Find the scum that did this to her and break them. She'd been so trusting, with Zorya and these people, and they'd taken advantage of it.

I can't talk. I've been taking advantage of her trust every damn day since I stole her from her home.

I chose my next words carefully. "Did these people have names?""

"Ethlyn was the woman from the café. The other two were Mabel and Resh," she said softly.

Fuck. Those names I knew, but I kept my recognition hidden. "What made you change your mind?" I asked, still circling my thumb on her arm.

"Resh said he was going to keep my song as payment. He asked if I knew the Red Knights, and I couldn't."

I looked into her face. Those trapped tears freed themselves and flowed down her cheeks, but something else hid within those dark depths. Pain. Regret. Guilt.

"I can't let anyone else have that kind of weapon."

Weapon.

Guilt of my own rose to the surface. I wanted to tell her not to think of herself that way, but I would only have been a hypocrite.

That's about the only thing you excel at nowadays, Dariush.

I stood and pressed my lips to her forehead, not entirely sure if I was giving her or myself space. Her shoulders relaxed again under my hands as I let the kiss linger. I moved my hands to hold her face and wiped away tears with my thumbs. The two dark marks on her left cheek warmed beneath my palm.

"I'll get you some Earl Grey," I said before walking out of the room, keenly aware of her eyes still on me.

***

Geira was waiting in the kitchen, her jumpsuit-clad legs dangling off the edge of the counter.

"Zorya is a piece of fucking work," I growled, pulling up a chair at the round yellow table like an actual adult. I would have pulled up my second for not using Hestia's furniture appropriately, but I needed someone in my corner.

Everything was turning to shit.

"What? Your princess scrape her arm in the big bad city?" Geira taunted, tossing a braid of gold hair behind her shoulder.

"It was a fucking gouge, Geira. And your little upir left her for fucking dead."

"You've told Zorya nothing. She's not the type to follow along with orders when she can't see shit at the end of the tunnel."

Her words directly contradicted the thoughts I'd had of the woman only moments ago.

"You're the squad leader. Not me." Geira jumped down from the counter. "And I'm not the one who's defending an unstable monster who hasn't exactly taken responsibility for her gifts. She didn't even try during my lesson with her."

"Jaz and Nate have no problem with her."

"That's because she's a bookworm. They're giving her history lessons. Try anything practical with her and she baulks," Geira said, making her way to a cupboard to produce two ceramic cups and a fat square bottle that hid behind them. After placing the items on the table, Geira pulled up a chair and poured me a double shot of whisky before pouring her own.

"You know I can't tell Zorya." I took a long swig, the burn releasing some of my tension. "Can't trust her to take care of anyone but herself. And now she's in the pocket of the White Guard."

"Bullshit. She's smart, she knows there's no place for her in their world. But that's all she has to aim for right now. Give her something else to fight for." Geira downed the shot and smacked the base down on the table twice. "Reminds me of someone," she taunted, voice husky from the burn. She rose and headed towards the door, leaving me to clean up the cups and lost drops of whisky.

The valkyrie was right. *She was always fucking right.* It wasn't that long ago I was running around for a spot on the White Guard, seeking to better my own standing. Only, that mistake cost the lives of four fara soldiers.

Still, I couldn't help but smile to myself. Geira cared for Zorya.

I felt bad over changing the plan when I found Annalise. After the death of our squad members, Geira and I had devised a plan to be paired together. The Tuath Dé were tactical with pairings. Solas fara were a prized commodity and some, like the valkyrie, possessed more dominant genes. All I'd needed to do was not piss off the Tuath Dé and there was a good chance Geira and I would have been paired.

There would have been no children between us. I didn't care much for that anyway. The Tuath Dé would have pinned our lack of offspring on my abnormal genes. They'd be fucking clueless.

Geira would've been as free as she could be under the Tuath Dé's thumb. Only now, the stakes were higher for her. The Tuath Dé boy would never force anything on her, but the council would ask questions when the time came.

I'd done the exact opposite of what I should have.

My plan had to work, for Geira's safety as well as Annalise's. Maybe my own.

CHAPTER SEVENTEEN

Zorya

"**I**'m putting you up for night shift."

Dariush had started questioning me the second I stumbled through the door. A puddle of blood had formed where I stood, trapped between Dariush and the door to Dubnos City.

His questions were thorough, but I was tight-lipped. Despite Hendrik leaving me wounded, I took my oaths of secrecy seriously. A little blood loss wasn't going to change that.

"You'll be patrolling the city every night till ascension. Geira will patrol with you for the first week. You'll be with me for the second. And when you're not on patrol, you're here. Cleaning, sleeping or doing whatever Hestia asks of you. Understood?"

Every night?

My body temperature seemed to drop by a full degree. Nothing happened on night patrol. The city only required half as many soldiers to patrol at night for that reason. And unless I could sneak out during the day, there'd be no way I'd be attending any more secret jobs for the council. I could just about kiss that white uniform goodbye.

"But I don't have dark vision," I said, eyes darting to two silent figures leaning against the staircase posts a few feet behind Dariush. Geira looked through me, and I shivered. It was clear I was getting no sympathy from her.

I looked to Jaz as if he might jump to my defence, silently pleading with him to corroborate my pathetic excuse. Jaz's gaze wasn't as cold as Geira's, but he kept a stone-like expression.

United front it is.

"Then I guess you'll need to rely on your *other* senses." Dariush took a step forwards as he spoke, the words a violent growl emitting a hidden message.

Glamour wasn't a sense, but my strong hearing was, and I definitely hadn't shared that information with him. *What else does he know about me?*

My tongue stuck to the roof of my dry mouth as the room swayed slightly. In one swift movement, the towering man slipped past me and opened the door to the city.

"I need to feed!" I called after him, my voice sounding more like a whine than a request for help.

"Ask your pair." His response was another growl, barely discernible as he slammed the door behind him. Geira moved towards me. Hope made me feel light as she stood an inch away, then it shattered to the bloodied floor as she slipped past me too and followed Dariush out into the city.

Jaz was by my side the moment they were gone. "I'll do it. Nate's sleeping," he said as he lifted my arm over his shoulder and carried me towards the kitchen. We passed the living room on our way, and I was sure Jaz deliberately slowed down enough so I would see Annalise.

The shadow dog cuddled her feet as she sipped a mug of something hot in an oversized armchair. It was the bandaged arm and white, stricken face that told me something was off. She looked so fragile.

What the fuck happened to her?

Dariush's anger was making more sense. Guilt washed over me for the billionth or so time that day, but I shoved it back as I hobbled forward. She probably got distracted by the will-o'-the-wisps again and had a bad fall. It was too late to do anything now anyway.

"Sleeping? It's a bit early to be in bed." Outside, late evening had given way to night, and the last lingering light of day had turned Dubnos City into a graveyard of silhouettes. Still, it was too early for bed.

"He's been having trouble sleeping. It's something to do with some nightmare that's going around," Jaz said as we entered the kitchen. A ceramic mug and a square bottle had been left on the table among spillages of something strong.

"Going around? You mean a dream that's . . . *shared*?" The room spun in front of me.

"Yeah, he didn't think it was possible either," Jaz said as he guided me to a chair and began clearing away the mess on the table.

"What happens in them?" I forced myself to ask. It could have been any question. I was deteriorating, fast.

Jaz pulled up a chair in front of me and rolled up his sleeve. My teeth sank into his skin the second he offered it to my lips, and he flinched. Warmth spread through me as I drank, pain shooting to my leg as the strange workings of my body healed the wound at a quicker pace.

"Darkness and tumbling," Jaz said through gritted teeth, turning his head from me. Jaz had always been squeamish around blood. I appreciated him volunteering now. "Screams. He didn't say much beyond that."

My mind drifted to a place hidden within the blood. I was in a small town somewhere on the outskirts of Dubnos City, running after a naked man with a white crystal in his ear. He was babbling strange things. I yelled for Nate and looked behind me only to see Nate frozen in fear. His eyes bloodshot, sweat beading at his forehead.

Before I could move to him, I was pushed to the floor. The naked man had doubled back and pushed past me. He grabbed Nate by the shoulders, shaking him. "You see it all. You know. They look like angels but they're not, are they. They won't help us. But you could." The man was manic. Recognition flashed in Nate's face, but before he could react, another patrol team arrived and began to pull the man away.

"Demons! Demons!" The man struggled against the grip of two soldiers. He was terrified of them.

I found myself back in the kitchen, my stomach heavier.

"Is he sure they're not his own dreams?" I said after one final gulp, wiping the excess blood from my mouth.

"You know the mora have no original bone in their body." Jaz laughed, allowing himself a moment of lightness before his face turned grim again. "He thinks the humans are dreaming it." He rolled down his sleeve, not looking at the patch of blood I'd smeared across his arm.

Ugh, that was messy. "How does he know?"

"A human man was caught running through the streets of Kil on our patrol today," Jaz continued. "Kept talking about angels and demons. Anyway, Nate said it was like he knew the dreams he was having were this man's dreams, but also someone else's."

"Let me guess, the man was naked."

"You did the thing?" Jaz said. "Oh, could you have not done the thing!? You could have seen anything just now."

I had to laugh at that.

None of it made sense. Sure, the mora's specialty were dreams. Depending on the individual mora's skill, they could view the dreams of whoever they touched. Even see a person they knew well and peer into that part of their mind.

It was useful for all number of reasons. Spying, health, but the Tuath Dé trained their mora soldiers to be exceptional decipherers of fear. In battle, that meant soldiers who knew the soft spots of their enemy.

Nate was an exceptional mora, but this was the first time I was hearing of his gifts manifesting in this way. I supposed we had both been keeping secrets of our true abilities from the world.

"Do you think the human had second sight?"

"Maybe. You'd hope he'd be used to seeing the fae by now if that were true," Jaz said with a shrug. The implications of his statement were clearly lost on him.

To lure a human beyond the veil was to give them the gift of agelessness and immortality. It was also to curse them with eternal imprisonment. Once beyond the veil, they could never leave.

It was an easy and cruel way to silence humans who knew too much about the fae, particularly humans with second sight. The practice had been made illegal since Dubh had taken the throne, and humans rarely stumbled beyond the veil on their own.

"He'll figure it out." Jaz shrugged, bringing the conversation back to Nate's dream dilemma. "But you should figure out where you stand with Annalise. What the fuck happened, Zorya? She was cut up pretty bad."

"Oh, and I wasn't!?" I accused.

Jaz got up from his chair and moved to a drawer by the sink. "The girl's never seen blood in her life, probably never been in a fight before. You know what the city is like. There are crazy people everywhere."

The details didn't slip past me. *Someone had attacked her?*

"She killed two people, Jaz. You all just assume she can't fend for herself. And she's alive, isn't she?" I said, unable to shake the defensive tone. Once again, guilt slammed into my chest, and I fought hard to keep it from showing on my face.

"Here, you're good enough to clean up the mess you trailed in," Jaz said as he threw me a towel.

I followed his eyes to the kitchen doorway. Sure enough, blood drops lined their way through the threshold and beyond.

Rolling my eyes, I stood, threw the towel on the ground and very lazily mopped up the mess with one foot.

I ignored Jaz's groan of annoyance behind me as I shuffled out of the kitchen.

***

Dariush woke me a little after midnight to demand that I show him where I'd been stationed with the White Guard. I didn't have time to pull on more than boots and pants, my oversized sleeping shirt half tucked in, before Geira kicked me out the door and returned to her bed. At least she was getting some sleep.

Nate wasn't.

I was more surprised by his bloodshot eyes and drawn face than the fact that he was to accompany us. He looked like he hadn't slept in a week.

My leg had almost fully healed, making the trip back to the grimy bar front quicker than it had been earlier in the opposite direction.

Dariush had taken my claim that I couldn't see in the dark seriously and warned me of steps and potholes that remained dull under the will-o'-the-wisps' starlight.

For a moment I thought about showing them somewhere else. Another hole-in-the-wall room behind a dingy bar, maybe? No one had actually told me to keep the White Guard's task a secret from other fara soldiers, but I was sure it was implied.

Nate's state set off my internal alarm. If what he was experiencing was connected, and Dariush seemed to think so since he'd brought Nate in the first place, I needed to find out how.

It would have been an easy choice to slip down a lone alleyway and then claim I was lost. But in my indecision, I found my feet kept their own pace, directly to the dishevelled A dangling above a grotty door.

I stared at it for a moment. Willed my feet to stop. Willed my mouth to claim that it wasn't a mission at all. That I had gotten into a drunken bar fight and lost, but an image of Geira flashed in my mind. The look of disappointment that painted her face the second I had arrived home to find Annalise shaking in that chair.

It was Geira's face that made me take that one extra step towards the alleyway and point to the hidden entrance.

This was it. Dariush would know that the White Guard was smuggling something in, likely on the orders of the TDE, and . . . and what? *What will he do with that information? What will it mean to him?*

Only, when I followed the two men into the dark space, there was nothing. Not even when Dariush called for a single will-o'-the-wisp to illuminate the room, and its small bright frame touched everything with light.

The hole in the ceiling had been patched with rotted wooden slats. They could have been sitting there for decades. The ropes used to pull the shipping containers into the space had been removed. The brackets rusted and dangling from their sockets. Even the threshold the White Guards had shoved the containers through was now solid rock.

"There was a hole in the ceiling!" I pointed to the wooden slats, unsure what to make of the room in front of me. "They lowered shipping containers into the room, and we fought off about a dozen sluagh. They dropped the city's wards around us! This whole space was open!" They had to believe me. I wouldn't be made a liar.

Of course, Hendrik would have left me stranded and without an alibi. Of course, the White Guards would have cleaned up after themselves. Of course, Dariush wasn't privy to whatever secret plans the council was enacting.

I wanted to blame them all, but I couldn't shake the feeling that I'd majorly fucked up.

I searched Dariush's face and wasn't sure what to make of it. He was angry. So angry, it looked to be smothering anything else he might have felt or thought.

I turned to Nate. "You believe me?" The words came out as more of a question than I liked.

"I—" was all he could come up with before his eyes settled on the space behind me. Nate moved to the threshold that was no longer a threshold quicker than he should have been able to, given his weakened state. He placed his forehead and a shaky hand on the solid rock and closed his eyes. His face strained as if he was listening for something only just out of earshot. And before either Dariush or I could ask him what was wrong, he said, "It's nothing. We should go home."

On our walk back to Hestia's home, silence amplified the tension that shifted between the three of us. I was ordered back to bed as soon as we returned and felt a pang of rejection as Dariush and Nate made their way to the living room to discuss their findings without me.

I tried to keep my distaste for Dariush front of my mind. I even thought about telling them both off for excluding me. But none of this was their fault. I had fucked up. If I were in Dariush's position, I wouldn't trust me either.

CHAPTER EIGHTEEN

Annalise

"**F**ocus," Dariush growled.

It never ceased to amaze me how little value the demand to focus actually brought to the table. I *was* focusing. Every little ounce of me was committed to getting this stupid light to form in my hands, and yet, I sat in an empty warehouse completely lightless.

Punching bags, a climbing wall and several tall structures that were expected to be jumped over, an impossible feat if anyone had asked me before I witnessed Geira's warm-up routine, surrounded the space Dariush and I were using.

This was the space Geira and I had used to train in hand-to-hand combat only a few days ago. I thought I had been making progress, but the attack yesterday proved otherwise. Under the threat of a knife to my throat, I'd gone completely still.

I was ready to beg Dariush to teach me how to defend myself this morning, only he beat me to it. Today was about learning how to bring forth the light that came so easily to fara, and fomóire, as I'd recently learned.

"What are you even thinking about?" Dariush barked with disappointment.

"Bright things, Hestia's fireplace, the wispy things," I said, rattling off whatever light came to mind.

"Wispy—?" Dariush stopped his question abruptly and sighed as he realised what I was referring to. There were so many new things down here, all with complicated names. How did he expect me to remember them all?

"Maybe I'm like Jaz. Maybe I just don't have one," I said, throwing my hands up and rising from my seated position on the floor. The practice of focusing was a little like Nate's attempts at getting me to meditate. And I was bored.

"Jaz isn't like us. You have a light, you're just not trying," Dariush said, rising to his feet too.

I wondered what my friend would have thought had he heard the prince talking about him like that.

"You say you don't know what else I am, but you seem to be pretty certain I can do this," I said with another huff.

"You *can* do this." Dariush's stern expression became a shade darker.

Why is he so insistent on helping me? I thought back to last night, to the way he had paid attention to me as he wiped blood from my arms.

"And what's in it for you?" My question seemed to catch him off guard, and he bent down to roll up the mats we had been sitting on. I could tell he was avoiding my eyes.

"I'm your pair. You die, I don't get another one," he said, casually repeating words I had heard before in the Glistening City. As if my death would be a minor inconvenience.

"You could live without me," I stated flatly, poking him to give a better response. His shoulders tensed at my words. "Why bring me to this place? Why lie to your leaders for me? I imagine you wouldn't be their favourite pet anymore if they found out." I tried to evoke an element of Zorya's venom as I spoke.

Dariush still wasn't looking at me as he walked to a shelf by the wall and packed away our mats.

"You're procrastinating." His tone returned to the controlled, low vibration I was used to with him.

"And you're not answering me." *Checkmate.* I could hold my own with this man. I would.

Dariush turned and walked up to me. He was a breath away, eyes dark, and towering over me when he said, "Produce a light and I'll share my secrets."

Damn. Scratch that.

My heart quickened at our closeness. I could feel the heat of his body rising from his chest. How could someone so rigid, so serious, inspire such a reaction from me?

"Well, then how did you learn?" I asked, finally finding my composure.

A small crinkle appeared at the corner of Dariush's mouth and vanished just as quickly as it arrived, as if my question had unlocked a moment of joy in his memory. "The light first becomes accessible to most of us from the age of eight. That's why the Tuath Dé collect fara at that age," he said, seriousness returning to his tone. "We're mostly useless before that."

I frowned. Children, especially ones so young, should be free to play and learn about the good things in the world. Not stolen for the *use* of a backwards empire. Not for the first time since I'd left home, I felt hatred for the Tuath Dé and a deep sadness for the world trapped under their thumb.

"I trained with the queen's guard. I was able to produce the light by the time I was seven and began teaching the new fara initiates when I was eight."

"Of course, you did. The spoiled prince with personal trainers got it before everyone else even started trying," I said dryly, folding my arms as I spoke. I winced at how childish my words sounded, especially since his situation had been far from spoiled.

Dariush tightened his jaw and let out a grunt of annoyance before his eyes widened. It was the most surprised I had ever seen the man. The look was gone in an instant, and he turned towards the warehouse exit without a word.

For a moment I expected him to call back to me, tell me to wait where I was or go with him. Tell me literally anything. But as he disappeared through the door, I realised I wasn't getting another word from him.

"What is it with people not telling me where they're going?" I whispered under my breath before running after Dariush.

***

It was a short walk to Hestia's home from the Fáilte warehouse. We barely saw a soul on our way back. For a moment, I thought we had reached our destination. Maybe he'd become fed up with me and I could steal a break to paint in my books while Obsidian kept me company by the fire. My hopes were crushed as Dariush continued his fervent pace through the hallway of the house and out through the backdoor.

The city was in stark contrast to Fáilte. People walked, biked, stole rides on trams in every direction. Some looked rushed, carrying bags and boxes to their destinations. Others moseyed along casually. As we neared the centre of the city, those moseying seemed to be mostly Tuath Dé. Tall, lithe people flaunting a flawless beauty, an impeccably lavish wardrobe and delicately pointed ears.

Like in the Glistening City, I couldn't help but stare at them.

Our pace slowed as we reached the castle. It was as beautiful as I remembered it, even better in the faux daylight. An hourglass of crystal structures, glistening and multidimensional. Today it boasted colours of blue and dark green, shifting like a seaweed-ridden tide across a white shore. Walls rose and encircled the castle in a wavy line, reminiscent of a ship's sails.

Standing tall at the palace entrance were grey-blue figures in black uniforms, all marked with the blue crosses of the queen's guard.

A flicker of movement along the left side of the curved wall snagged my attention. It was as if someone had walked out of the castle from the side of the wall.

"What are they doing?" Dariush said, as he caught sight of the movement.

A man in a white uniform with a purple mark on his chin appeared out of nowhere beside the wall. I thought I was seeing things, or that maybe some soldiers could do that. *Is teleporting real?*

It wasn't long before another man in white appeared from a space where the wall folded in on itself like a curtain. A dark patch on his forehead and a brown bag at his hip, stark against the uniform.

Without so much as a glance around them, they turned and begun skirting the wall towards the back of the castle. Resuming their patrol as if they'd been circling it all along.

Where had they come from?

Dariush moved towards the men immediately, never once looking away from the place they appeared. There was a fury in his pace.

The wall of crystal sea breathed and danced as we moved closer to that spot. It was hidden in plain sight.

I wouldn't have noticed the opening had a solid block of white light not shifted over it.

There. Where the wall wiggled outwards and folded in on itself, there was a gap big enough for one person to slip through.

Dariush was first to move into the tight space. I followed, feeling my way as the wall bent backward. The texture of its surface felt rough and granular against my fingers. Bending again and again, the space was like a short labyrinth, ending at the start of a staircase.

There were no wispy things in this cave, but my eyes didn't need time to adjust to the darkness. I had attributed that skill to the years of walking to Lucknow's lake every morning before dawn, but now there were other possibilities. With questions of what I was circling through my brain, I mentally stored that observation as another potential clue.

Dariush had disappeared ahead of me. Grunts of anger echoed upwards through the tight space. Twenty-seven steps exactly, and I was standing at the mouth of a crystal trove. A mine.

Cloaked by the darkness, the cloudy stones appeared dormant. Like they were sleeping through a cold night.

I could make out faint colour. Red specks in a span of white. They clustered around each other, and large work benches and pickaxes littered the spaces where some had been removed or sawed back.

Heavy breathing from Dariush alerted me to where he crouched. The man I had begun to associate with composure and unrivalled focus, to a fault, held his head in his hands. Something bubbled beneath the surface. Whatever it was, he was working hard to keep it down.

I knew we were underneath the castle. Beyond that, I could only guess as to why Dariush had wanted to take me here, or why the guards' presence in this place evoked such a reaction out of him.

"This place is important to you," I said, not really knowing what to offer beyond that. It was clear the crystal trove under the palace was supposed to be a secret. And someone, the guards in white, had desecrated it.

"This is where the fomóire trained me." Dariush's whisper was one of mourning. He rose and walked towards a cluster of white stones. A large patch smoothed as if a saw had cut away some small, jagged pieces.

"These are the sister stones. They talk to each other," he said as he placed his hand upon the space. It was so absurd a statement that, if Dariush hadn't sounded so broken, I would have laughed. Instead I kept quiet. "The red stones awaken the white stones and give them purpose. It's how we keep the kingdom protected from the sluagh.

"Dubh gave them a few hundred once because she had to. Kept the rest of them hidden here." He waved to the expanse in front of him, pain etched on his face. He didn't have to tell me who *they* were.

"When it was obvious they had more, she thought they'd managed to duplicate them or create fakes but . . ." Dariush was
rambling now. I still knew too little about this world, about the
politics, but even I understood the horrific impact the Tuath Dé's
knowledge of this place would bring.

Or had already brought.

My hands clasped the crystals that were trapped in silver around
my wrists. The thought that these were the white sister stones sent
a chill through me.

"They're stealing from us. They're always stealing from us and
it's never enough." Dariush's voice cracked. The man I had come
to care for looked defeated. "They're after the stones, all of them,
so they can gain more control. Over everything and everyone
till the entire world kneels before them." His pained voice grew
into a rageful growl. It bubbled upward, threatened to spill over
into something destructive, monstrous. But the man breathed in
deeply, demanded the storm within himself to quieten, and after
a few moments of silence, he'd regained the control I knew him to
hold.

It dawned on me, after all this time, that Dariush was just as
much a desperate prisoner of the Tuath Dé as I was. *How long has
he wanted his servitude to end?*

Without being asked, I sat cross-legged on the floor of the cave
with my hands in front of me. Taking from Nate's meditation
lessons, I breathed deep and found a sacred place within myself.

It too was overflowing with pain. Resentment for the hand I'd
been dealt, for how little I'd been trusted with the direction of my
own life. That deep well pulled to the surface a terrible grief, one

that came with the overwhelming thought that maybe I shouldn't be trusted with the kind of control I sought.

The song inside me was too violent, and I was too fragile, too quick to anger to be the vessel it needed. Maybe Dariush could be the key to that. Maybe I just needed someone to guide me away from the destructive monster I'd already started to become.

I drew air into this place, fanning flames and exhaling from it. Focusing on the energy it provided. It took four deep breaths, in and out, in and out, before that fire demanded to be released.

A spark came to life in front of me. Just a single blue ember that flickered before being snuffed out like a candle, leaving the softest waft of smoke in its wake.

"Did you see that!?" I spoke finally, my voice cracking with excitement. I'd done it. The thing I was so sure I'd never be able to do.

I looked to Dariush. His eyes were wide, unreadable, and then he smiled. "You did it."

We sat there together, and he watched as I practiced. Offering words of encouragement, asking again about what I had been thinking of. Only this time his words held an air of curiosity. I told him about the place of power within myself as I worked to find it again. I wasn't sure how long we'd been sitting there before I produced another light. It was the same size as the last, the same flake of fire that snuffed out within a second, leaving the same wisp of smoke in its wake.

It didn't matter to Dariush how big or how long I could hold that ember, the simple fact that I had achieved something was enough.

And for the first time in my life, I felt that small achievement was enough for me too.

CHAPTER NINETEEN

Zorya

Will-o'-the-wisps glittered high among the city's ceiling pillars. Pinks, purples and oranges twinkled high above. Too high to really throw projections of light on the floor, but low enough to tell that it was late dusk.

The air in Dubnos's hospitality quarter buzzed with excitement. There was a reason we had been stationed here. It was a classic Friday night, and it seemed everyone in the city had come to this quarter to eat, dance and drink the stress of their week away.

For most soldiers it was the end of their shift. Some would join in on the frivolity. Most would turn in for the night, orders of their squad leader. On a better night, I would be among them.

Tonight was not a better night.

Geira and I began our patrol at the centre of the quarter, meeting with other soldiers unlucky enough to receive night duty. Three squad leaders stood in this meeting place ready to relay the information of the day.

Nothing dramatic.

A bakery owner was reprimanded for displaying a breadbasket lined with a red-and-white linen cloth in their front window. The colour of the Red Knight rebels. Also the colour of the kingdom's former dictator. To use excessive amounts of red in any way was

frowned upon by the people of Dubnos. It showed a disrespect to
their queen, but a red-and-white cloth was nothing to faint over.

The bakery had been searched for propaganda and weaponry,
but the soldiers came up short.

Even to me, someone who appreciated being thorough, it
seemed excessive.

After the squad leaders moved out, Geira and I worked towards
our first area for patrol. Food stalls peppered the streets, just like
at the Samhain festival, and revellers moved between them. Some
danced to music played by street performers, others relished art
displayed for the public.

The street was lively. On any other night the energy would have
bolstered me along. I would have let it take me over.

But *exciting* and *night shift* were words that soldiers didn't want
to hear together. On nights like this people got drunk, they got
cocky, and worst of all, they let themselves get complacent. A
well-mannered grandmother could get arrested just because she
felt she could vent about the Tuath Dé at a restaurant after one
glass of rosé too many.

"So, when are you going to tell me what actually happened?"
Geira's words ran through me like a knife. Of course she didn't
believe me. Why would she? I had tried so hard to become the best
soldier I could possibly be. To become as well respected as she was.
And not only did I fuck that up, I lost her trust in the process.

I couldn't keep my hurt from bubbling to the surface as I said a
little too loudly, "I already told Dariush what happened! I wasn't
lying!"

A sharp-toothed fae woman with green-tinted skin and a human selling her fabric flowers at a nearby stall each shot me an incredulous look at my outburst. I ignored them.

"Not that," Geira started, choosing to ignore the judgement wafting in our direction. "You're denied a spot as squad leader, get called a slut—on a regular basis apparently—and then you go do the bidding of some guy who looks at you like a piece of meat. What's up with that?"

"Ugh! I didn't do his *bidding*." The words stumbled out of my mouth stupidly.

"He chose to give you the letter. He knew you'd do anything to gain back the Tuath Dé's faith. Probably got you to do all the heavy lifting too." Geira jerked her chin, as if to point to the spot on my leg that had been ripped open only a few nights earlier.

It had mostly healed, but I still walked with a slight limp.

"You don't think the Tuath Dé authorised the job?" *How did she know I received a letter?* I shook away that question.

"Oh, they were the head orchestrator, I'm sure. But that doesn't matter does it." Geira's blue eyes held me in my place. A fire shone in them and glowed with the steady heat of a furnace. "Why did you agree to it when all the TDE have shown you, all those soldiers have shown you, is contempt and rejection?"

I could feel tears pricking behind my eyes. Threatening to break through to the surface and spill down my cheeks, but I forced them back, setting my face to a practiced look of focus.

"W-why," I stammered. I didn't know what question I was asking, but Geira answered. Her lips moved so slightly, her words so soft I almost thought I had imagined them.

"Because we're in the middle of a war, and I give a shit about the person you'll be when it's all over."

War? We'd won the war against the rebels. Our job in the under cities was to protect the Tuath Dé from sluagh attack and arrest the last remaining rebel sympathisers. There was no war beyond the veil or in the hidden cities above. War was a human thing now. Something that had been recently eradicated among the fae.

I searched her eyes again. She was being sincere, stern, but they held no more answers.

Noise erupted one hundred metres down the street. Geira and I sprinted and were there in a heartbeat. A jewellery stand lay in pieces on the ground. Jewels and chains scattered in every direction, and in the centre of it all were Dylan and Cynthia, a woman I had trained with at the college, being arrested.

"Get off her! She didn't do anything!" Dylan kicked a White Guard in the groin, and the man went down. His knees hit the floor at the same time as Dylan was body slammed into the wall of the nearest building. It took three guards to keep him pinned in place.

They didn't have this under control, but I didn't dare get involved. Fara getting arrested for any reason was never good.

"I'll handle this." A tall figure walked over to the struggling bodies, holding a piece of red glass attached to a sharp, long pin in his hands. It was Hendrik. Behind him, leaning slightly on her twisted walking stick, stood Councilwoman Neeta.

For a moment I thought he might plead Dylan and Cynthia's case. With the confidence in his walk, I was sure he'd succeed. Until I noticed the cold flicker in his eye. The small upwards tug in the corner of his mouth.

Hendrik placed the red stone against Dylan's wrist, muttering faintly. Dylan stilled. It took the three guards a second more to realise that Dylan was incapacitated.

With a whisper from Hendrik, Dylan turned to reveal dead eyes. I shivered.

"Kneel before our councilwoman, Dylan." Hendrik's tone was so condescending I almost thought I heard Tierney's voice. Dylan moved towards Neeta and did as instructed, both knees hitting the ground with solid impact.

The other arrestee had remained entirely silent. It was only when Hendrik turned his attention to her that she broke her frozen state, choosing instead to fight. Or beg.

"No. Not that, Hendrik. They'll kill me. No—" The woman struggled to pull her wrists away from the red stone, kicking a guard in the shins in the process, but the arms detaining her pushed her forward.

With the impact of red stone on white and a few muttered words, the woman stilled before walking towards Neeta. She kneeled by Dylan's side.

Hendrik, a breath behind the two captives, made his way towards Neeta. The woman looked at him, waving her hand towards Cynthia expectantly. Hendrik moved quickly, taking the red stone and placing it again on the woman's cuffs.

My hands clasped the metal at my own wrists as I considered with horror what that small red stone could do to me.

"Cynthia, you admitted to me that you and Dylan have committed a crime, and as a loyal soldier of the Tuath Dé I cannot let such an admission go without further investigation," Hendrik said, a smug tone coating his words. "You are in the presence of our councillor and are expected to answer her questions truthfully."

My mind whirled. What would Cynthia have possibly done, let alone admitted to Hendrik? She never stepped a toe out of line at the college, and he wasn't known for being a close confidant of hers. Had they formed a friendship since graduation?

"Cynthia!" Neeta barked immediately. Her voice shot fear through my spine. "Outside of the council's approved birthing period, and in spite of your sacred pairing to Victor, are you carrying the child of Dylan?"

My body went cold, thinking back to my last encounter with Hendrik and the pills he offered. Had Cynthia asked Hendrik for help only for him to betray her? How did she know he had access to that stuff in the first place? I silently begged for Cynthia to answer the councilwoman with any answer other than the one that was given.

"Yes." Cynthia's single, lifeless word seemed to suck the air out of every fara soldier, every underdweller who'd come to witness. She produced no further defence of herself; she continued to kneel in a trance. Nothing more than a shell.

There would be only one outcome in this situation.

"There are always two dumb enough to think they can get away with it," Neeta said to herself. "Thank you, Cynthia. For setting such a fine example for your peers." Mockery coated her words. "The arena" was her only direction to Hendrik before she turned on her heel and disappeared into the crowd.

Hendrik stood behind Dylan as he had with Cynthia and whispered low in his ear.

Dylan's body, void of will, rose to its feet and moved farther into the bustle of people, towards the centre of the city. The three guards who were seconds earlier struggling with the arrest, nodded to Hendrik and walked behind the captive.

Hendrik then returned the red stone to Cynthia's wrist and spoke. "Follow Dylan to your death, Cynthia." Hendrik's words held heat this time. Hate.

Cynthia's body obeyed. One foot in front of the other. The guards shooed the small crowd that had gathered out of the woman's way.

I followed. Followed even though a firm hand gripped my upper arm. Even though my head screamed that this was a bad idea.

I followed till Dylan and Cynthia stepped onto a podium in the middle of the square. My feet finally froze in place. A hand tried to pull me away. My mind tried to force my eyes shut.

Knees hit wood. A neck placed itself on a curved stone table obediently.

Words echoed through the square, but I took in none of them. Only the slicing of blade through flesh and bone.

Only the thud of a something solid falling to the road beneath the podium. Only the gushing noise of hot liquid breaking from an enclosed space. Fear and desperation, the remnants of a silent scream filled my nostrils.

My mind begged me to turn away. Begged me to shut my eyes. A word breathed in my ear with almost the same desperation.

Knees hit wood again. A neck placed itself on a curved stone table. Blade through flesh. A red and wet scream.

And then I saw it. Saw the mess in front of me. Only, to me, it wasn't Cynthia's head on the floor of the city. Bloodied, dirty and cold.

It wasn't Dylan's head that had fallen before hers.

It was my mother's. It was my father's.

It was their shared screams heard only in blood.

Hendrik's eyes met mine from a space in the lingering crowd of underdwellers and fara soldiers. They flickered with amusement before resting upon the hand that held my right arm. Geira. It was Geira who had been trying to pull me away. It was the grip of someone who cared that I was one stupid decision away from getting in the middle of an unwinnable situation.

Still, I didn't dare look to Geira. Didn't dare let Hendrik glimpse what was still unknown to me. My heart pounded in my chest.

How close are we all to the same fate?

He twirled the long pin decorated with the red stone between his fingers and turned on his heel—away from the mess he had created in the centre of Dubnos. Like he'd done nothing more than spill water on the rocky streets.

***

Geira chose to end our patrol early. I stayed quiet the entire way back to Hestia's home. Hendrik's actions played over in my mind as Geira filled Dariush in on the night's events.

I couldn't shake the cold that had set into my bones after seeing Dylan's dead eyes, hearing the scream on Cynthia's blood. I imagined Dariush with the same look on his face. I imagined Annalise like Cynthia, begging for help and instead receiving betrayal and death.

I imagined Geira . . .

No.

I couldn't imagine Geira like that. Dead eyes. Obediently walking to her end.

I shook my head, forcing back tears. A blackened realisation dawned on me. This is what it would mean to force Dariush out, to take his place. This is what it would mean to win back the Tuath Dé's trust.

Was that what I'd wanted all this time?

I needed to throw up. I was seconds from leaving the room when my mind was pulled into the conversation before me.

"Tomorrow. I'll take her to the Nine Daughters tomorrow," Dariush said, one hand massaging his temples, jaw locked.

"Good—" Geira started to say, but I jumped in.

"The Nine Daughters? You're going to talk to oracles when two soldiers have been murdered?! Little fucking late!" My words were hot.

Dariush stared at me for a moment, turned and walked towards the kitchen without further explanation.

"Wha—" I began after him, but Geira placed a warm hand on the space below my neck. The world stopped. She didn't take her hand away.

"What happened to Dylan and Cynthia wasn't right. But right now, we need to plan for what's coming," she said.

"What's coming?" I repeated, entirely confused. What was this woman hiding?

Geira dropped her hand and my chest felt abnormally bare in its absence. "If you really want this, I'll talk to him about filling you in, but not right now. Tonight was—a lot." Geira nodded to the stairs. "Get changed. I'll bring up food."

CHAPTER TWENTY

Annalise

Long figures moved elegantly between the swirling, rising heat of the large pool. Even from afar, these creatures were near identical to the gruesome pictures in my mother's book, which lay heavy in a leather satchel by my side.

I'd brought it on a whim, feeling the need to be closer to her. I didn't dare reach for it now.

Two of the Nine Daughters of the Sea, creatures who featured heavily in that old book, sat among a cluster of rocks surrounding the waterfall's base. Their torsos elongated into two-pronged tails. At first, the half-human beasts looked to be skinless from the waist down. With a longer gaze, I noted they had adorned themselves in a collection of skeletons. Shark teeth, bleached coral, crab claws—treasures from a watery grave decorated a cascading frame of human-like ribs. Opalescent scales glinted under that haunting web of white bone.

I shuddered, thankful that my feet refused to bring me to the water's edge.

Dariush had warned me they'd look different from me and my mother, they weren't really sirens after all. These ancient creatures had prowled the deepest depths of the seas for millennia, godlike and ungoverned by the current powers of the fae world.

One story in my book told the tale of Dröfn, the middle sister of the Nine Daughters who'd fallen in love with a sailor she'd only ever seen from a distance. Dröfn had a beautiful voice and liked to collect shiny things that fell off the sides of ships into her waters, but she wanted nothing more than to raise a family with her sailor. She made a deal with the gods; they would let her have his child, and in return, they could take any one of her precious things. The next time she saw the sailor, she sang to him, and he was instantly infatuated with her. He dove into the water to embrace her, and afterwards she brought him down into the depths of the sea to show him her collection of precious shiny things, but the human man couldn't breathe underwater, and he drowned. Nine months later, Dröfn gave birth to the first siren.

The chapter Dariush had given me to study confirmed the details of this reproduction myth.

An illustration that sat underneath the text was that of a seaweed-covered skeleton surrounded by old gold vases and coins. A younger me had given the skeleton a pirate hat and an eye patch. It was the kind of story that should have readied me for seeing one of these beautiful monsters up close.

It didn't.

Neither had spotted my presence. They were too busy in their own worlds.

One lay on a low rock, head tilted back to allow her long, yellow hair access to the steaming water. She was keenly observing something gold and small, biting it every now and then like the action might make it open. Until the other, the personification of a translucent lake, rose from her perched spot above and dove into the water inches from her sister. The lazing daughter jumped and growled at the transgression as a small wave covered her. Multiple rows of sharp teeth bared in a foul display of hostility. The silver daughter returned quickly only to snag the gold piece from her golden sister's hand and swim off.

Laughter echoed throughout the vast cave. I looked to the shoreline to my right where the sound seemed to originate and spotted a mass of red descending into the depths below. It wasn't much of a shoreline. There was no sand to sink toes into. No shallow waters to wade through. Only rock and a sheer drop into darkness. Dariush had told me the underdwellers had built a collection of shallow pools to the west side of the lake, but I couldn't see any of those from where I stood.

"I am Blodhadda." The eery words, closer now, startled me, and my head snapped to see a red-haired figure floating in the water two metres from my feet. "And these are my sisters, Himinglaeva and Hevring." Her voice rose and fell like a rowboat in the middle of a swell as two heads rose sluggishly from the water, each emerged as their names were called. Water ripples drifted from wicked smiles that revealed sharp and stunted teeth. The smiles brought a stark contrast to the smooth and unblemished skin of their faces and torso. Even Hevring's speckled, sun-kissed complexion looked to be made of polished stone.

These were three of the Nine Daughters. Nine sisters, each born from gods and embodying one of nine waters. Only, in the book they were portrayed as women full of life and beauty. Had I known their true image I wouldn't have painted the margins of their pages with soft, pinkish clouds and blue swallows.

I shuddered at their age, the ancient knowledge that swam in the depths of those terrifying eyes.

"Where are your sisters?" I asked, looking at each of them.

"The stupid girl knows of us at least," said the yellow-haired half-woman on Blodhadda's left. I ignored the insult, more out of fear than emotional maturity.

Hevring.

"She knows of us and not herself. But we could play mirror—just this once," Himinglaeva responded with unblinking eyes, white light snaking coldly under her skin.

The three laughed a manic shrill, and I recoiled as the sound bounced off the cave walls. The sticky blackness of it stuck in my ears.

"Hmmm, what fun. But what shall she give us in return?" Blodhadda's question was met with another unified cackle.

"What do you want?" I said with feigned firmness. Though I didn't understand what it was they were supposed to give me. Dariush hadn't told me anything, not that I expected anything else from him.

"That depends on what you have." Blodhadda's red eyes pierced the satchel by my side as if she knew what it hid.

"You can't have the book," I said with real firmness now, sliding the strap across my shoulder so the satchel was mostly hidden behind my back.

"Oh, you'll give it up eventually." A bony elbow hit the side of Hevring's face faster than the words had come out of her mouth. The clearly younger of the three recoiled slightly from her reddened sister but eventually brought her attention back to me. A trickle of gold slid from her nose, catching in her tangle of teeth.

I didn't know what to make of that information. I hoped it wouldn't cost me.

"What do you have to offer us?" Blodhadda repeated.

I couldn't hold back my huff of annoyance. Of course Dariush didn't tell me I needed to bring an offering. Judging by the sisters' hungry eyes, I was going to get my answers seconds before they feasted on my still-beating heart. My hands rummaged through the folds of my bag. Maybe there was something hidden in there and I just hadn't found it. The book, a palette of water paints, two brushes, a dirty cloth. Nothing I wanted to give up, or anything the sisters might accept.

My fingers fumbled a few seconds longer and a pit opened in my gut. I ran my hands over my loose fitting, and pocketless, pants. Clearly, in misplaced hope.

"I don't suppose you'll take my siren song," I said, voice barely audible.

"WHAT!? THE DAUGHTER OF DRÖFN OFFERS HER SONG!?" Blodhadda's arms whipped about, causing waves to splash against the rock platform underneath my feet.

"THE GIRL HATES HERSELF! DOES SHE HATE US?" Himinglaeva and Hevring joined in with their own admonishments, yelling over each other in an angry swell.

"Kidding! It's a joke. The humans do that sometimes. It's a bad habit I picked up. Sorry." I rambled on as I backtracked on my request. It was stupid of me to not think of how they might take that, and I wasn't fond of the idea of getting on their bad side.

The water stilled again. Ripples around the sisters' necks slowly moved outward. Blodhadda licked her sharp teeth. An act of frustration or a threat, I wasn't sure.

"My cuffs!" I yelled in relief. "Yes! Take my cuffs, just don't cut off my hands in the process." I took two steps towards the water and laid my wrists before them. My excitement over the possibility of their removal outweighed my fear.

"There is something that binds you." Blodhadda spoke low and steady now. Her voice brought forth images in my mind of a stagnant, black place at the bottom of the sea. "We will give you the answers you seek and in return you will allow us to take your bindings."

"Yes" had barely rolled past the tip of my tongue before I was pulled into the water by my wrists. Only, the hands didn't let go. They pulled me farther down into the inky blackness, and every ounce of my being protested. I tried to kick and scratch and swim upward, but the grip of the sirens was too strong.

They stopped and I swam upwards again, only to be pulled down by my ankles. Over and over this repeated. My lungs burned. I was running out of breath.

Finally, I relented. I opened my eyes to a still blackness and barely suppressed the urge to scream.

"She is host and hostage, she is friend and foe,
A collision of hands; of mind.
To reveal the darkness, where the black soul sleeps,
Blood and heart awaken, truth's pull.
Weapon of a king, will you seek Sacred Tree?
Bloodsong, amplify in the depths.
She speaks to unspoken; she is the silent.
A queen of dark places, be light."

The words echoed in my mind as figures darted towards me. Scraping and grasping at my clothes, my shoes, and my satchel. I was tumbled and pulled in every different direction. Bubbles escaped my mouth and danced sideways.

My chest was empty. Soon I would have to breathe in, and only water would be there to fill my lungs. Losing the book was the least of my worries.

***

Water spluttered from my mouth. A metallic sound clanged through the cave as I pulled my naked body onto the stone floor, and my knees and palms scraped jagged rock. In those dark depths, surrounded by cruel beasts, I had felt the water trickle into my lungs. I'd felt them burn as my body protested to the very last moment.

Dead. I should have been dead.

And then, my head was above water, my hands had reached for stone. The silver cuffs still firmly attached to my wrists mocked me under the cave's low light. I'd nearly drowned, and it was for nothing.

Regaining my breath, I crawled away from the water's edge. Dariush couldn't pay me to go back into those waters. Not even if he paid me in all the secrets I knew he was keeping from me.

Fear rose in my chest as something catapulted out of the water towards me, landing inches from the water's edge.

The spine cracked on the rocky surface, and the book fell open to a page I hadn't seen in a long while. There'd been a reason for that. The last time I'd seen this page I'd been so terrified I smothered it in an entire palette's worth of paint.

Now, all that paint had washed away, forcing me to witness the willowy figure with two heads, holding a flaming torch and a bowl. Black, terrifying eyes stared back at me from the book.

Unease crept over my skin. It was like looking at a reflection of something. The familiarity of it distorted by truth, or more lies, like ripples on the surface of a pond.

Sensing a trap, I sucked in a breath and inched closer.

Dammit, Annalise. If they pull you back in, you deserve it.

My fingers reached for the book, arms groaning in protest. The moment I felt the tacky fibres of wet paper on my fingertips I slammed the book shut and snatched it towards me, moving fast to get myself on my feet and hobble to the door. I wasn't going to give the sisters a chance to pull me back in.

This part of the Temple of Waterfalls was deserted. That fact only made me more terrified for my safety, but I was thankful no one else was around to see me naked. The water had been warm. Steam drifted upwards and around my ankles but melted away with the distance I put between myself and the sisters. By the time I'd reached the giant temple door, I was shivering, my drenched hair and the less-than-temperate air drifting through the cracks in the threshold added to my discomfort.

"Eh-hem," I grunted angrily at Dariush while cranking my head through the small opening I'd made in the door, carefully hiding behind the width of it. I was glad to see him still standing where I'd left him.

"What did they tell you?" Dariush asked a little too quickly, pushing back off the wall and moving towards me.

"Oh, how kind of you to consider my safety!" I raised my voice. "I'm so glad you value my life above half-baked riddles from flipping fish! Give me your clothes!" He flinched backwards as I reached for his shawl and missed.

"Why do you need my clothes?" Dariush said, oblivious.

"Because they stole mine and nearly drowned me in the process! *Give me your clothes!*" My shrill echoed through the temple's main entrance. I didn't care that we might not be the only ones in the space.

Dariush smirked and began removing his shawl. It was the same short, blanket-like cloak that he'd worn over his shoulders on the night of Samhain. Kindness looked slightly condescending on him, and it only infuriated me more.

I snatched the dark piece of fabric and slammed the heavy wooden door in his face.

After wrapping the fabric around my chest and tucking a corner tightly under the wrap by my left arm, I opened the door again and moved through it with a quick jump, eager to leave the Nine Daughters and their lake of doom behind me.

From the way Dariush looked at me, I might as well have left the house wearing nothing but a towel.

Laughter erupted from him. A bellowing sound echoed through the temple entrance as he bent over, steadying himself with hands on knees.

"What? They took my clothes!" I said, hugging my book close to my chest for extra protection.

"Get back inside," Dariush said, leaning into the handle behind me and opening the door again. My mouth opened in protest but his body, dangerously close to mine, made me step backwards into the damp chamber.

Standing in the threshold, Dariush slipped his grey shirt over his head, revealing a toned chest that glowed slightly beneath an even tan. I could see now that the sharp mark of black by his left jawline extended down his neck, over his shoulder, and connected with the dark fur that covered his left arm and hand.

Heat seemed to pulse off him in waves. His physical body was such a juxtaposition to those icy, invisible shadows he commanded with his mind. My cheeks flushed as I caught myself staring far too late.

"Put this on. I'll leave the door cracked so the *bogeywomen* don't get you." He made no attempt to hide his smirk, and handed me the grey fabric. I almost protested, giving his bare chest another once-over.

What the hell is he going to wear?

My absolute terror of the beasts prowling the water behind me won out. I snatched the shirt from him and handed over the book, moving behind the door for privacy.

Putting on the shirt proved difficult. I hadn't done a very good job of securing the shawl around my chest, and as I quickly lifted my arms over my head, too eager to get out of the damp chamber, the sheet fell to the ground.

In that moment I was thankful for Dariush's large frame, at least his shirt covered my arse. I picked up the cloak, careful to not reveal too much skin to the ancient sirens I could feel watching me from the water. They had seen it all as they stripped me in those dark waters. Revelled in my humiliation. I didn't want to give them that satisfaction again.

I wrapped the cloak around myself and poked my head out the crack in the door.

"Hold this," Dariush said with a frown. He handed back my book. Removing the brooch that had secured his cloak from a pocket in his loose black pants, he placed the metal between his teeth. With his free hands he pushed himself farther into the room.

I gulped and stepped back.

"Just— Let's go," I whined, wrapping the cloak tighter around me. My words came out more as a plea than I wanted them to.

Dariush pulled the cloak from my shoulders with one easy movement, then wrapped the fabric twice around my waist before taking the brooch from his teeth and fastening the makeshift skirt in place.

My whole world stopped as he placed his hands on my hips, looking up and down my body to observe his work.

With a satisfied nod he pulled back, his hands lifting off my hips, leaving them cold. Before he could turn to the thick wooden door, I leaned in and his eyes snapped to mine, a question in them. My entire body tingled with our proximity. The thumping of his heart, or maybe it was mine, steered me closer. His arms encircled me without hesitation.

I didn't know what I was doing. I couldn't quite pick the moment when contempt in his gaze began to feel more like adoration. Maybe it was the moment I'd leaned into him for protection from his brother at Samhain. Maybe it had always been there, and I'd been wilfully confusing it with something else up until now.

I couldn't ignore it any longer.

His hold on me was loose, our bodies separated by the book in my arms. It was as if he was waiting for me to pull back. Waiting for me to run.

I let the book fall to my side, reached on toes and kissed him. It was soft, short. But as I pulled away, hands gripped my upper arms and pulled me closer to him. The kiss deepened. A growl of satisfaction erupted in the back of his throat. I wanted to hear that sound on repeat.

When he finally pulled away, I thought I saw the flicker of uncertainty wash over him before he turned for the doorway and stepped through.

I reached for my lips, and they felt cold in his absence.

Plop.

Movement in the water behind me woke me from the strange stupor Dariush's kiss had left me in, and I jumped once again through the threshold without looking back.

"So what did the *half-baked fish* tell you?" Dariush said as I caught up with him. For a moment I thought I could have day-dreamed the entire encounter, but his lazy grin told me he was still thinking about the feel of our bodies so close to each other.

We moved through the temple's entry chamber. The space was brightly lit with the wispy things that danced in blues and whites among rising waves of steam. Large showers that fell in a constant stream lined two opposing walls. The other two walls were lined with cupboards and towel-stacked shelves. I really should have taken a towel into the temple.

"Why do you want to know? Why take me here in the first place?" I asked.

"To find out what you are."

He'd only answered my second question, and I waited in silence for him to answer my first. "A riddle," I said after a moment. "They told me a riddle. I've forgotten half of it already, but it was something about seeking the Sacred Tree, something called a blood song, and that a friend and a foe will reveal darkness. Or was it a friend and foe in one? I *was* drowning when they told me."

Dariush stopped. "I send you to oracles and you forget what they've told you the minute you've stepped out of their temple?"

He turned back to look at the large doors as if contemplating sending me back in there with a pen and paper.

"I won't do it!" My voice boomed around the room. I was relieved to realise the place was empty, excluding us.

"If you went back in there and asked them to repeat themselves, they'd skin you alive." Dariush was rubbing his temples now. It took a moment for him to collect himself, but when he did, he turned away from the doors and continued walking. "Tree. Blood-song. Friends and foes. We can work with that." He said it more to himself than me.

"Care to fill me in on what all that means," I asked. Anger was building up inside me. I was the one to nearly drown gathering these pieces of information, but he seemed to be the one who understood what they meant.

"I'll let you know when I find out," he said simply. I didn't push, but it felt very much like a lie.

CHAPTER TWENTY-ONE

Zorya

I should have been asleep, but how could I sleep when Annalise was being taken to the Nine Daughters? Annalise was having the very secrets of her existence shared with her, and I was lying in bed, trying to pretend it wasn't the middle of the day. I felt lazy, and it made me furious.

If she were a valkyrie, there'd be no reason to take her to the Nine Daughters. I glanced at the braid of gold that stretched half the length of the bed next to me. Valkyries didn't believe in knowing their future. They were true warriors. They stepped into the battlefield of life fearlessly. To know your future was to cheat life. To play unfairly.

Upir, the non-fara types that couldn't step into the light of the sun, had different opinions depending on the tribe. Some were known for their blood divination. Others held no opinion either way. As the last daywalker, I didn't know what my tribe had believed. It didn't matter anyway.

The Tuath Dé didn't allow fara to seek prophecy or visit oracles for personal reasons. Which made Annalise's visit to the oracle sisters all the more unusual.

If they get caught, they deserve to have their heads roll.

It was the undercurrent of jealousy that pushed my thoughts into that dark direction. I didn't really mean it.

My mind was still reeling after what happened to Dylan and Cynthia. I was torn between wanting to defend an empire I was sworn to serve and knowing that something was deeply wrong.

I'd barely known the two soldiers, but their deaths felt personal. A betrayal. It was worse that Hendrik had been the one to hand them over. He'd turned his back on all fara for a place on the White Guard.

My stomach twisted. Wasn't that what I'd been aiming for this entire time?

I shook the comparison away.

My thoughts swam as I tossed in my sheets. Sleeping during the day had always been exceptionally difficult for me.

Even though I'd nailed a dark sheet to my circular rainbow window, the vibrant glow of Dubnos edged around the corners, making it impossible for me to imagine that it was night.

Geira didn't seem to find it too hard to fall asleep. Her heartbeat had slightly slowed. Even when she slept it sounded even, strong. The rhythm was like a steady, commanding war drum calling for all within earshot to keep in time to it.

If I left now, I could sneak into the Temple of Waterfalls. Maybe I'd hear Annalise's prophecy myself. At worst, I could wait them out and then interrogate one of the Nine Daughters afterward.

It was a stupid plan, but I couldn't lie here any longer.

Kicking the sheets back, I let my feet find the floor with the intention of tiptoeing past Geira's bed.

A hand caught my wrist after two steps.

"Don't." The command was firm. Geira yanked me towards her bed, the sheets pulled back and my knees collided with the mattress. "Get in." It wasn't a suggestion.

I froze. Geira's hand a death grip around my wrist.

"Well, if you don't have the willpower to keep out of trouble, I'm going to make sure you stay here." Geira let go, only to snag my other wrist. She rolled over, keeping my hand close to her chest, and I fell on top of her. "Get. In," she said again, this time through bared teeth.

I did as she said, mostly because my mind had frozen, and slid down behind her. My head hit her pillow, and I tried desperately to keep some distance between my front and her back. She flipped a corner of her blanket over me with her free hand.

We lay there in silence for a few moments.

Was I supposed to sleep like this? Was I supposed to say something? Both would be impossible at this point, because every nerve in my body was on alert, and my brain was completely empty except for the dreaded thought that I had no idea what to do with my hands. I grabbed the pillow under my head with one and tried to angle the other away from the thin, soft fabric that covered her chest.

"You know you're going to have to breathe at some point, Zorya."

An involuntary puff of air escaped my lips and ruffled her hair. I instantly sucked more back in. My thoughts turned solely to the effort of breathing.

Geira turned over, her eyes snapped to mine. Her hand pulled my hips closer to hers, forcing me to abandon my pursuit for distance.

And then her lips were on me, tongue pushing its way into my mouth. In one quick movement she pushed my body flat against the bed and was on top of me. She moved her knees to either side of my hips, her lips never leaving mine.

"You don't have to do everything by yourself you know," she said as she pulled away for a breath.

I flushed as the thought of what other women did in the safety of their own beds flashed through my mind. Privacy wasn't a thing at the college, even in the women's bunks, though that hadn't stopped some. *Does she think I do that?*

She caught my trail of thought, took my wrists again and pulled them above my head. "I wasn't talking about that. But I'm surprised you don't. Every woman should know their own body and what they like." She leaned into me as she said the word *like*.

How does she know I don't do that? My breath caught in my throat at the idea that she'd paid that much attention to me, and I squirmed.

"I'm talking about what you were planning on doing just now. Does squad mean nothing to you? We're a team, Zorya, and I've been at this longer than you. If you have questions, doubts—If you need help, you should know you can come to me." She kissed below my left ear and whispered low, "Do you want this?"

An involuntary moan escaped my lips, and she chuckled. "I need you to use your words, Zorya." The raspy heat had left her voice, replaced by a clarity. She pulled back to look at me.

I wanted her to keep going, to keep making me feel these things. I nodded, before realising that wasn't using my words either. "Yes. Yes I want this," I finally let out.

Holding my wrists in place with one hand, she pushed up my nightshirt. A single finger brushed a nipple under the fabric, and that sound escaped me again. She pinched the little knob harder, testing some sort of boundary before she twisted and pulled. It was like she'd pulled on some invisible string connecting my nipple to a place low in my gut. Pleasure and pain shot through that connection, and something close to a breathy squeal sounded through the room. She let go with a snap, replacing fingers with soft, slow kisses.

Her body pressed into mine as she shifted off the weight of her knees. She took a moment to kiss me deeply. The fingers of her free hand moved downwards to the hem of my underwear and slipped beneath it. Pleasure ripped through me as she found the other end of that string. A spot I'd never known was there, or had been too scared to entertain its existence.

She moved lower, her mouth leaving a trail of gentle bites and kisses down my neck and across my chest as her fingers found the wetness that had pooled between my legs. She slipped two fingers inside me, and I gasped. Then her slick fingers moved out and upwards and found that spot again. They rocked and slid as her mouth teased every bit of bare skin she could find, both sensations coaxing more moans from my lips.

"Promise me. When things get dangerous, when you need help, you'll come to me." Her lips were by my ear again, whispering low and heavy, but she pulled back to meet my eyes.

I nodded as the pressure built with every flick of her fingers. I didn't trust myself to speak.

"Say it," Geira commanded. Her eyes pierced mine, drinking me in. Watching my pleasure reach its peak.

"I promise." It came out as a pathetic plea, voice shaking as the waves ripped through me and tore past my defences. Commanding my body and mind to release weights I hadn't even known were there.

Geira's fingers kept moving, slower as the last waves of pleasure rocked through me and stole the last of my strength.

"I hope you took notes, because next time I'm going to watch you do that to yourself."

My eyes were fluttering closed, but I could hear the satisfied grin in her voice.

Geira released my arms and gently moved them to my sides as she shimmied in behind me. Her arms wrapped tightly around me. I was sure her hold was the only thing keeping me pinned to the bed. The only thing stopping me from floating to the ceiling, through the mountain and high into the clouds above.

For that moment at least, it didn't matter where Annalise was or what Dariush was up to or what anyone else was doing. No one else even existed.

Except Geira.

In her arms, I slept.

CHAPTER TWENTY-TWO

Annalise

I slipped into the shared bedroom with every expectation that Geira and Zorya would be asleep.

They were, just not in separate beds.

I stumbled over my own feet and dropped my wooden book while trying to steady myself on the door handle. The book fell with a thud, waking the two women.

My face flushed as they jolted awake, Zorya pushing Geira's arms off her with haste. I instantly felt like I should be anywhere else.

"You're back," Geira said sleepily, shrugging off Zorya's embarrassment about the state I'd found them in. It was enough to stop me from turning around and leaving.

"Yeah" was the only word I could find.

Geira hopped out of her bed and moved to the wardrobe. "I need to talk to Dariush," she announced as she shoved on a pair of tracksuit pants under the baggy top she'd slept in and headed for the door.

"Go back to sleep," she said over her shoulder, presumably to Zorya. Zorya just scowled in response and made her way to her bed.

I moved to the wardrobe, desperate to get into my own clothes and thinking Zorya would ignore my presence anyway.

"Could you maybe keep this a secret?" Her voice made me jump.

"Of course. It's not really any of my business anyway." I offered her a small smile, not expecting one back, and sifted through my drawers.

"So is Dariush wearing your clothes now too?" Zorya said. Her voice held humour, but it was strained. Uncertain.

I turned to her with a tattered oversized shirt, and blue lacey knickers scrunched in my hand.

"What?" I wasn't sure if I was dumbfounded by her question or that she had chosen to continue the conversation.

"You're wearing his clothes. That pin has his royal symbol." She pointed to the piece that held the shawl around my waist like a skirt.

"Oh yeah. He's walking around without a shirt on. I got wet."

Zorya raised an eyebrow and bit her lip. It looked like she was trying to stifle a fit of laughter.

The sentence I'd had in my mind rearranged itself till it looked more like what had actually come out of my mouth.

"Oh— I did *not* mean it like that. I was naked—but it wasn't my fault! I was at the Temple of Waterfalls and these fish women pulled me in." The more I tried to explain myself, the more my sentences came out backward.

A snort exploded from Zorya, and her hands found her knees as she tried to steady her breathing. My hand reached for the threshold of the walk-in wardrobe as tears of laughter clouded my vision.

It wasn't long before I realised who I was laughing with though, and I let the moment die abruptly. Zorya picked up on it.

"I'm sorry."

Those two words, words I never thought I'd hear, hit me out of nowhere. Zorya stood between her bed and Geira's bed, eyes shifting. Her fingers fiddled nervously with the cuticles of her thumbs.

"I treated you like just another soldier, but you're not. You don't know this world. I betrayed your trust and put you in danger. It was really, *really* shitty of me." Zorya looked like she'd just bitten into a lemon, but every word felt genuine.

I didn't know how to respond.

"I get that you hate me—"

"I don't," I said quicker than I had time to think, but in that moment, I knew I was telling the truth.

"Oh." A long pause stretched between us.

I was the one to break it.

"I had a close friend when I went to university. I was studying fine art and she was studying contemporary music. She was obsessed with my voice, and we'd record samples to put into her projects. This was before everything started to happen." I didn't know why I was telling her this, but Zorya let me finish. "I got carried away with my singing one day. I was feeling a lot of intense things. I was angry at her, I don't even remember what for, but she got hurt, badly. She had to drop out because I had taken away her hearing."

I paused for a moment, trying to piece my next words together.

"I guess it was safer to let myself think that you and I would never get along, than to actually try and be a friend," I said finally.

"I get it and that sucks," she said simply. "But you didn't choose to hurt your friend, Annalise. Remember that."

Her words should have lifted a weight off my shoulders. Instead, it became heavier. If I'd known my voice would steal her hearing, her dreams with it, I would have superglued my mouth shut. But that didn't change the fact that, in that moment, I'd wanted Orla to hurt.

"Besides, I'm a bit tougher than a human," Zorya said. "Smarter than one too. What are you really?"

I raised an eyebrow at her jab but didn't remind her that I'd spent my life among humans, and she was definitely wrong on that last assessment. We were making progress, and I wasn't going to sabotage it.

"I'm a siren," I breathed out. If this was a real truce between us, a chance to wipe the slate clean, then I wouldn't muddy it with half-truths. "Half siren."

"That—that's impossible." Zorya looked to be churning through a thousand theories, deciding whether any of the ones she held stood up against this new information. "Sirens can only reproduce with human men. *Only* human men. There are no half sirens."

"Here I am." I shrugged, trying to push past the reminder that my existence was an anomaly. The chapter Dariush had given me and the story in my book had both signalled a dead end in my search to discover what I really was.

I changed the subject. "I'll ask Dariush to take you off night shift."

Zorya didn't look too pleased to hear that, and I was certain it had everything to do with the woman she spent those night shifts with.

"It must suck trying to work in the dark when you can't see anything. I thought vampires could see in the dark." I was prodding. Shifting the conversation further away from me.

"It's not that bad," she said, dismissing the idea. "And it's upir, not vampire."

"But Jaz told me you drink blood, right?"

"*Jaz* is a snitch," Zorya huffed. I'd hit a nerve, but she was doing well keeping her anger in check. "Yeah, but we don't use that term. And it's mostly just a once-a-month thing, or if I'm badly injured."

I thought about the state she'd been in that night. She was hurt worse than me, but I never saw the healer tend to her. If that was some form of extra punishment Dariush had put on her, he and I were going to have words.

"How's your leg?" I asked. A purple scar peeked out from under the baggy top she'd worn to bed.

"It's mostly healed. Not the worst state I've ever found myself in." She pulled the top up slightly to reveal three very new scars tracing the length of her thigh. "Left a decent scar though." There was a brightness in her voice.

"You sound happy about that." I was horrified.

"Scars are the closest thing to a badge of honour the fara ever get." She smiled, but there was a flash of pain in her eyes before she quickly changed the subject. "I heard you made a spark the other day. It took me a while to figure out my light too. If you need help just ask." Her offer sounded genuine. "And maybe we can go over some of the things Jaz has told you, sounds like he's filling your head with bullshit."

The comment came off as a slight, but I knew it sounded harsher than she meant it.

"OK, let's make a deal," I said, moving around the beds to make her shake on it. "I'll actually try with the whole 'learning how to use my gifts' thing, if you try to be less mean."

"Fine, but I have to teach you how to swear."

Our hands collided and the world went black.

CHAPTER TWENTY-THREE

B lackness.

A young woman with wavy black hair that curled around her face squealed with excitement. "I can't wait to graduate! Do you know how long I've been dreaming of this?"

As if she was talking to someone.

Us.

The woman faded and a man, slightly older, replaced her. Skin tanned from the sun, hair a dark mahogany, eyes kissed by red flecks. He was kneeling before us, yet still larger than life.

"My girl. You'll be safe here so long as you do what they tell you to." His voice was strained. Tainted with fear. "You are my little truth seeker, and in better times I'd never ask you to dim your light for anyone. But I need you to keep your gifts a secret. I need you to become the soldier they ask you to be. I need you to survive. Can you do that for me?" The man's words were cut off by the reappearance of the woman.

Her demeanour was different now. She was frozen in fear. Disbelief and terror warred with each other in her eyes.

Then her fingers grasped at her ears. A blood-chilling scream erupted from her throat. Her wailing and pleading grew and grew till—

The man's head lay detached in a dirty pool of blood and mud. Above him, the neck of a woman lay on a guillotine. Red hair half spilled over her face. Red-flecked eyes peered through the strands. They stared into us. Screams echoed through the room as metal sliced—

The black-haired woman collapsed onto dirty, blue carpet. Red dribbled from her ears as her hands relinquished their hold and fell limply beside her head.

Two lines of blood rolled down her neck, one crossed her chest to meet the other on her shoulder. It pooled and rippled there, wanting to leap off the woman's skin. Wanting to be closer to us.

CHAPTER TWENTY-FOUR

Zorya

The city was mostly quiet. Blackness was broken by the silhouette of buildings and faint sparkles of stalagmite pillars. The will-o'-the-wisps bobbed too high on the city's cave ceiling to be more than bright specks in the distance. They could have been sleeping like the rest of the kingdom.

All the will-o'-the-wisps except the unlucky few that floated through the streets and illuminated the city like dull streetlamps. I found myself especially thankful for their small glow after the disturbing dreams I'd woken up from.

They were fractured, the stories made a mess as they collided into each other. I couldn't make sense of them. Some I knew. They were memories, near replays of the executions I'd witnessed the night before. Others were like I was viewing the world through someone else's eyes. I was yet to shake the unnatural feeling that accompanied that. It was like my soul had spent the night soaking in a bath of brackish water.

A consistent pitter-patter of water on stone echoed through the city. Dubnos had a few cracks in its ceiling that liked to leak on occasion, and with the heavy dampness in the air it was like the faux sky was trying to rain.

As Geira and I moved through narrow walkways and crossed the main square, the shuffle of our shoes on granite and stone, and the rhythm of Geira's heartbeat, met that watery percussion with precise syncopation.

The timing was annoyingly convenient. I needed to mess it up. Dislodge that rhythm from my mind, along with all my thoughts of Geira and what we'd done only hours ago. What I desperately wanted to do again.

"Why are you walking so fast?" Geira whispered after noticing our change in pace.

"Nothing," I snapped, too embarrassed by the truth to share it.

Geira's warm fingers wrapped around my wrist, pulling me towards her as she stopped.

"We couldn't have changed anything," she said. Her tone told me what I would have viewed in her eyes had I been able to see more than her towering silhouette. I took a moment to consider what she was saying and flushed with guilt.

Had I just been more preoccupied with Geira's heartbeat than last night's execution?

"You don't believe that," I accused. "And what about now? We could go to the council. Tierney will be here in three days. We can tell him—"

"What? That two fara soldiers were executed for a crime without proper trial. Without their cases being heard? That's as good as it gets for us."

"But they were innocent. You saw them. They were blindsided. Cynthia had more to say!" My words had picked up volume, and I winced as the last word echoed faintly through the silent square.

"No trial, Zorya." Geira's tone darkened, her voice so low I wouldn't have caught what she said had we been standing in the same spot during the hustle and bustle of the day. "That's how it is. And that's what we will get if we bring this up with Tierney."

My gut turned over. Geira was right. Her fingers became chalky before she let go of my wrist.

"We're better off focusing on what we *can* do," she said, focusing her attention on the buildings and alleyways surrounding us.

"And what is that?"

"Right now, it's patrolling the city."

"There is literally nothing happening here." I had let go of our commitment to whispering.

It looked as though Geira was about to say something, then she went still. A distant light somewhere illuminated her face enough to reveal blue eyes fixed on a space behind me.

I turned.

At the other end of the square, a cluster of will-o'-the-wisps moved brightly in unison. Following obediently was a girl not much younger than myself.

Her short, curvy frame and the lack of point to her ears told me she was likely human.

A human with eyes as dead as the grave fixed on a cluster of will-o'-the-wisps.

What are will-o'-the-wisps doing with a human?

The thought was like frost settling on bones, but it lifted in a second. A blink from the girl sent the will-o'-the-wisps scattering. Another blink and her eyes livened, only for a horror to settle in them. I recalled the vision I'd pulled from Jaz's blood of the human man who'd behaved strangely and jumped into action.

Geira was a breath behind me, and we were by the girl's side in an instant.

"Are you all right?" Geira said, putting on a voice that was softer than what I'd heard from her before.

"I-I don't know where I am," the girl stammered.

"You're in the city square of Dubnos City," Geira's said. "Can you tell me your name?"

"Uh." The girl furrowed her brow and gripped her dark hair at its roots with both hands. It took a moment, but she found what she was looking for. With eyes closed, as if she had to walk a labyrinth in her mind to find the answer, she said, "Ettie. My name is Ettie . . . Ettie . . ."

As the girl struggled to remember her last name, I paid closer attention to her clothes. She wore baggy, dark blue jeans, and a men's brown button-up shirt left open like a jacket to reveal a T-shirt that was probably white at one point in its life. Her canvas shoes were ready to fall apart, and her rounded ears were littered with silver studs and rings. A silver chain with a white stone bead sat on her neck like a choker.

Humans stuck beyond the veil kept up with fashion trends loosely. They preferred to dress themselves in styles that reminded them of home, of their time above. In Dubnos it wasn't strange to see Victorian-era gowns, bomber jackets, or double-breasted suits, altered only slightly to keep up with fashion trends that made their way underground.

This girl clearly belonged on the surface. Not in a kingdom that had signed a treaty to end the practice of luring humans into its borders well over a half-century ago.

"Ettie . . ." With her eyes still tightly shut in concentration, Ettie began to twirl a finger around a dirty strand of bleached hair that had been hiding behind her ear. ". . . Silang. My name is Ettie Silang."

I looked to Geira's ashen face as she took in the sight of the dishevelled human girl and deduced what I had.

"We'll take her to Dariush," she finally managed.

***

There I stood. In front of the treaty breaker. Once we informed Dariush of the girl's strange encounter with the will-o-the-wisps, there wasn't much of an argument. The prince insisted on taking her to Queen Dubh, and Geira silenced my attempts to go to Neeta or another council member residing in the Tuath Dé district.

It wouldn't surprise me if he was in on the queen's ruse.

The feeling that I shouldn't be here was stifling. These people were crafty, there was no way they'd let anything slip in front of me. Not while they thought of me as loyal to the TDE.

I tried to not consider the recent events that had sliced at that loyalty like a . . .

Guillotine through flesh.

Forcing air into my lungs, I zeroed in on what the queen had to say for herself.

"We've been investigating the influx in human population. It's jumped over fifteen percent in the past six months." The queen spoke from her place at the end of a large oval mahogany table. As usual she wore a classic, black suit with twenty or so rings adorning her fingers. Today it seemed she had spared us the formality of her crown.

"Well considering they can't reproduce down here, *any* new humans should have sounded the alarm," I said. "Why haven't you alerted the council?"

The queen removed her attention from Ettie, who'd not stopped gaping at the woman since we entered the large room designed for official meetings. Before that she'd been fixed on Annalise, watching her every move like a doe suspecting she'd been spotted by a wolf. When Annalise got too close, she'd flinched.

"And what do you expect the council to do, dear?" The queen's tone was low and precise, intimidating even, but I held her gaze as she spoke. "Take my kingdom away from me?"

I considered Geira's insistence that Dylan and Cynthia wouldn't have gotten a fair trial regardless of Tierney's involvement.

No, the queen was right. They'd have this kingdom already if it wasn't for the treaty, and they'd relish any suggestion that it had been broken. For some reason, the idea of the TDE gaining full control over this territory sent a shiver through me.

"I'll inform the leeches once I'm sure of the culprit."

I almost gasped at the queen's casual slight towards the Tuath Dé. Geira snorted at my reaction, and suddenly I felt childish.

Why was it so important now that I defend them? I'd called our rulers worse in front of Nate and Jaz plenty of times.

"It's kind of obvious, isn't it?" I said as I both doubled down on my stance and interrupted Dariush. "There were will-o'-the-wisps right in front of her. Her attention was glued to them."

"I'd say the will-o'-the-wisps were just as confused by the situation as Ettie was," Geira jumped in, giving me a look that said, *What are you doing?*

The queen let out an exasperated breath and side-eyed Dariush before answering me.

Yes, I was being a pain, but I needed answers.

"See this?" she said holding up her right pointer finger, bending it at the second knuckle to show off a gold ring with a spherical diamond placed on top. The stone glinted with several different colours, all reflecting its many faceted sides. Within a few moments three will-o'-the-wisps travelled into the room from the door behind me and danced around the queen.

"This allows me to communicate with my, less-vocal subjects." She leaned towards me, her eyes darkening in the same way I had seen Dariush's do before, and I felt the threat they projected. "I can assure you the will-o'-the-wisps are not responsible for this attack against the treaty."

Thinking over what the queen was implying, that she could speak to the will-o'-the-wisps directly, I fell silent.

Who would go to the effort to make it look like the will-o'-the-wisps had broken the treaty? The Red Knights hated the Tuath Dé more than they hated the queen, but if the treaty was broken that's exactly who would take over the Kingdom of Dubnos—the Tuath Dé.

"Hestia, if you approve it, we'll keep Ettie safe at your home." Dariush's words broke my thoughts. "We'll need to use the door so as to not attract any spies to her location. We might have already risked that by taking Ettie here first," he said, looking to Hestia and then the queen. The two women nodded to each other before

Hestia removed a black ring from her left hand and leaned across the table to give it to Geira.

As Geira placed the ring firmly on her left thumb, I noted the symbol stamped across its oval, flattened top. It was identical to the brooch Dariush had worn at the Samhain festivities.

Why the ring? What door?

"Annalise and I will stay behind," Dariush said to Geira. "Do not come back through that door. If the house becomes compromised, go to Fáilte."

"We might need the assistance of Jaz or Nate," Hestia chimed in. I frowned, feeling completely left out, but with only a glance at each other Nate and Jaz had decided who would stay.

"I'll stay behind," said Jaz firmly. It always puzzled me how they were on the same page about everything. Ever since I'd met them, they rarely needed to talk things out.

Another pang of exclusion shot through me. They were supposed to be my friends too, but a distance had grown between me and them since graduation. I thought it had been because of Annalise.

Geira stood from her seat beside Dariush, and Nate and I followed suit. Ettie, having done nothing but stare at the queen during the entire meeting, needed to be told by Geira to follow us into the room behind the queen's throne.

The solid mahogany door slid open at our arrival to reveal a circular room filled with elaborate, free-standing doors arranged in rings emanating from its centre.

As we moved into the room the mahogany door slid shut behind us. Geira passed a door made of faceted, white crystal and stood in front of a simple black door. It glowed with a green hue at her presence.

Geira knocked on the door three times. A golden hand appeared in the space where a doorknob should be and Geira took it in hers, giving it a firm shake. The door swung open to reveal a bedroom drenched in emerald green and luscious velvet furnishings.

CHAPTER TWENTY-FIVE

Annalise

M y cheek and ears buzzed with Hestia's magic as we approached the large and ornate double doors. The streets behind us were bustling with people, mostly humans and non-Tuath Dé fae, going about their day-to-day business. They all clearly had better things to do, but every now and then eyes flicked my way, lingering too long. At first, I thought they could see through my glamour.

"Stop touching your cheek. You're supposed to be Tuath Dé," Jaz whispered loudly in my ear.

I'd seen my appearance in the mirror before we left the castle for the Sacred Tree. There was something very wrong with my reflection. Something had yelled at me from within that this was not how I was supposed to look.

Fraud.

Hestia had elongated my ears, letting them round off ever so slightly at the tip. My skin glowed with an ethereal radiance, and while I could feel their weight on my wrists, the cuffs had vanished. My birthmarks were the most surprising.

In their place was nothing but smooth, radiant skin and a prickling itch that wouldn't go away no matter how much I fussed over it.

I decided I hated it. The woman walking to the Sacred Tree, far a soldier at her side, was not me. The clothes she wore were excessive even for my standards. A floor-length, sleeveless, light blue gown with a matching cloak. The hems of both embroidered with silver moons in all their phases. The neckline of the dress plunged to just above my belly button, making the metal latch of the cloak, an ornate full moon, a centrepiece on my chest.

I had never shown so much cleavage. I'd never looked so regal.

"Stop slouching," Jaz whispered to me again. We had ten steps to climb before our conversation would be overheard by the two White Guards standing by the double doors.

Taking one hard look at Jaz, I let him know how I felt about his bossiness. "Tell me what to do again, and I'll feed you to Obsidian."

He looked at me with a harsh seriousness that cracked almost instantly. A smile spread across his face, and we both let out a snort of laughter over the absurdity of the shadowy lapdog doing anything but laze about.

"Do you remember what we went over about the Tree?"

"The Tuath Dé have a birth chart that revolves around the Tree's branches," I said. "I need to touch the branch that would have been my birth branch."

Jaz frowned.

"What?" I asked.

"I know you have to try, but the Sacred Tree has only ever been for the Tuath Dé."

I met Jaz's eyes and found a pang of sadness there. It wasn't right that he should help me do this. It felt wrong to stand in front of him, looking the way I did, when he'd been denied his own identity since birth.

"When the Tuath Dé take the pilgrimage beyond the veil to touch the Sacred Tree, their gift is amplified. Sometimes a little, sometimes a lot. Sometimes they receive a new angle to the gift they already have."

There was a pause from him, and his eyebrows rose as if he'd had an intriguing thought. He didn't give voice to it. Instead, he said, "Touching the Sacred Tree is considered the greatest honour in any Tuath Dé's life. Play the part."

"Pretend to be a spoiled princess? How will I ever manage that?" I feigned a damsel's faint, and he responded by poking his tongue out at me.

We continued up the stairs, the power my nerves had held over me broken.

As we reached the ornate doors, I noticed a story played out over its surface. One of the Tree that lay within the chamber. Symbols of fire, water, air and earth were spread out to the four corners. In between them, four more symbols which I recognised from my painting in Hestia's book on the Sacred Tree. Scattered between the larger symbols were flowers, leaves, fruits and nuts. These were painted with gold.

I flipped a strand of my flowing white hair, tamed by magic, behind my ear to reveal the pointed shape. The small movement signalled the guards to give me entrance to a holy place that was my foreign body's birthright.

They opened the doors for me.

I lifted my chin a little higher as I entered the round room. As promised, a long trunk followed by a system of branches hung upside down from the ceiling. Each branch twisted outward, away from its brothers and sisters and towards the line of Tuath Dé surrounding it.

The leaves on each branch were different, and some bore the fruits, nuts and flowers that decorated the door. Where the branch stopped reaching outward, the wood extended into a flattened platform with a symbol etched on it. Like an offering plate.

I retraced my memory. What symbol was I looking for?

Dariush, the queen and Hestia had all argued over where I should touch the Tree. Since the Nine Daughters hadn't been specific, they decided it was best it I stuck to what would have been my birth branch had I been born a Tuath Dé. The symbol was intricate, jagged in places and curved in others, but all of them looked intricate and there were over twenty to sift through.

"Between the pentagram and the one that looks like a stick," Jaz offered calmly.

I readjusted my shoulders and began walking over to the branch. I had almost started to hold out my hand when someone else's grabbed my shoulder.

I jumped and spun around. We had been caught out after only a few steps inside the room.

"I know you're eager to receive the Tree's blessing, dear. But you'll have to wait your turn," a greying Tuath Dé man said and pointed to a space in the outer circle of the room. "Stand over there and watch what the others do. It's quite simple."

"Th-thank you," I mumbled.

He looked down at the wooden item I held close to my chest. Dariush had told me to bring something that held a lot of meaning to me. I considered keeping the book a secret, but Dariush seemed distracted enough that he'd probably never consider the importance of it.

"Ah, my sacrifice was a book too. Most give jewels, gold, but I believe the Tree loves books the best. Of course, that was quite some time ago," the man said with a distant smile. It was then that the reality of gifting a tree a collection of pulped and dried tree parts stuck me as a bit violent, and I hoped the thing didn't have consciousness.

"May the blessings be ours." He bowed his head slightly and waited, then he frowned.

It took a moment for me to realise he was waiting for me to respond.

"May the blessings be ours," I said quickly and hurried over to the space he had pointed out.

As the ceremony went on, it was clear that not every branch was utilised at the same time. The Tuath Dé only approached the Tree in fours. There wasn't much to make out between the heads of Tuath Dé in front of me. Most fara guards stayed by the outer circle, but I noticed I wasn't the only Tuath Dé-looking individual with guards only a mere step from them.

Each time a Tuath Dé placed their sacrifice on the plate and their hand on the wood, a golden light erupted in front of them, swallowed their sacrifice and flowed into their body.

I was suddenly very unsure about this.

My hesitancy was short-lived as my turn arrived.

"I'll be right beside you," Jaz said over my shoulder.

As I stepped up to the branch, I noticed there were no etchings on the plate. Rather the branch had entwined itself in intricate knots to form its symbol. I thought placing something as large as a book on the branch might have snapped it, but the branch stayed sturdy. Seeing the book on the plate, I felt panicked at the realisation that my only connection to my mother was currently being sacrificed.

Knowing there was no turning back I placed my right palm under the flattened wood. A single desire running through my mind. *Third time's a charm.* I had to make this work.

It took a moment longer than I anticipated. Like the Tree was thinking. It knew I wasn't Tuath Dé. Still, it had something for me. Something different.

Light erupted from the branch, encasing me in white. Blinding me. I felt the wood beneath my hand begin to morph. I tried to pull my hand back, maybe see what the wood had to give me. But my fingers stuck to the wood. Like the Tree wanted to keep me there for a moment longer. Electricity pulsed through my fingers, and they moved into the shape of an almost fist, clasping something solid.

I only saw what I held in my hand for a brief moment before another light erupted beside me. The light was too close to have been the Tuath Dé to my left.

As the light faded, I saw.

Murmurs and gasps echoed through the room. Guards rushed forward, pushing me away from where the light had been, and wrestled Jaz to the ground.

On his face, a five-petaled flower branding burned an angry gold. The heart of it stretched from his left eye, turning the once-blue iris a shimmering gold, and knotwork twisted in every direction. Over the bridge of his nose, down to his mouth and lower jawline, past his temple, high onto his forehead.

Where Hestia had changed my face to look foreign to me, the Tree had changed Jaz's to look more himself. Like it had removed a glamour he'd been cursed with for a lifetime.

Get off him! I felt my words rise in my throat, but they didn't come out. The White Guards pulled Jaz to his feet, his arms bound behind his back.

"Apologies, ma'am!" The man nodded my way, ducking his head as if all this was his fault.

Let him go! The man didn't see my mouth move soundlessly. I was desperate to get the words out. Desperate to convince them he didn't do anything wrong, but Jaz's eyes were fixed on me. They went wide as he realised what I was struggling with, then they darkened with purpose.

"Go home!" Jaz yelled. "Get the fuck out of here!" There was so much venom in his voice, if I didn't know Jaz's truly golden soul, I would have believed his projection of hatred.

Still, I couldn't look away as the guard pulled him down a hallway and out of sight. I was moving towards the hall's double door entrance when a second White Guard stopped me.

"Ma'am, I'm sorry about your guard's betrayal. You really need to get back to the district. We've set up adequate protection for all Tuath Dé there, but the rest of the city—" The man paused. "The council has finally moved for a takeover. Come dusk it'll be unrecognisable. The queen's had it coming."

An attack on the city? I felt weak.

"Move quickly. I'd send one of the White Guards to escort you, but I have none to spare from the front line."

It took everything in me to give the guard a smile and a small nod before I fled the hall. If he was expecting me to thank him for that information, or recite that strange blessing, he didn't stop me.

I kept my pace even, my chin up, till I was out of sight of the Sacred Tree Temple and the guards protecting it.

On a street bustling with people, I stopped to look at the wooden object the Tree had bestowed me with. A bat. The Tree had *blessed* me with a wooden baseball bat.

I felt myself begin to slip into a panic. Tears spilled over my cheeks as I leaned against a brick building. That feeling of something solid at my back was the only thing that kept me together. The only thing that kept me focused on the now instead of how completely I'd failed. I allowed myself a moment to breathe deeply.

And then I ran.

CHAPTER TWENTY-SIX

Zorya

"You know those don't work down here," I said, interrupting Ettie's solitude in the living room. She had been sitting cross-legged on one of Hestia's green lounge chairs, staring into the fireplace like it was another will-o'-the-wisp. Her attention on the flames only broke long enough for her to check her mobile. The long screen remained black and unresponsive no matter how many times she tapped it or held down the side button.

Ettie's head snapped in my direction. She gave me a grimace that said, *I already know that,* then proceeded to stare intently at the fireplace again, tucking her phone into a pocket in her loose jeans.

The others had tried coaxing information from her, but so far, she'd offered nothing but scrunched-up facial expressions and silence.

Geira had left for the kitchen to make coffee and speak with Dariush once he had returned through the door on his own.

I shoved down jealousy. Annalise and Jaz were off doing far more exciting things than I was, and Dariush and Geira were planning something without me. Again.

I knew she was trying to convince Dariush to involve me. Even after I apologised to Annalise and carried out night duty with barely a grumble——*OK, a lot of grumbling*——he hadn't forgiven me for what I'd done.

Only Nate seemed content that he'd been left out. His sleeping form took up the entirety of the couch on the other end of the living room. There were deep bags under his eyes. He needed some restful sleep, but from the crease in his forehead and irregular twitches of his body, it was clear he wasn't getting it.

"Up for a game of mancala?" I asked, my voice barely above a whisper, and lightly shook an old, light brown box to steal her attention again. The pebbles inside shifted quietly in their wooden frame.

"Sure," Ettie said, flicking her eyes to Nate.

"I can run through the rules," I began, placing the box I had found in Hestia's library on the coffee table in front of her and then pulling up an ottoman to sit on.

"I know the rules." She scrunched her face as if she was trying to recall whether she really did know the game, and where she might have learned it.

The box unfolded to reveal a board. Each side held wells, and underneath the board was a compartment with a green velvet drawstring bag with playing pebbles tucked inside.

I opened the bag, rummaged through the pebbles with my right hand and removed a closed, but empty, fist from the bag. I repeated the process with my left hand, only this time I stole a pebble in my fist before I removed it.

"Which hand?" I asked, giving her the opportunity to win first go.

"Left," she said with certainty. I revealed a pale pink glass pebble and handed her the drawstring bag, making a mental note to have her close her eyes next time.

Ettie took the colourful glass pebbles and placed them into their allocated wells, pausing only a moment before she made the first move.

The first game was quick, and I won, making her scrunch up her face again and demand another round. She won the second and third game, before accusing me of letting her win.

As the rounds rolled on, we fell into a silent rhythm. Her shoulders relaxed, and she became more focused on winning than on her lost memory or the fact she was in a house full of strangers.

After losing twice in a row she became more focused on winning and made a noise of triumph when she did. Nate shifted and let out a deep groan in response but didn't wake. Ettie found that funny, and she snorted before quickly covering her mouth in a show of silence. Giggles came out muffled behind her hands.

I was glad we could bring out some of the brightness in her soul, even if Nate had done it in his sleep. Part of me wanted to just keep playing, let her have this moment of joy, but I knew I had to push. I had to steal this moment from her to get even an ounce of information.

If someone had broken the treaty, I needed to know. It was my duty, and not even small acts of kindness were supposed to get in the way of that. Right?

My attention fell on her choker. Small silver links sat close to her neck. A white, round crystal pendant slipped over them like an afterthought. Ettie was constantly fussing with the crystal, returning it neatly to the notch of her neck when it slid too far to the left or right.

The stone reminded me of the ones embedded into my cuffs. Only, Ettie's stone held more lustre. It glowed, refracted the light of the fireplace. Like it lived. Like it had purpose.

"Ettie—" I began, but she cut me off.

"I can't remember anything. There's when you found me with the lights. There's a tumbling darkness and screams." Ettie squeezed her eyes shut and shook her head like she could drown out the sound. "And then there's nothing. Not a single fucking thing."

A loud thundering from the backdoor broke our attention, and I knew I'd lost my chance to push any further.

The clatter of rushed footsteps and something solid hitting the lower parts of the walls moved towards the kitchen.

Nate woke up abruptly, and all three of us headed into the hallway, then towards the dining room that connected to the kitchen as the noises moved. At the kitchen's entrance stood Annalise, back facing the three of us. A bat in one hand, the other pointing at her throat.

At least, I thought it was Annalise. Instead of the blue dress she wore when we left her in the queen's war room, a floor-length, light blue cloak swept off her shoulders. Her hair was twirled back at the sides and held together with a silver comb to reveal—*pointed ears*?

I blinked twice, and the pointed ears vanished.

A glamour, I decided. There was no Jaz with her.

"What are you trying to say? Are you choking?" Dariush said, his hands gripping her shoulders, panic lacing his words.

Nate was the one to use his head, handing her a piece of paper and a pen from the mahogany chest of drawers by the dining room entrance.

Annalise took the items and pushed her way to the kitchen table and began to write.

Where is Jaz? I stepped back into the hallway, taking a moment to check the backdoor. He couldn't be far off.

No one.

Ettie.

Ettie, whose small steps and fast heartbeat had followed me towards the banging, was now absent. Had she gone to sit in front of the fireplace again?

I glanced back at the dining room. Not there. Then took one step towards the living room before I heard it. So faint I might as well have imagined it.

A lopsided pitter-patter that signalled nothing good. And it was on the other side of the backdoor.

I sprang for it. Moving quickly through the threshold and towards that familiar heartbeat. A few steps towards the labyrinth of Dubnos City and a second heartbeat came within earshot, the one that I needed to hear. Ettie's.

There was no one on the main street. The heartbeats I keenly listened for moved at a steady pace behind the first row of buildings. Out of sight.

They could have been running, or on a tram. I needed to move fast, or I'd lose them.

I looked back to the door in stone that I'd left open.

Geira might have my back, but the others wouldn't.

I didn't know when the TDE had become more important than doing what was right, but I knew that if I walked back into that house without Ettie, their trust in me would be irrevocably broken.

Ettie has no one, except me.

Trusting my gut, I focused on the two heartbeats weaving through the streets of Dubnos and set off at a sprint.

CHAPTER TWENTY-SEVEN

Annalise

I scrawled furiously over the paper as my mouth moved. Nothing came out of it. When I'd asked the Tree to take my siren song, I hadn't thought it would take my speaking ability with it.

And at the worst time too.

Dariush needed to know what happened to Jaz. He needed to know of the Tuath Dé's plans to take the kingdom.

They took Jaz. Guard said to stay in Tuath Dé district. Planning on taking Dubnos before dusk. Streets not safe.

It wasn't eloquent by any stretch, but the message needed to come out quickly.

Dariush, who had been peering over my shoulder as I wrote, spoke before my pen had come off the page. "We stick to the plan. Geira you're here with the girl and the squad. Annalise and I will take this information to the queen and return with an updated strategy. No one is to leave this house or heed the command of the TDE or any other fara. Our priority is Dubnos and keeping the girl safe. Then we see what we can do about Jaz."

A pit opened in my stomach. Any number of things could have happened to Jaz by now. Execution by decapitation had been the punishment of that fara couple who'd been arrested. I had no delusions that Jaz would escape the same fate. But with everything else happening around us, how did Dariush imagine we'd get to him in time?

"So, we mutiny?" Nate said from across the kitchen table after deciphering my message that he'd read upside down.

Dariush shot him a glare that said *I dare you to question me* as if expecting some kind of push back.

"Nothing wrong with that, just making sure we're on the same page," Nate said quickly, throwing up open hands in a gesture of surrender. Panic tinted his words, and I knew his concern for his friend outweighed any loyalty to the Tuath Dé he might have been clinging to.

"We don't have much time," Geira started. "The Tuath Dé could execute their plans early, and it's midday now. We should decide on a place to evacuate the queen to—"

"She'll die before she leaves her people unprotected," Dariush interrupted. "Where's the girl?"

I looked around the yellow-toned kitchen to see three focused faces morph into a display of worry. Geira walked out of the room abruptly. A guttural roar of frustration emanated from the hallway before she returned a moment later. She shook her head. "The backdoor is open."

My stomach went queasy as I considered the lack of real protest against Dariush's plan. I thought of Zorya's apology, the promises she'd made. I'd been so stupid to believe her.

There was no way she'd ever been capable of trusting Dariush. She'd gone behind our backs and taken the girl to the Tuath Dé the second we were distracted.

"Zorya." The first word I'd spoken since touching the Tree escaped my mouth. Again, the faces of the fara in front of me changed. This time, into confusion.

I clasped my hands over my mouth in excitement for a moment before trying again.

I can speak, I mouthed. No words came out.

"You said *Zorya*," Nate said. "Do it agai—"

"We can't wait for this," Dariush interrupted. "Geira, Nate. Find them. We're going back through the door. Now!" Dariush grabbed my wrist and pulled me from the kitchen, up the stairs and towards Hestia's bedroom. His heavy breathing startled me.

You're angry, I wanted to say. But again, the sounds failed to leave my mouth, and with his attention fixed on a black door nestled between two mirrors on a large black wardrobe, my attempts to communicate were lost.

I didn't have time to take in Hestia's private room aside from the wash of green-and-black-accented furniture.

Three knocks with a black ring, it looked identical to the one Hestia had given Geira, and a golden hand-shaped doorknob appeared from the dark wood. We stepped through the threshold and the door swung closed behind us. It locked with a resounding click.

"What did you do!?" Dariush fumed through his teeth, jaw clenched. His eyes pinned me against the black door. My back leaned into its solid frame, and I almost wished it was the golden portal I had walked through in the forest. Maybe then I could drown in it and not have to face the anger that radiated off him.

"You were destined— The Tree was supposed to make you stronger. A weapon. And you come back with a stick and no voice!" He pointed to the baseball bat I held clenched in my hand.

My whole body stilled as he admitted pieces of his plan for the first time.

Weapon of a King.

Snippets of the Nine Daughters' prophecy fell into place in my mind, and my heart shattered. I had been nothing more than a pawn to this man. A thing that could break his chains and give him power.

The way he'd taken care of me after my run-in with Resh. When he'd shown me the secret place under the castle. He'd protected me from the Tuath Dé's demands for my execution.

Had it all been a ploy to get closer to me?

First Zorya, and now Dariush. These betrayals were too much. Tears threatened to spill to the surface. I needed to speak. To tell him exactly how I felt, my side, but the man kept talking and my frustration grew as the words vanished in my throat.

"I should have never trusted the Nine Daughters when they told me you would be our saviour. I should have never sought you out in that fucking backwards town. Do you even know what you were supposed to be? Everything we've worked so hard for is gone now, Annalise!" Dariush breathed, his tone little more than a growl.

I jolted at his admission.

"They will be at our doorstep in minutes, and they will spare no one! Especially not you—"

My hand covered his mouth as I leaned in towards him. His words muffled against my palm; my eyes bored into his.

He'd been working some sort of plan this entire time, a plan that involved me. No, worse than that. His plan had fallen to pieces the second I lost my voice.

I *was* the plan, and he hadn't bothered to let me in on any of it. My mouth moved.

You dragged me into this world. You've been playing a game the whole time. Treating me like a chess piece, but I have no idea what's going on. I don't know what's wrong, how to help, what you want from me. I have no choice here. None. You hold all the cards and it's not—"fair!"

The last word was the only one to escape my mouth. The fist of my left hand shook as it choked the wooden bat by my side. Dariush's body released tension as he caught my meaning, and anger.

I kept my palm on his mouth. Feeling his hot breath against it for a few, silent moments more before he took my wrist and entwined my fingers in his.

"Fair," Dariush repeated, a softness in his voice. I took a moment to look deep into his eyes. Something heavy, but true, sat within their blue-grey mist, like he'd understood every word without needing to hear it. Like he felt guilt for his hand in all this, and all the things I felt in this moment.

He led me through the thicket of doors that surrounded us till we reached one door at the edge of the room. There was no knocking with rings this time. The door opened at our approach, and we moved towards the queen's oval mahogany table beyond.

It was just the two of us in the room. His guilt, my pain, our silence making it feel all too crowded.

Dariush moved to the queen's large chair and pulled open a drawer hidden under the table. From it he removed a pen and two pieces of paper and placed them on the table. Each item was marked with a sigil identical to his brooch.

"You first," he said, handing me the pen. "Tell me what happened."

I placed my hand on the Tree and—

It wasn't something I would've been able to say aloud. I could barely acknowledge to myself the weight of what I'd done. But there was something freeing about writing the words out. It lightened them.

*I asked the Tree to take my siren song. Just like I asked that man to take it. I don't—*I paused, then scratched out the last word—*didn't want it. I think I might need it now.*

"What happened to Jaz?"

I flicked my hair out of my face and raised an eyebrow, giving him a look that I hoped said "really?"

He clenched his jaw and with a huff, held out his hand for the pen.

What happened to Jaz, he wrote, forgetting the question mark, before handing the pen back. I took a moment to note his messy handwriting. The smaller letters were as large as the capitals and they ran into each other, making the sentence look rushed and loud. I smiled to myself at how it matched him so well.

I think he touched the Tree too. There was a white light. The Tree marked his face, and they arrested him. My hand shook as I wrote the next words. *I could have stopped them if I'd had my voice.*

Dariush stole the pen from me with clawed fingers and set it down on the oval table, then wrapped both his hands around mine.

There was a long stretch of silence as he seemed to consider his words, flipping through sentences in his head, weighing up their truth against their potential ramifications.

"When Dubh told me she is dying, she swore she'd never let my brother have the crown. It was either me or no one. I told her she'd have to find a way to live forever because I wasn't going to take it."

A sad laugh escaped his lips, but the edges of his smile failed to reach his eyes. He dropped the attempt at humour.

"You've felt my shadows. That's not even a drop of what I can do, but you know what happens when powerful people are allowed to run loose. You know, probably better than me, just how deadly even seemingly good people can become.

"I went to the Nine Daughters. I told Dubh it was to find out how to break my bonds with the Tuath Dé. Instead, I asked them what would happen if I refused my mother. I'm not sure why they told you your prophecy in words, but when they spoke to me, it was in images that floated just beneath the surface.

"I saw my home burning red, and when I asked them how I could ever hope to be this kingdom's saviour, they showed me you, singing by the lake. You were beauty itself, all light. Then I saw you turn into something else, something old. I saw you standing against the Tuath Dé, defending this city."

When he spoke of that change within me, a change that had caused the deaths of two innocent men, it wasn't with disgust or malice. A sliver of hope edged his words. His faith in me and subsequent betrayal mixed in a caustic concoction that pulled my soul downward. I was back at the house on the hill again, listening to my mother tell me things that were too painful to hear in that moment and had come too late.

He seemed to see me as the answer to his problems. Had Dariush shared what those problems were from the start, and how I could solve them, maybe Jaz would still be with us. Maybe I wouldn't have given away so much of myself to a flipping tree.

I inhaled a sharp breath and counted to four.

"I've thought about telling you, all of it, but I was afraid you might see the monster in me. See how broken I am. I was afraid you'd see how perfect they are and choose them instead. I couldn't risk that."

I stared at the hands that clasped mine, one black and clawed, the other callused and sun-kissed, and exhaled to another slow count of four.

"I don't deserve to be king of Dubnos, but the people need someone, and I can't let it be the Tuath Dé. Dubh gave me to them so one day I might find a way to break their hold over us. But after all this time, after all this planning and searching, the only plan I have ever had that was worth a fuck is you.

"You haven't lost your voice, I'm sure of it. You've said two words since the Tree. We can figure this out. If we survive whatever they throw at us tonight, if by some miracle he's still alive, we'll get Jaz back. We'll save as many fara from the Tuath Dé's grasp as we can. Together." He spoke as if he held a fragile butterfly between his fingers and the faintest breeze might blow it away. His voice held no anger, no harshness. Just a promise, one that I felt deep within my fractured soul.

Dariush, with his beast hand, slipped a loose strand of hair behind my ear and rested his palm against my cheek.

I was torn. His words shone with truth. He'd lived a prisoner, watching things get worse and worse for his mother, this city he called home, the soldiers he'd come to see as family.

But was it enough that he'd told me the truth now? Did all his pain and feelings of failure and the weight of *his* world on *his* shoulders make up for the fact that I'd been led blindfolded into the middle of a battle, my only weapon long discarded because I thought I was safe? Because I thought that with it, I was the problem?

Weapon of a King.

Weapon of a King.

The words of the Nine Daughters swam in my head. They sank into my lungs like the waters that failed to drown me.

A war erupted between my heart and my head. Was he really holding out hope that I'd find my voice again, like it just needed a good rest and a mug of camomile tea? This heat that I felt swirling between us, pulling us together as it had done since the day we met, was it all part of his grand plan to keep me on hand in case I became useful again?

Heart or head, I couldn't distinguish between the two, screamed at me that Dariush would never use me like that.

But he had.

I leaned into him. And with all the things I still felt. All the hurt. I pressed my lips to his.

And he kissed back.

I savoured the taste of his lips, soft and tainted with floral tea leaves. The kind, I realised now, he probably only started drinking since he'd met me.

Warm hands found my hips and urged me closer. The hem of my skirt lifted as his fingers moved upwards to my waist.

The bat dropped to the floor with a thud, but neither of us relented or paused. I rested my palms against his chest, sucking in gasps of air as our mouths collided with more fever and fury.

Clenching his shirt with two fists, I arched my back and exposed my neck. His mouth was on it in an instant, trailing kisses from a spot beneath my jawline to the place where my neck and chest met. A heavy breath escaped me involuntarily at the feel of his complete closeness.

He growled in response. After some time of soft touch and long, sweet kisses—teasing—Dariush grabbed my arse and lifted me to sit on the edge of the table.

Taking the hem of my dress in both hands, he lifted the fabric to my mouth.

"Open." That one word, and the gleam in Dariush's eyes, was the hottest thing I'd ever witnessed. Heat flushed my cheeks and pooled low in my stomach. I couldn't help but obey. He forced the fabric into my mouth, leaving my stomach and underwear exposed for him.

Dariush sank to his knees and kissed that spot between my legs that was stubbornly shielded by fabric. I squirmed in frustration and Dariush responded with an infuriatingly smug chuckle and a firm grip on my thighs.

"Still," he commanded.

I was about to drop the dress, about to pull him to his feet for being such a tease, but as quickly as he'd spoken, a finger pulled that fabric aside like a curtain and his tongue was on me.

Long sweet strokes glided over that spot, teasing silent moans from my gagged and unhelpful mouth. Only the rocking of my hips and my inability to keep my head from lolling backwards would have told him that I needed more.

He gave it. Pleasure overwhelmed me until that was all I could think about. I knew the hem of my dress was about as soaked as my underwear.

I rocked harder, torn between my search for release and wanting to be lost in this pleasure forever.

Dariush stood abruptly, halting both.

He flung a hand into my hair, wrapping the long strands around his beastly fist. Pressing himself closer to me before he angled my head inches from his face.

"Eyes on me."

That spot between my legs pulsed. I felt far too naked and far too clothed at the same time.

With my attention on him completely, he dipped his free hand into my underwear.

I sucked in a breath through fabric as his fingers, warm and pressing, slowly worked that spot between my legs.

For a moment I closed my eyes, biting down hard. I sank into the feel of his fingers on me, but his fist held tighter, and my eyes opened with the pain. Good pain.

My chest heaved. The storm of his eyes told me what he wanted. Demanded it of me. He wanted to see this moment. The moment he undid it all. Unravelled me.

His fingers moved faster, flicked and pinched, but his eyes never left mine. My dress nearly slipped from my lips, and for a moment, he blurred in front of me.

Even if I were able to speak, the waves of pleasure that rolled through me again and again would have made delivering anything coherent impossible.

I gave him what he wanted. My body shuddered violently before his hands cupped the space between my legs, palm pressing into my core. Forcing more waves of pleasure to rock through me. He released his hold on my hair, and his hand made its way to the back of my neck.

"Good girl," Dariush said, so low and soft in my ear, before he pressed his lips to my forehead.

After a few moments longer gently kneading the last pulsing pleasure out of me, Dariush pulled back and removed the dress from my mouth. It was as damp as I thought it would be.

Both his hands moved to my cheeks. I did my best to catch my breath as he wiped away some of the wetness from my face.

For a split second, the harshness of his typical expression was gone. Replaced with pure satisfaction, joy. Awe.

But that look only held for a moment before fear blemished the edges of his eyes again, and his smile faltered.

He held my face in his hands.

"Annalise."

My name sounded like sugar on his lips, and I didn't stop myself from leaning in.

"The next time I stand in front of the queen, she'll ask me to take the crown. She'll ask me to become king of Dubnos."

For the faintest moment his words caught in his throat. He paused as if what was to come out of his mouth next was a final betrayal.

Instead, he said, "And when she does, I'll ask something of you."

I knew now what he still wouldn't share. Dariush needed to control everything. He was drawn to me, and I to him, but he was too fearful of my autonomy to let me in.

His secret prickled over my skin, danced in my stomach.

This was my chance to free myself from the Tuath Dé and take the means for my own survival. And if he was willing to keep things from me again, deny me time that was paramount to my choice, I would keep this revelation to myself too. I forced the butterflies down, kept my gaze vacant and gave a questioning frown when his next words came.

"I need you to say yes."

CHAPTER TWENTY-EIGHT

Zorya

I had begun to worry when I arrived at the top of the staircase. I'd lost the two heartbeats some time ago, but I was so sure this would be where they'd take Ettie. The cold stone stairwell was silent.

Still, I ventured down. Hoping.

My thoughts raced back to the promise I'd made Geira after what happened with the security job. She was going to be pissed.

I moved deeper into the stairwell and relief flooded me as murmurs bounced off the curved walls. I made my footsteps lighter, trying to keep my pace at the same time. If Ettie was in any real trouble, I needed to act fast.

The murmurs turned into a conversation between men. Three different voices, broken every so often by the soft voice of a smaller figure. The voice sounded like Ettie's except it was dull. Like her heart wasn't really in it, or her mind wasn't in control of her mouth and she was simply speaking on autopilot.

The voices grew louder with my descent, and eventually, I could see light spilling around a corner. I stopped before I could see in, instead choosing to listen to the conversation before planning my next move.

"We know you went to the castle. Tell us what the queen looked like." A masculine voice, less gruff than the others, spoke. It ebbed and flowed in its pitch, and I had feeling of dread that I'd heard this voice before.

The man was using Ettie for information, but why would he need to know what the queen looked like? I'd visited Dubnos City a few times before. Spotting the queen walking through the streets wasn't uncommon, but if these people had never seen her before, they could simply ask any underdweller what she looked like, and they'd answer freely.

"A ball of light. Every colour. Shining like the sun. Like a star," Ettie babbled, and I almost exhaled a breath of relief. She was talking nonsense. That couldn't possibly mean anything to these people.

I glanced ever so slightly around the corner, making sure to not let my head stay in the light for too long.

A desk sat against the wall farthest from the stairwell threshold. The man with the familiar voice stood near it. He was looking towards the other end of the room. I could only see his back. I felt confident that he was looking at Ettie, but where were the other two men whose voices I had heard earlier?

I steadied myself against the wall. I needed a better idea of the layout of the room. My view was too limited. Those other men could be anywhere, and even though I had a few knives on me, I couldn't possibly take all three of them down.

Maybe I could—

I almost jumped at the sound of loud footsteps entering the stairwell. A metallic piece of their shoes clacking and echoing off the sides of the stone walls. They seemed to be walking faster than I had, not hindered by the necessity of stealth.

Too late to consider my options, I clung to the opposite wall. The one I knew would lead me to the closest part of the room where I was sure Ettie was. With a deep breath to steady myself, I thought of the wall at my back. I thought of the creatures that lived in the cracks of the unsmoothed rock. I thought what it might be like to hunt them. To hide within the cracks and wait for my prey to walk into my home. I thought what it might be like to crawl over these walls knowing I was the apex predator and nothing could capture me.

Slipping deeper and deeper into the image I had carved in my mind, I let my body vibrate with static, felt the glamour take hold and stepped out into the light. I made sure to keep to the wall. Keeping myself small, thinking about the way I might seem to hide in one of the cracks should one of the men look my way.

I could see Ettie now. Her face was pale and robotic, like she was still in a trance. They'd tied her to a chair, her arms angled behind the backrest. I didn't dare look at the men. Instead, I focused on keeping my glamour and getting to the girl.

Ettie's chair was a metre and a half away from the wall behind her. The room wasn't an even square shape either. The wall curved in towards the girl and rounded off behind her, leaving an awkward pocket in the room where no desk, shelf or chest could sit without looking misplaced.

Perfect. I decided in an instant that was where I was going to hide and bide my time.

The footsteps in the stairwell reached the room, and the room's attention shifted to the new presence.

I took this as my chance to close the distance between my spot on the wall and the space behind Ettie's chair.

From my hiding spot behind Ettie, I had a full view of the room. The person who had entered was Prince Aed. I wasn't surprised by that fact at all. Neither was I surprised to find Hendrik dressed in white and leaning with one arm against the other half of the desk. There was another guard that I had only ever seen a handful of times, mostly as a close guard to Tierney.

It shouldn't have been a surprise to see Tierney himself, but it was. That familiar voice with the strangely jagged pitch clicked with his face. I'd be lying if I said I ever liked Tierney, but his position symbolised everything I had committed myself to. He commanded the fara army. He wrote the laws that I had kept for the longest time. But I wasn't keeping them now.

I was outright rebelling against them. Breaking them.

I could have turned myself in then and there. Changed my tone. Asked how I could serve the Tuath Dé in this moment, but Tierney's plan involved using Ettie. Involved *compelling* Ettie.

He was probably the one to put the crystal collar around her neck and lure her beyond the veil in the first place.

How could I let this girl's freedoms be taken away like that, when everything else, everything she had loved, had been stolen from her. She would never again see the sun. Never again feel the warm embrace of her family, because of the people who stole her away to this place.

A pang sounded in my heart, and I mourned for the things the girl had lost. And for what *I* had lost.

There was no way I was leaving her to endure whatever they had planned for her. Saying that the queen was a ball of light didn't mean much to me, but it clearly meant a lot to Tierney. I was suddenly afraid for more than just the girl. I needed to make sure they couldn't pull more information out of her.

I inched myself closer to Ettie's wrists, sank my teeth into her arm just above the rope, and drank. She flinched ever so slightly but seemed zoned out by whatever spell she was under. I was counting on that.

Images flooded into my mind. I tried to reach the time before I met her, to see what her life above had looked like, but there was a wall there. The wall took shape. I was on the inside of a large box. The walls tumbled around me, and the dark silhouettes of people crashed into me. Their screams drowned my thoughts. It was getting hard to breathe. The world was stuffy. Only darkness.

I forced my mind to the familiar parts of Ettie's memories.

The girl had seen plenty of the world down here in her short time in it. But it wasn't what she saw that stopped me in my tracks. It was the way she saw the fae.

I knew what the girl was talking about now when she said the queen was a light. When Ettie gazed upon the queen, she saw no features. Just a blazing light bent into the shape of a person. The light swirled and moved, flicking through every different colour of the rainbow as she spoke, as if the light were revealing her mood.

Ettie had second sight.

My mind drifted across more faces as I drank. Most looked the same as they were with only minor changes that revealed a hidden nature. Geira was imbued in a gold light, the outline of a weapon always at her fingertips regardless of whether she held one or not. Nate's eyes were like mirrors reflecting everything he saw.

For a moment I wished I could pass memories of my own through blood. Jaz would have liked the way she saw him.

Then I found myself. I had seen myself in the eyes of others plenty of times before. Often the blood of the person I drank from wanted to show me how that person saw me. Or maybe it was me searching for my image in their memories.

But the image of myself I saw in Ettie's memories was vastly different from those I had seen in other blood.

My mind clung to that image.

I wanted it so badly to reflect the truth, but the moment the Zorya in Ettie's mind stepped towards Annalise, both of our forms changed. At first, Annalise looked to be shrouded in a neon blue hue. It blackened as I stepped closer, and her face became gaunt. Her eyes were gone, and in the space where they should be—blackness. A blackness so deep that it threatened to pull your soul towards it and swallow it whole.

My eyes were gone too, and in my hands was a bowl.

Annalise and I had been drawn to each other from the start. Threads of black reached and drifted over everything in the space between us. They pulled us together, only for us to resist and pull the threads in the opposite direction. This happened over and over. Two boats rocking towards and away from each other in the tide.

"And the girl. Annalise. Tell me what she looks like." Tierney's voice inched towards Ettie.

I flinched. *Why would Tierney want to know about Annalise?*

Ettie responded. Her voice calm and obedient. Robotic.

"Eyes that see into black... Two heads... A..." Ettie was fading.

Two heads? I flicked through Ettie's memories of Annalise. No image of her depicted two heads.

"A what, girl!?" Tierney's voice rose with frustration. He shook the girl violently and I released my teeth to stop them ripping open her arm with the movement.

"Eyes . . . eyes . . ." Ettie was slipping further into unconsciousness. I was glad that I had stopped Tierney from getting more information out of her and hoped he couldn't make sense of everything she had already said.

"No worries. I know how to kill the queen now. We'll get you the girl after that." The voice was Prince Aed.

My hopes vanished. He'd at least figured out the queen's secret, whatever it was, and to make things worse, he was willing to use that information to *kill* her.

I listened as the prince retreated up the stairs. I needed to get us both out of here and get that information to Dariush. It wouldn't surprise him that his brother was out for the throne, but at least he could do something about it.

"You." Tierney's voice zeroed in on me like an arrow. I didn't have to look at him to know that my glamour had failed me.

I stood. There was no way I was going to run and leave Ettie. Not like I'd get very far anyway. Tierney would be no match against me, but Hendrik and his guard friend would be a problem.

The guards moved towards me. Not needing Tierney's command to know he wanted me restrained.

"String her from her feet." Tierney flicked his wrist towards a bracket in the stone ceiling. Casually waltzing towards the desk.

I didn't bother struggling. I was in no position to make demands either. And there was no way I could run up those stairs, Ettie in my arms. My stomach was heavy with blood, and I felt the weight of it on my mind. Everything I did felt slow. Sluggish.

I let the men tie my feet together and hoist me from the ceiling. They tied my hands in front of me. Big mistake. I still had so much movement. Clearly Hendrik hadn't paid attention to my morning pull-ups in the gym.

But I feigned restraint. Twisting my wrists, bending my back in effort for show.

"Has anyone told you how incredibly nosey you are?" Hendrik quipped. He pressed his finger against the tip of my nose, grinned smugly and walked back to the other end of the room with his guard friend. Both of them chuckled at some joke I wasn't privy to.

I wanted to rip his fingers out of their sockets one by one.

Now that I was hung from the ceiling, Tierney waltzed back over to me. His face still and cold. I decided I preferred this expression over his smile. At least with this expression I knew what he wanted. Answers and blood.

He took my ponytail in his hand and pulled tightly so my face was almost in line with his. I would be lying if I said it didn't hurt, especially with my full weight pulling me downwards and my body contorting in an ungodly way. But as far as hair pulling, it wasn't that bad at all.

"Zorya, is it?" His cold eyes bored into mine. I squirmed, this time to pull myself away from him as much as possible. Every inch of this man exuded an aura of grime. Of tarnished and bruised morals.

"Dariush sent you, didn't he?" That awful smile returned and curled his face into something cruel.

When it became clear to him that I wasn't going to answer, he continued. "Do you know what I'm going to do to Dariush,

Zorya?" His voice pitched upwards again in that way it did when he was excited by a brilliant idea he had concocted. "I'm going to kill his mother. I'm going to take her kingdom. I'm going to make him watch as I destroy his beloved city and then I'm going to rebuild it. Not the way it was of course. I'm going to make it a Glistening City beneath the earth." He leaned closer, his whisper sinking deeper into my ear with his hot breath. "And then I'm going to feed your friend to the sluagh. They should be breaking through the wards any moment now. Don't worry. You won't live long enough to see it."

My mind became numb. All sound muffled by the shock of Tierney's confession. There was no real threat to my life here. I'd already made the calculations. I could escape this. I could fight my way out, maybe even save Ettie while I was at it.

But there was a certainty to Tierney's words. He'd collected the information he needed to put his plans into action. He'd found a way to bring sluagh into the city. Aed was already on his way to kill the queen.

It was too late. Regardless of what happened to me in this dungeon, there would be bloodshed. Humans and fae and fara alike, those who'd already suffered too much under the Tuath Dé's thumb, would die. And I was powerless to stop it.

He would get away with it too.

I took my chance. His face was so close to mine. I mustered every ounce of strength, twisted my head upwards and sank my teeth into his neck. It took a second for him to react. For his hand to pull me away, drop me and leave me swinging from my rope.

But a second was all I needed to reach my hands up towards his chest and retrieve the hackberry pin attached to his green coat.

Tierney stumbled backwards and clasped his neck, the guards coming to his aid.

I pulled my arms above my head and secured the hackberry pin into the back of my hair in one quick movement. If anyone had bothered to look, it would have appeared as if I were bracing my head for an inevitable attack.

And I would have been right to do so, for Tierney's guards were quick to move. Hendrik's friend punched me square in the middle. My arms reached for my stomach, and I swung, spitting Tierney's blood onto him.

That move was a mistake. Hendrik was next to act. This time his fist met my face. I wouldn't know if they continued with their beating. I was out cold to the world.

CHAPTER TWENTY-NINE

Annalise

A voice from the doorway sounded through the room. "Be careful what bargains you make with this one, cousin. She has a cunning way of slipping out on her end."

I pulled away from Dariush to see who had caught our moment. Embarrassment heated my cheeks before I even laid eyes on the intruder.

Pale blue skin and a crown of horns that framed milky white eyes. The man from the café leaned lazily against the doorframe, a familiar knife held between his right hand and a fingertip.

How much had he seen?

My hands went clammy, but I squared my shoulders and offered him what I hoped to be a repulsed glare. I wouldn't reach for the space under my neck that had once felt the tip of that blade, even though it felt compromised in his presence.

I took that moment to pick up the baseball bat by my feet.

"Get the fuck out," Dariush growled low. His voice was menacing, and a chill crept up my spine. When Resh chose to smile rather than respond, Dariush removed the sword at his back and pointed promisingly at the intruder. A guttural noise emanated from Dariush's throat. "Get out! Before I remove the horns from your head and make you an exile!"

"Calm down, Dariush." Resh straightened, moved into the room and waltzed around the oval table. "I'm only scoping out my new home. Your mother's done an awful job of decorating." He tutted, the point of Dariush's sword followed him. "Your grandfather may have been a false king, but at least he had flair. I wasn't there for his reign, but I remember the stories. He'd have humans brought in to fight sluagh for his amusement while everyone else stood for hours on end, watching." He chuckled, as if telling a relatable joke rather than a man's twisted display of power.

"You'll never sit on this throne," Dariush snarled through a clenched jaw as he positioned himself between the man and his mother's chair. His back stiffened.

I looked at the chair Dariush protected and noted how simple it was. It was made of sturdy mahogany wood, a black velvet cushion nailed into the seat. No embellishments, and only its tall back signalled it out as different from the other chairs in the room.

"We could fight it out here and now. You'd certainly make it easier for me to claim the throne when your mother is dead."

He was here to kill the queen. Now? Did he know about the Tuath Dé's planned attack on the city, or was this just a timely coincidence? I didn't hold a lot of faith in that last thought.

"You'd need to do more than just kill me, Resh," Dariush spat.

"But your brother isn't the ruling type, is he? No matter how much he wants to be," Resh mocked. "Can't even kill his own brother without help."

Dariush flinched at the man's admission of his brother's betrayal. It was slight and short-lived, but I saw it. Resh must have seen it too because his tongue traced over his sharp teeth, as if he could taste the emotional wound his words had delivered.

Dariush jumped onto the oval table and sprinted towards the intruder.

Resh pulled a second dagger from his leather jacket and the twin blades met Dariush's longsword with a violent clang followed by the screech of metal on metal. The longsword was pushed to the side, leaving Dariush open to Resh's next move. Resh jumped on the table and barged into his cousin, tackling him onto the table's surface. Dariush spluttered in pain as his back violently thwacked into the hardwood. The impact didn't slow him, and a half second later he'd brought the hilt of his sword down on Resh's spine.

Resh fell off the table and stumbled backward. It was enough time for Dariush to jump to the floor and regain a handle on his sword.

With three quick steps, his feet barely lifting from the stone floor, Dariush slashed forward, backing his cousin into a tight spot between the curved wall and a cabinet. The muscular beast of a man looked to be losing against Dariush. Still, he swiped with his blades and skillfully dodged Dariush's attacks. In a moment where it looked like Dariush might land a blow, Resh leaped high into the air, somersaulted over Dariush and sank one dagger into the soft tissue between Dariush's shoulder and collarbone.

Resh landed between Dariush and the table, looking over his shoulder to give me a foul, toothy smile.

Dariush held a firmer grasp of his longsword, only acknowledging the blade in his body with little more than a grimace.

"Pity I have to kill you to get the throne, cousin. I would love to make you watch as I returned this city to its original glory," Resh teased. "What do you think? Humans strung up by their feet.

Fed to an army of sluagh. The will-o'-the-wisps burning red at my command." He waved his dagger in the air dramatically.

Resh's words were so at odds with what I'd seen from him before. The way he'd moved to Mabel's side the second she'd hit the floor. I didn't know much about what I was, but I was sure my song wouldn't have affected her so easily if she really were a fara like the mark on her forehead suggested. He was in love with a human, or at the very least cared about one.

With one quick movement, Resh plunged a hand under his leather jacket, retrieved a gun and pointed it at Dariush's chest.

Ice formed in my lungs, in my veins, and my entire world stopped.

"Tuath Dé wouldn't dare step foot in Dubnos again. I guess I could always make her watch." Resh's smugness grew. I could feel the anger rising from Dariush. It looked like he'd stopped weighing up his choices. Like he was seconds from taking a bullet to the chest just to feel Resh's neck snap between his hands. All because he'd threatened me.

Then Resh made the mistake of taking his eyes off Dariush and turned his head in my direction.

Dariush sidestepped, slicing his sword upwards into flesh. The gun fell from loosened fingers and thumped on the wooden floor. Dariush pulled back his longsword before piercing Resh's shoulder creating a wound that mirrored his own. Then, the short blade still wedged in his own shoulder, Dariush pulled the longsword back and swung it high above his head.

A shatter sounded to my right, and I covered my head as glass rained down on me. Something giant and cold hit my stomach and pushed me backward. I flew through the air. My back hit the wall with a loud thud, and I fell to the floor. I couldn't tell which was worse, the pain of my knees hitting stone or the overwhelming stillness of being winded.

I gasped air back into my lungs and managed to look up in between strained breaths. A beast of shadow, with a birdlike head and too many talons to count, had crashed through the window and thrown me across the room. It roared in my direction, the deep sound vibrating everywhere.

I steadied myself and grabbed my bat that had been flung a metre from me. This thing was going to come at me again.

I thought to sing. To just try it, anything. But I knew the song wouldn't escape my lips. A giant clawed paw hit the stone floor, followed by another, and another. Four legs moved slowly but surely in my direction. Glass crackled beneath those shadowy pillars.

Breathing deeply, I closed my eyes and searched for the place within myself. The one where fire erupted and sang when I couldn't. It was the smallest sensation, but it was something.

Brightness shone through my eyelids, and I opened them to see a blue flame, neon and cold, flicker longer than any flame I had produced before. It sat atop the baseball bat. Only, it wasn't a bat at all.

It was a torch.

The bluish flames licked upward. Once, twice, then snuffed out completely.

The beast took one step backwards before it hesitated in place, assessing the threat. It was long enough for Dariush to steal the beast's attention.

Standing between the throne and the beast, Dariush held out his clawed left hand. The longsword held loosely in his right. A dagger still wedged in his shoulder.

The beast stilled momentarily, then offered Dariush a deafening roar. I flinched as a talon sprung forwards and stopped inches from Dariush's hand.

A smaller growl emanated from the beast, like it was questioning its target. The beast moved backwards and pulled his talon away with force as if Dariush had some invisible hold on it.

Another low, uncertain growl and the beast leaped out the window, talons forming wings in its retreat.

"Are you OK?" Dariush asked as he rushed to my side and lifted me to my feet. I found myself silently mouthing the word *yes* despite wincing as I rubbed my painful knees.

"Let me see," Dariush said as he helped me to a chair by the oval table, flipping it upside down once to let shards of glass fall before I sat. Dariush kneeled before me and lifted my dress to reveal angry red knees. They'd begun to swell. He placed a hand gently on each one as if feeling the heat rise off them.

"That was a sluagh. They're beasts that live below the kingdom." His cold shadows, usually invisible, took on a black, wispy form. They wrapped themselves around my tender skin, offering relief. "Our wards keep them out—when they're working."

Dariush winced and I looked to the blade embedded in his arm before frantically scanning the room.

How had I forgotten about Resh?

"He ran when the sluagh crashed through the window," Dariush said as he wrapped his fingers around the hilt of the blade. "Not the courageous type, my cousin."

With a breathy grunt, Dariush pulled the blade from his body. I tried not to throw up as the blood-stained metal was lifted into the air, revealing it had been embedded halfway in.

Red gurgled slowly from the wound. I looked away immediately and failed to hold back a dry retch.

Dariush dropped the blade to the floor and worked quickly, removing his blood-stained shirt before taking the hem of my dress in his hands.

With his claws he tore a slit in the side of the fabric before ripping two or more inches off the length of the dress. Blood gurgled with his movements.

"Can you tighten this?" he asked after he'd wrapped the lush light blue fabric around his bare shoulder. He leaned in towards me so I could work on the makeshift bandage.

Why couldn't you use your own clothes to do that? was what I wanted to say as I pulled the fabric tighter and secured it with a double knot. Instead, I made a face that let him know I didn't appreciate my dress being ripped up like that.

I thought I caught a glimpse of mischief reach the corner of his mouth.

When his arm no longer gurgled uncontrollably in front of me, I leaned across the table, grabbed the pen and a second piece of paper that hadn't yet been written on.

Why? I'd stopped caring about adding context to my written words.

"A decoy, maybe," Dariush replied, understanding the question. "They would have wanted to keep the queen distracted long enough that she wouldn't notice the wards being tampered with. Only they got me." Dariush considered something else. His jaw set tightly as he spoke. "They might have intended to keep us both distracted."

Dariush picked up his shirt and stood. Sweat beaded against his chest and blood leaked, slower, into the makeshift bandage. I shook my head and stood too, needing to keep my focus on current events rather than his body.

"We need to alert the queen's guard," he said as he stopped and stretched his black hand out towards me.

I looked at it for a moment. Hesitating. Not because of the way it looked. I had grown fond of the way his warm fur felt against my skin. The way his nails worked so hard to avoid accidentally piercing my flesh whenever he was near me.

Dariush never seemed to think of his arm as a curse. It made me feel a little more accepting of the two dots on my face that I'd held responsible for the rejection I'd experienced all my life.

I hesitated for other reasons. The truth he had kept from me. The lies he had told the people around me. The power within his veins that he had used to keep me silent in front of the Tuath Dé. It meant so much more now that I couldn't actually speak.

It may have been out of protection, but it had eaten away at my choice.

Dariush's actions were at odds with the way he seemed to feel for me. He was using me, that was undeniable, but nothing he'd done so far told me he'd leave me to fend for myself against this chaos.

As I took his hand, accepted his protection once again, two questions sounded in my mind. *What more will his protection cost me?* And, *Will I ever be ready to protect myself on my own?*

CHAPTER THIRTY

Zorya

Nauseating motion welcomed me as the dungeon blinked back into my vision and my head throbbed with pressure.

"Looks like she's awake," a drifting blur of white said from my periphery. I didn't turn my head towards the voice. I was looking directly at my target.

Hendrik.

Only, he was upside down and swaying. Drifting closer to me, then farther away, then back again but slightly off centre. Never once returning to the same place.

Is he drunk?

No. I was swinging from the ceiling by my feet.

Where is Ettie?

My eyes darted around the room, but it all remained a blur. Save for Hendrik walking towards me. Swaying towards me.

"Back for more pain? I thought you'd keep playing dead," Hendrik taunted. His finger found my stomach, the momentum of my body pressing into it slowed the swaying ever so slightly. A sharp breath left me as I recalled how much blood I had ingested. I could have burst then and there.

"And I thought you'd actually kill me by now." The gibe came out quicker than I had time to think.

I moved my hanging and bound arms to shield my face, but I had predicted his reaction incorrectly. A fist slammed into my stomach, and I curled in slightly as bloody vomit pooled in my mouth. A little dribbled from the side before I could swallow it back down and a sticky, warm sensation began to travel slowly towards my nose.

Eww.

I was swinging again.

A flicker of movement from the stairwell caught my attention. I wasn't quick enough to hide my surprise because Hendrik whipped his head to the place I had been staring at.

"Don't play with me," he said through gritted teeth when he found nothing there. He was ready to punch me in the face again when his guard-mate made a strained sound and hit the floor face first.

I almost didn't believe what I was witnessing when Obsidian, in a puff of shadow, stood on the guard's back and sank his teeth into the guard's neck. The sight was sickening. Bone crunched. Blood and muscle squelched. It was almost impossible to look away from the mighty beast's kill, but I needed to make the most of Hendrik's terrified stupor.

I slipped my wrists from their pathetic bindings before bending my back and legs. I reached for the rope at my feet and climbed, ignoring the swinging. Ignoring the near-bursting pain of my stomach. Once I reached the hook in the ceiling, I was able to undo the ties at my feet and let the rope drop.

I looked down to see a head separated from its body, drenched in a pool of blood. Hendrik stood in a fighting stance, longsword out. He'd forgotten about me, head darting between various points in the room where Obsidian appeared in a dash of shadow, then disappeared only to reappear somewhere else. The sluagh dog was playing with his food.

Now was my only chance.

I pulled the hackberry pin from the place it hid underneath my ponytail and jumped to the floor behind Hendrik.

He must have heard me because he'd already started to spin around, but as I jammed the sharp end of that pin into his left temple, his arms went slack. His sword clattered to the ground.

His eyes held the same lifeless sheen Cynthia's and Dylan's had when they'd been forced to walk to their deaths.

I didn't know how much time I'd wasted. I might have never left that spot, staring at Hendrik's still body, had Ettie not let out a groan. She was still tied to the chair, blood dribbling from the two holes I'd left in her arm.

I tore a strip of fabric from Hendrik's White Guard cloak and secured Ettie's wound. Leaving her tied to the chair, I searched the room for my daggers and throwing knives. They'd been lazily left by the desk, and I made a mental note to never be so careless if I ever had to interrogate someone like this.

After securing my weapons, I turned to collect the sharp stick of the hackberry pin from Hendrik's head.

My hands shook.

Hendrik's eyes held nothing in them. No hatred. No self-satisfied smugness. No spark of life. I pulled the needle-like pin from the soft space in the side of his head, and I felt myself hoping that the action would undo it all. It was a stupid thought, but the weight of what I'd done slammed into me with another heavy blow when the hole didn't magically close up and his eyes remained glassy and dead.

I'd never killed anyone before. No amount of training could have prepared me for what I'd just done.

I wiped the pin in the crook of my sleeve's elbow and secured it in my hair again with its circular brooch piece.

Obsidian had left at some point, but I had a feeling he'd be back. I rummaged through the desk for a piece of paper and pen and hastily wrote as many details as I could about what I'd learned from Tierney before shoving it in a pocket.

Then I freed Ettie from her restraints and set out on the task of getting us both up the winding staircase. I carried her in my arms, her legs hanging over my left arm and her back resting on my right. It was harder than I expected.

I was a strong woman, but the weight of a near adult was a lot to carry, and the stone stairs were worn in odd places. As she faded in and out of consciousness, it became more difficult to keep a good footing. The weight of her was painful against my bloated stomach. I felt like an overfed leech.

I wanted to curse out Obsidian. Clearly, we weren't friends.

Maybe if I called out to him, he'd come running from the shadows. Maybe that was how Dariush did it.

Though I had never actually seen the prince call for the sluagh dog at all. He just sort of, showed up.

"He knows . . . I didn't mean to tell . . . He knows." The girl was fighting to stay conscious. I started to worry that I might have taken too much from her. Even though I knew I had been careful. Had Tierney cut her during his interrogation? Was she bleeding elsewhere?

"Tell me what he knows." I didn't need her to tell me anything. I could see the memory of her interrogation shattering through my mind, intertwining with what I'd glimpsed when I bit Tierney and what I'd seen firsthand. It was the clearest and most detailed memory I had witnessed. But having her explain was better than her losing consciousness completely.

I had never drunk from someone for the purpose of making them pass out before, but I imagined too much sleep after that much blood loss was not a good idea. I needed to get her to a healer.

My mind shook with the scattered memories of both Tierney and the girl. I tried to focus in on the latter. The way the queen looked to her; the way Annalise looked to her. The two couldn't have been more different. One shone so bright it was almost impossible to look at her. Colour peeking through the rays of white light, here and there.

The other, had no eyes. Only black sockets in their place. Yet it felt like that empty space saw everything.

And the familiar face that stood next her, mirroring her image as if they were one and the same. I knew now why Ettie had mentioned two heads in her delusional ramblings.

I shuddered.

"He knows what she is. He's going to use her..." The girl drifted again.

That was different. What I saw in Tierney's mind had nothing to do with using anyone, save Prince Aed. Knowing what the queen was, he would let Aed kill her. Imprison him for his crimes and claim her kingdom in the name of the Tuath Dé. The prince was a fool.

I needed to get this note to the queen, or Dariush.

Where the fuck is Obsidian?

Footsteps echoed above in the stairwell. I braced myself on the stair and considered placing Ettie down so I could defend her. I wasn't sure whether I even had enough strength to fight off attackers on my own, but I had to try.

A bark sounded, followed by the pitter-patter of paws.

Thank fuck.

Obsidian rounded the corner, and without hesitation, I dropped Ettie's feet. They fell to the stairs with a louder thud than I intended, but there was no time to worry about her feet. The queen needed this letter.

"Obsidian, take this to the queen. It's important." I found the piece of paper I had scrawled on in my pocket and handed it to the dog. He took the paper from my fingers, delicately holding it between his black, smoky teeth, and vanished. Wisps of shadow drifted momentarily in the place he had stood.

The instant he was gone I wondered if the beast could understand the word *important*. Maybe I should have said *now* or something simpler.

There was no time to think of that because Geira and Nate were rounding the corner. Finally, I would have help carrying this girl. I didn't think I had made it up more than one-third of the stone staircase.

"Nate, get the girl out of here," Geira said with a straight tone, keeping her eyes fixed on mine. Her stare told me one thing—I was in trouble.

Geira leaned against the wall to let Nate pass her. The stairwell was wide enough for two people to walk up side by side, but not comfortably and definitely not when Nate was one of them.

Nate took the girl from my arms. I had lifted her to make it easier for him. He didn't need the help. I started to walk behind him, but once he was past Geira, she stopped me, blocking my way with her whole body. Her entire being pulsed with anger. She waited till Nate was somewhat out of earshot before she made her next move.

Suddenly, her arms took my shoulders and slammed me against the wall.

"What the hell did you think you were doing?" Geira's voice was low and guttural. Her mouth inches from mine. Her hands tightening against my upper arms.

I was in shock. I knew she would be mad. This was all my fault after all. If I had just done what I was told and kept an eye on the girl, she wouldn't have been led away from the safety of Hestia's home. I just didn't think she would be this mad.

"I-It was my fault." There was no point attempting to evade blame. "They found her, and I wasn't looking. They took her away, but I had to keep following. I didn't have time to tell you."

Geira stilled, breathing heavily.

Maybe it was her silence. Maybe it was the desire to break the swell of anger that rose within her.

Without thinking, I closed the space between our lips and kissed her. Only once. Only enough to let her know I was here if she wanted me.

I hadn't completely pulled back before she pulled me into her. One hand moving to my hip, pressing me against her. The other caught the side of my face, fingers brushing the back of my neck. Her kiss was harder, more desperate. An answer to the question mine had asked.

My hands moved to her neck, wanting to be as close to her as possible. For our skin to touch in more ways than just this. Geira took my wrists. Lifting them above my head and pinning them there with one hand. She kissed me again. Harder. Her other hand digging into my hip again. Then she pulled away with a groan.

"Zorya," she panted. A smile broke her stern face, and she shook her head. My hands were still pinned above my head, but that was the only place we were now touching. I wanted her lips on mine again, but I knew why she had stopped.

I'd broken her foul mood, and she hated that.

"You made me worry," was all she could come up with.

"I can take care of myself."

"I want to take care of you." Geira was an inch from me again. Our body heat mixing. Static trying to close the distance between us. I squirmed under her grip, leaning in towards her. She pulled back, keeping her hands where they were.

She raised one eyebrow now, but her smile was not gone. I knew what that look meant. *Behave, Zorya. We have a job to do.*

I took a deep breath, in and out, and straightened my stance. "Tierney has plans to kill the queen and destroy all of Dubnos."

This time, Geira did let go of my wrists.

CHAPTER THIRTY-ONE

Annalise

We didn't get a chance to warn the queen's guard. A furious Dubh stormed into the throne room, followed closely by Hestia.

"There's a break in the wards. Sluagh are piling into the city." Anger rose in the queen's voice as she walked over to the window, shoes grinding the remaining shards of glass in satisfying snaps.

"Who would do this?" Hestia squeaked.

"Aed," Dariush answered. "It's likely he's been working with the Tuath Dé. He sent Resh into the castle to assassinate me, or you," he added to the queen. "Both maybe."

"He must be desperate if he's working with Resh," the queen muttered, all distaste in her throat.

As the two spoke of what this meant for the kingdom, what the Tuath Dé could possibly want with Dubnos, I stood there in silence. Nothing more than a sword waiting to be wielded by some knight in shining armour. Only, I was blunt. Banged up. Useless.

"She can't speak. The Tree took away her voice," Dariush said protectively.

"She can still be of use. It needs to be done now," the queen said, not bothering to even look at me.

I crossed my arms and stomped my foot. *Yes. I stomped my foot.* It was the only thing I could do to get their attention. Even a huff of annoyance produced no sound.

"If you want to be involved, now is your chance." The queen opened her arms as if giving me a moment to add to the conversation.

I hadn't decided how I felt about Dariush's mother. The few times I'd seen her, she'd flicked through emotions, different sides of her personality, quicker than a rotating disco ball that only slowed when she found an angle she liked. Right now, it seemed she'd landed on mockery and quick gibes.

I shot her a silent glare. A smirk slipped over her lips before she turned and made her way to the plain throne at the head of the oval table. Hestia moved to the entrance and closed the door.

A knock of one of the queen's many rings on the throne's left hand rest and the room spun. Will-o'-the-wisps descended from the ceiling to encircle us, and the oval table disappeared with its chairs, leaving three of us to stand on a sea of darkness. The queen was seated on a throne woven out of shadow and orbs of light.

I grabbed Dariush's arm to steady myself.

Where are we?

I squinted my eyes, trying to see past the blackness, but there was nothing. Just Hestia standing beside a throne that morphed with the movement of light and darkness.

The queen was haunting on that throne, commanding and regal. She had never looked as much like a ruler to me as she did in that moment. The chair's back stretched upward. She leaned back into it as if she was listening to the shadows.

"Annalise." Dariush pulled both my hands into his and broke my fixation on the queen. "I know I haven't shared everything with you. You should hate me for bringing you into this mess, but please, for the good of my kingdom, for the safety of my people. Please. Please say yes." His voice cracked unevenly as he said the words. They came out in almost a whisper, as if he was too afraid to ask. As if my rejection would bring about the end of his world.

"Annalise. Today I shall accept the throne of Dubnos, handed down to me by Queen Dubh. Will you help me achieve my responsibilities to the Kingdom of Dubnos and stand by my side as queen consort of this kingdom?"

There it was. The real reason he'd stolen me away. I'd figured out the truth when he told me he'd be king, but it still hit like a tonne of bricks.

It must have seemed like I didn't hear him for Hestia chimed in. "When Dovey—when *our queen*," Hestia corrected herself, glancing at her friend on the throne.

The queen rolled her eyes and leaned back farther into her chair.

Hestia continued, "Took the throne from her father, she was forced to marry in order to keep her title."

"I was so pissed off I made parliament amend the rule so that it applied to male successors as well." The queen gave a hearty laugh, shattering the queenly image I had built up in my mind.

"And look where that's gotten us," Hestia chided.

"It was hard enough getting them to agree to it. I wanted to abolish the rule altogether," the queen said in defence of herself, sounding more like a child than a ruler.

"I remember. *Anyway*, my dear, we need to pass the throne to Dariush, but to do that he needs to marry."

I looked to Dariush as he spoke again. "Will you marry me, for real this time? Will you be my queen?" Dariush stared into my eyes for a long moment, and I wasn't sure if he was searching them for my answer or he'd simply forgotten I couldn't speak. I felt it was the former.

For real this time.

I knew what he meant. Our pairing? That wasn't real. We'd both been forced into that. Our choices taken away from us. There was nothing binding about it, no matter how much the Tuath Dé wanted to claim it was.

But this time, we had a choice. Both of us. And even though we were backed into a corner. Even though he had so much to lose, I clung to the fact that he had handed me the reins all the same.

Everything I had learned since my first night in this kingdom, since Dariush had stolen me from my home, thrashed around in my head and mixed with the Nine Daughters' riddle.

There was so much at stake. I could change my life in this moment, or I could fall into a very clever trap, spun by someone who had kept truths from me time and time again.

In that moment, I knew what I needed to protect myself.

"Regent." The single word croaked out of my lips. My surprise stopped me for a moment. I tried again, to formulate a full sentence this time. To explain what I needed in all its terms, but no sound escaped my mouth as my lips moved.

The queen leaned forwards in her throne, confusion written on her face, as a small, waist-high table of shadow appeared to my right. On top of it lay the pen and pieces of paper I'd used to communicate to Dariush. It seemed that the throne room wanted me to have my say.

I ripped a blank square from the paper and scribbled violently.

I, Annalise Elizabeth Rhine, will only accept the proposal for the marriage between Prince Dariush—

I lifted the pen for a moment before continuing with my demands, making sure to leave a space for his last name and any middle names to be filled in later.

—and myself to be made formal so long as I am made queen regent and hold equal title and power as Dariush over the Kingdom of Dubnos.

I folded the paper and tried to hand it to Dariush.

"Whatever your terms are, I accept." Dariush held up his hand, refusing to look anywhere except my eyes. I searched deep within them. He'd gathered my meaning from that one word.

"Well, I should know the terms if I'm giving away my crown." The queen stretched out her arm, and I handed her the piece of paper. After reading my scribbled handwriting what must have been three times over the queen looked back to me, eyes unblinking. There was utter silence, before a wicked grin pierced the corners of her cheeks and a small cackle escaped her thin lips.

"It shall be done," she said with finality. Her eyes met Dariush's for the briefest of moments before she turned to Hestia.

"Hess, you'll be our witness," the queen said as she stood from her throne and waved her hand. The small table sank into the blackness beneath our feet. "You two. Kneel." She pointed to the nothingness that was the floor between us. "Quickly, I haven't got all day."

Dariush held my hand in his, the tension in his body had left him. We kneeled in the nothingness, and I didn't need to glance his way to feel the relief radiate off him. But I did. The moment our eyes collided, the weight of my decision pressed in on my chest and a building pressure rang in my ears.

I was ensuring my survival.

But with it I was accepting a crown, a kingdom, a people, an imperfect man. I was entwining our lives. Making it so my pain, my joy, my accomplishments, my failures, were his—and his, mine.

I hoped the trade-off was worth it. It would have to be.

Snap, snap.

The queen clicked her fingers towards the sky, and the throne behind her morphed again. This time, to something smaller. White stars broke off from the ring of will-o'-the-wisps that encircled us and wove themselves into the shadows. The two danced their way to her head and together formed a crown.

The moment the crown took its incorporeal form, the queen removed it from her head and pulled at its edges.

The shadows and light stretched, ripped away from each other. Untangled until there were two crowns. One of shadow and one of light.

"Accept, within your very being, the Kingdom of Dubnos, the throne of shadow and light, the crown—crowns that rule this land beneath." The queen spoke with clarity, only pausing to correct herself. "Accept within yourselves these responsibilities, equally, to rule fairly and to serve the people of Dubnos, or may these crowns reject you where you kneel."

Reject me?

My breath hitched for a moment before I steadied myself, keeping my focus on the blackness beneath me and the warm hand that gripped mine.

Almost as quickly as I'd taken control of my own fate it had been snatched from my grasp. My life was in the hands of an inanimate object's acceptance, and there were only two outcomes if they saw me as unworthy.

The crowns could accept Dariush without me, and I'd be married to the man who would use me as a weapon. It didn't matter that he cared about me, he'd choose his people over me. I was sure of it.

Or the crowns could reject us both. No one would take the throne in Dubh's place. The kingdom would be stolen by the Tuath Dé, and I would have nowhere to hide. Those lithe people had proven how little they valued my life. There was no place, bar Dubnos, that would keep me safe from them.

My head warmed and I closed my eyes. I didn't need to look at the queen to know the crowns had made their choice.

"Be united in this gift, King Dariush and Queen Annalise." Dubh paused. "May you rule as equals. Rise!"

I stood and faced Dariush, who was still holding my hand. A mighty tangle of shadows knotted on top of his head. The breathing thing was pointed in six places, talon-like and fearsome. His eyes danced too, as if shadows hid within them, and I knew he was made for this moment. To be crowned a king of shadows.

But it was the image reflected in his eyes that caught my breath. The flicker of lights as he looked towards the warmth that sat upon my head.

What did I look like to him? The awe written on his face, was it the look a soldier might give a weapon that could tip the odds of war in his favour? Or did Dariush see a woman before him, one who would do everything in her power to survive even if that meant tying herself to a man blinded by duty.

"Long live the king and queen, regents of the Kingdom of Dubnos!" As Dubh spoke, a cunning smile split across her face as the room appeared from the blackness again.

"Long live the king and queen!" Hestia repeated. I looked over to the woman. Tears swam in her eyes as she looked to her friend and former queen. Happiness tainted by the fear etched across her face. She held so much love for her.

"I believe you require the crown's ring collection. They've served me well over the years, so please clean them regularly," Dubh said nonchalantly. The informality had returned to her voice.

"I request that Dariush, my King Dariush." Dubh beamed at her son as she said the word *king*.

I suppressed a laugh as Dariush let out a sharp exhale and set his jaw. It was refreshing to see such a human interaction between Dariush and, well, anyone.

"You should take this one." She pulled a golden ring with a faceted orb stone off her pointer finger and handing it to him.

His eyes went wide. "But this is—"

"Yours now," Dubh said simply as she slipped it on the only finger that would fit the ring, his pinky. The stone shone in stark contrast to his clawed hand covered in dark fur.

"Now, how do we do the rest of these?" she continued, brushing off Dariush's shocked expression.

Dubnos's former queen settled on giving Dariush the ten rings from her right hand, including the orb ring. Which left the eleven rings from her left hand for me.

Most fit, but some were clearly designed to be worn closer to the nail. Upon each hand sat five rings. Most held stones in them, except two. One displayed the royal sigil etched in gold. The other held a strange knotwork across the length of it.

"This ring here needs to be replicated to share between the two of you," Dubh said, holding up the knotwork band from her left hand. I recognised it as the ring she'd used to access the throne. "Since I'm no longer queen, I don't have the authority to do that."

Dariush took the ring from Dubh and held it between the pointer finger and thumb of his clawed hand. "Will you do me the honour of sharing this ring?" His grey-blue irises swirled as if the shadows within him were trying to find a place to hide in the depths of misty colour. I saw them all.

I pinched the ring between my fingers, as he did, and as we pulled a second ring was formed. Dariush took my left hand in his and placed his ring onto my left finger, and just as I had done in that council hall, I held his left hand in mine. But instead of a shackle around his wrist, I willingly placed a ring on his wedding finger.

"Don't do that more than once. They don't like to be stretched too thin," Dubh said.

It took me a moment to realise she wasn't talking about getting married twice. Too late for that anyway.

"Hess has the twin ring to this black one here," Dubh said, pointing to the black band I'd placed on my right middle finger. "You could ask her to give her one back, but then she'd have to walk the long way home." Dubh chuckled, giving her friend a wink.

Hestia rolled her eyes and rubbed her temples. "Stop playing, Dovey. We have a threat to deal with."

"I've ordered my closest guards to take the tunnels to the gap. A small group of them will make their way to the wards while the rest bring as many civilians into the castle as possible. I have a handful stationed at the entrance to make it look like we've locked ourselves inside," Dubh said, her queenly demeanour returning. "Tierney is materialistic. He will keep his focus on me and this palace."

"I'll join the guards in the tunnels. They'll need someone who can handle the sluagh while they get people inside. Our people can't be left defenceless," Dariush said. "Maybe I can give your guards a clear line to the wards while I'm at it." Dariush looked at me for a long moment, taking in the two spots on my cheek, then my lips, then my eyes. It was like he was trying to memorise my features, keep a piece of me locked in his memory.

I looked away. As intrigued as I was about where this *marriage* could take us, I wasn't ready to call it love, and his eyes burned with too much passion, too much intensity for my liking.

"Hestia. Keep her safe here."

And then there was this increasing habit of talking to others like I wasn't there or couldn't take care of myself. I'd have to pull him up on that when all this chaos had settled.

Hestia gave a slight nod and Dariush headed for the door. As he disappeared around the corner, I found myself mourning his absence.

CHAPTER THIRTY-TWO

Zorya

We moved with speed through the city streets, Nate carrying Ettie as she wove in and out of consciousness. The streets were oddly vacant. Every now and then a racing heartbeat followed by a flicker of movement in the corner of my eye would signal a panicked underdweller fleeing the city's centre. With every step towards the castle, screams, explosions and a bellowing voice filled our ears.

A scene of death and destruction played out before our eyes as we cut through a side street and rounded our final corner.

Several sluagh hung from half-toppled buildings and stalked terrified underdwellers through the streets. One had taken flight, dive-bombing the city's citizens. Playfully picking one up and up, only to let go of their victim once they had reached the cave ceiling. It was a cruel scene.

And in front of the castle, protected beneath a translucent dome of light and bellowing out to the screaming city, stood Councilman Tierney, Prince Aed and the White Guard statuesque beside him.

"This is a shit show," Geira said from behind me. We'd tucked ourselves back within the alleyway to keep hidden from the sluagh and the small army that stood in front of the castle.

"I don't see Jaz," I noted, my voice wavering. I wasn't sure if that was a good thing or not.

"They wouldn't have killed him yet."

My eyes snapped to Geira. *Is she saying that just to make me feel better?*

"Dariush had our cuffs replaced with fakes before graduation," Geira said. "They'll be too busy trying to find out why their red stones don't work on him."

Torture.

The word swam between us unspoken. Neither of us needed to say it.

"What is he saying?" Nate asked me. Maybe it was the need to change the subject, the need to not think about where his best friend might be right now, that made him ask such a stupid question. I thought to glower at Nate for revealing an upir secret on my behalf, but since I had just made out with Geira for the second time and the life of the queen depended on my skills, keeping familial secrets wasn't high on my priority list.

I closed my eyes, allowing my hearing to drift past the screams and clatter. Zeroing in on the cacophony of heartbeats in front of the castle before mentally stepping back to take in the words of the deceptive man.

"What ruler leaves you to fend for yourselves in your darkest hour? First, she spits on the treaty by allowing innocent humans to be lured into your city, taking over your homes, your businesses, through no fault of their own. Then she spits on you, failing to secure the wards, hiding in her castle as you are slaughtered!" His words registered in muffled tones. Warped by the even pulse of the protective light that swam around him.

"He's talking to the underdwellers. Blaming the queen for the humans and the sluagh." I relayed his message in my own words.

"Come out, lazy queen! Give yourself up! It is time a new ruler took the Dubnos throne!" Tierney's message shifted. It sounded louder, clearer. And a close heartbeat jumped with excitement at this message.

"He's taunting the queen to come out. He wants to take her off the throne," I said. "Aed seems happy about that""

Geira grunted with disapproval at Aed's name. "She's safe for now then," she deduced. "We either take out the welcome party now or make our way into the castle. Help them fortify the entrance. Then come up with a plan to fix this mess."

Both were impossible options. While the idea of taking on a small army and several sluagh at the same time made my pulse race in the best way, I couldn't see how the three of us could survive that and keep Ettie safe.

"There's no way we'll get past Tierney," I started, considering the second option before my eyes widened with realisation. "The ring—"

"Dariush took it back through the door with Annalise. They're inside," Geira said without a glance in my direction, deflating my hope. "I know another way in. I just hope Aed doesn't know about it." She ducked back through the alleyway, Nate and me moving behind her closely. "Tell me if anyone is following." Geira caught my gaze as we wove through alleyways that I recognised encircled the castle.

I thought to tell her off. I was always listening to the heartbeats around me, sneaking up on me wasn't possible. But she had figured

out my secret, and I found myself unable to give more than a curt
nod.

***

It took some time for Geira to lead us to an unassuming tunnel.
It was separated from the castle walls but only a short way from
the main entrance. We'd had to circle the entire castle to evade the
White Guard's detection.

The tunnel opening was wedged between two buildings and
looked more like a garage that serviced the shop beside it.

Geira wasn't the only one who'd known of its existence.

People rushed in from everywhere, their panic palpable. Dariush
and two of the queen's guards were doing their best to usher people
through, but a cluster of sluagh had found them.

There wasn't enough time for me to consider the crown of
shadow that sat on top of Dariush's head.

In spite of my aching body, I jumped into the fight.

CHAPTER THIRTY-THREE

Annalise

"We need to gain a better view of the city," Dubh said. "Somewhere less—*messy*."

I followed her gaze across the room. Along with the gaping hole where the window had been, the floor and every surface near it was covered with shattered glass, a chair lay broken by the far end of the oval table, and slashes marred the face of a wooden cabinet propped against the curved wall.

The space looked more like the inside of an abandoned office building than a throne room.

We left, heading down the corridor and up a flight of stairs, towards a bedroom with three long slits for windows that looked out over the city and the castle's entrance. The room had the hallmarks of Hestia's handiwork. Pink velvet upholstered armchairs sat around an unlit fireplace at the end of the room, their backs to an all-white four-poster bed. The large boxy frame stood on a red-and-white rug that looked like it could have been pulled from a 1930s-themed movie set. Crystal-flecked walls were decorated with floral canvas paintings. The kind where the paint was spread on thickly and left to dry to enhance dimension.

Hestia moved to the window; a worried look settled on her brow. I followed her gaze. Three shadowy beasts rampaged through the streets. From our position, we could see where they had broken into the city. Rubble and splintered buildings laid out the path to a dark space of blackness at the far end of the street.

Screams wafted up the sides of the castle as I watched people, little more discernible than specks from this height, scatter across the kingdom floor. Light appeared among the cluster of people and vanished like lightning. Fomóire guards tried to protect the people, or fara soldiers, I couldn't tell. For the first time, true horror settled into my bones.

What have I left Dariush to face?

I hoped Nate and Geira weren't among those fighting the beasts. I even hoped Zorya had gotten herself and Ettie out of harm's way.

"We need to be down there with them." Hestia spoke the words I wanted to say, but before she could turn to convince her friend to make a new plan, a bang and click sounded.

The door was closed and Dubh was nowhere.

Hestia was the first one to move. "Dovey! You conniving—" She tried the door handle. It didn't budge. She stepped back, waved her hand over the handle. It morphed from a long and ornate silver handle to one that was round in shape. She tried again. It wouldn't budge. "You promised me!" Hestia yelled, pulling and pushing at the handle. Banging the door with clenched fists.

"You promised! COME BACK!!" Hestia's voice became a manic shriek. I moved to her. Pulled her from the door. Her hands had begun to redden.

I tried the handle myself, but the door wouldn't budge.

Dubh had locked us in.

CHAPTER THIRTY-FOUR

Zorya

"Zorya!"

My name sounded like an alarm, but my focus remained on the shadowy talons in front of me.

"Zorya, you're hurt." The voice, strained and low, stole my attention moments after my twin blades sliced flesh made of smoke and mist.

I looked to my side. Geira swung her axe high above her head and brought it down on the beast's neck.

"You need to take Ettie through the tunnel," she said as shadow dissolved in front of her.

"Nate's got it. I'll stay and fight. You need me," I said as I scouted our next target.

Geira stepped in front of me, daring to place her back to a sluagh one hundred metres away that was fighting two fomóire guards and winning.

"Damn straight I need you," she said. "I need you to survive." Her words were low and desperate.

It was like her words, and the sudden pause, made me aware of how much my body had endured. My stomach, stretched and bruised, protested with my every movement. My head still stung from the blow that had knocked me out. Each swift slice of my daggers had made my brain feel like it was bouncing around in my skull. I wanted to throw up.

"Take. Ettie. Now." Geira's eyes became too intense, and I had to look away.

Nate caught my attention. He was no longer holding Ettie in his arms. Instead, her body sat still against a wall of the tunnel's entrance. Nate stood over her, bow at the ready. His giant frame and focused gaze promising to protect her.

"Fine," I said to Geira.

Silence.

For a moment I thought she might have disappeared, but a snap of my head in her direction revealed that my single word had thrown her off.

"I can take orders, you know," I said gruffly, folding my arms across my chest.

"Only when I'm giving them, it seems." A crooked grin spread on Geira's face. I blushed and chided myself for wanting to step into her. To press my body against hers. Hear her whisper that same sentence in my ear.

I took a step towards her, and her face straightened. I read the unspoken message upon it.

Not right now. Soon.

I smiled, hoping she caught my message too.

Soon.

"All right, brick wall! My turn!" I shouted to Nate, who was preoccupied with scanning the length of the alleyway for more sluagh.

He took the hint as I drew closer, stowing his weapon away and picking up Ettie so as to easily place her in my arms.

"Don't drop her." He was serious.

I gave him one long look before I rolled my eyes and moved farther into the tunnel with Ettie.

The space was dark, but not silent. Others moved deeper through the space, most rushing past me in panic. Their heartbeats as erratic as their calls for friends and family.

My body groaned at the extra weight I was carrying. The sharp pains in my stomach increased.

This girl weighs a tonne.

"Zorya!" A familiar voice rang out above the panicked noises of the throng. "*Zorya run!*"

I turned with weak movements to see Geira tackle a cloaked figure at the tunnel's entrance. His hand was outstretched. And barrelling towards me, towards the belly of the tunnel, was a silver ball.

My feet swivelled. Legs and arms burned as they carried Ettie and me deeper into the tunnel. Away from the destruction about to befall us.

A loud crack, followed by a deafening silence, made everything around me stop for what seemed like an eternity. Then, a force so quick, so strong, threw Ettie from my arms. She was flung farther and farther away. The momentum catapulted her into the stone wall of the tunnel.

Thwack. Crack.

I reached out my arms to her as she scraped downwards towards the floor. As if they could stretch that far. Break the fall.

That soft but steady heartbeat I had been listening to intently ever since Tierney's hide out, quietened.

CHAPTER THIRTY-FIVE

Annalise

Muffled voices echoed through the window. It was enough to capture our attention. Someone was yelling, but what they were yelling about was anyone's guess. We were too high up to hear much other than the city's cacophony of screams and beastly roars.

"What is she doing?" Hestia gasped. She pressed against the window. I thought the woman might have broken the glass and stepped down from the castle's height if it meant being by her friend's side.

I narrowed my focus.

Dubh was walking towards Tierney and his soldiers in white. A circle of light kept him, and his men, protected from the swarms of sluagh.

What is *she doing?*

A voice boomed, and it sounded like Tierney was saying something, but I couldn't make out the words. Then another figure stepped up to the former queen. Aed. He held both arms out wide as if to embrace his mother. She moved forward, her arms still by her sides, each step cautious.

All her carefulness was not enough to protect her from what happened next. Aed leaned in for a hug that he wouldn't receive.

At the last second, he reached for something hidden at his back, then plunged the object into Dubh's stomach.

The world slowed.

Stopped.

One moment Aed had given his mother an unrequited hug. The next, Dubh's skin illuminated. Blinding white light collided with every colour. Dubh's form morphed until what stood in her place was one large ball of light. It stretched away from Aed as if in pain, as if retreating from a threat. Only, the thing that Aed held in his hands seemed to suck the light into it.

There was a short struggle between Aed and the light. Dubh fought to hold on, break free, but more and more of her became swallowed by the object. As the last sliver of white disappeared, I could see what Aed had struck his mother with. A blade the darkest shade of black I had ever seen.

A muffled gasp sounded beside me.

Hestia was frozen. Her eyes fixed on where her friend had stood. As if waiting for something else to happen. Waiting for Dubh to reappear like some magic trick.

I put my hand on her arm. The touch awoke something within her, and a panicked wail escaped her lips.

"*Dovey?*" Hestia choked. "Dovey!! Dov . . .ey . . ." Her screams were muffled by sobs, her body heaving uncontrollably. Tears sprang from eyes that were fixed on that same spot, and her fists pounded the window, making her hands red again.

She shrugged off my first attempt to pull her away. Relenting only when I used enough force that I nearly toppled the both of us.

I spotted a chair and sat her down, moving fast to retrieve a blanket from the bed and wrap it around her shoulders.

Hestia's body was still heaving, rocking even, but sound no longer accompanied her sobs.

It didn't feel right. Could fae die from shock? I needed to get her out of here, somewhere safer.

I walked to the door and held my baseball bat, my torch, in two hands. I'd barely been able to produce a flicker of a flame the size of candlelight. I didn't know why I thought I could produce one big enough to blow the door off. Even just a flame big enough to break the lock would have been a stretch, but now wasn't the time for what I *thought* I could do.

It wasn't the time to lament a life that increasingly felt like it wasn't my own, or a queen who'd died trying to save her people. A city was falling into ruin at the hands of shadowy beasts and a deceptive enemy who'd proven they had no limits when it came to getting what they wanted.

I didn't blame Hestia for breaking in this moment. I couldn't fathom what Dubh must have meant to her, how much they must have shared for her to react this way. She was completely broken.

But Dubh had died to protect her people and that job wasn't done.

I breathed in deeply and searched within myself. A song. A spark. Rage. Burning coldness swam in front of my closed eyes as I leaned further into that feeling.

Rage.

I dug through every ounce of anger and pain within me and threw it into that fire.

The Tuath Dé's claim upon my life. Taking Jaz away. The truth of who I was withheld from me by my mother, by Dariush. Zorya leaving me for dead in the city. That girl's expression the first time she laid eyes on me. That same look on the faces of children as they ran from me in the playground. The horrified faces of those two men. Orla's bleeding ears—

"Annalise!" a voice gasped behind me.

I opened my eyes to a sphere of blue flame threatening to engulf my face. With an exhale I imagined the flaming orb flying into the door and burning it down.

The flames hit the door with a deafening *boom*. I barely had time to shield my face with my hands as wooden shrapnel sprang back at me and dust clouded my vision.

"What did you do!?" Hestia coughed.

I didn't mean for it to do so much damage, I started to mouth before remembering my lack of voice. I was coughing along with her. As the dust cloud settled, I saw the full scope of my work. Large chunks had been taken out of the stone wall and what was left of the door was shattered and scattered into the hallway. Black smudge marks were everywhere.

I might have some issues I need to work through.

"Uh, warn a girl before you throw a fireball her way!" The familiar voice came from within the hallway just outside of view. Zorya stepped within sight, carefully tiptoeing around the debris, and holding a very still Ettie in her arms.

"What happened to her!?" Hestia pushed past me. Again, speaking the words I wanted to say. The closer Zorya got, the more I realised the answer wasn't good. Tears had left clean streaks down

Zorya's dirt-covered face. Her entire body looked defeated, and she was struggling to keep the girl in her arms.

Zorya's eyes met mine, then widened as they took in the lights upon my head. Recognition registered on her face and then, something else. For a brief moment I saw words there that hadn't yet formed on her lips. *I'm sorry.*

I nodded and offered a small smile.

It was enough to release some tension from her defeated stance, but only slightly. This was where Zorya had been instead of helping me, instead of helping Jaz. She had been with the girl.

Hestia, who'd seemed to recover from her bout of shock, took Ettie's upper body in her arms and helped Zorya move her into the room and onto the bed. Both Zorya and Ettie were covered in dirt, blood, and scratches. Ettie's wrist wrapped in a bloody white rag.

I watched as Zorya's arms shook by her sides once the girl was on the bed. How long had she been carrying her?

"We need to find the queen, she's not safe—" Zorya stopped as she caught sight of Hestia. The woman had just placed her blanket over Ettie before the mention of the queen sent her into a panic again. Her face whipped back to the window as she tried to steady her breathing.

"She's—she's—*gone.*" The last word was a whisper on Hestia's lips.

"What? What do you mean *gone?*" Alarm crept into Zorya's voice at the edges.

Hestia began relaying the events to Zorya, fussing over Ettie's still form as she spoke. I stole the moment, turned on my heel and stepped through the broken threshold.

"She locked us in here and walked out into the street, and Aed—
WHERE DO YOU THINK YOU'RE GOING?" Hestia's shrill
made me jump. "Oh no! You're not going out there too!"

Hestia took two steps forward, but I was quicker. I formed a ball
of blue flame on top of my torch, as big as the last, and focused it
on the threshold in front of me. Hestia backed away, horror etched
on her face.

I let it fuel me.

Instead of breaking through a wall, I used my flames to create
one. I imagined the fiery ball floating to the floor, stretching along
the base of the threshold and rising to meet the roof.

I couldn't let either of them stop me from what I was about to
do. Both of them had given up so much already, I wasn't going to
let them give up their lives too.

Weapon of a king.

Weapon of a king.

Weapon.

Survival looked different from what I'd imagined. Maybe I'd
confused it with immunity, the kind that human royalty and po-
litical leaders got to wield. But I wasn't human, and this crown
wasn't made of solid gold and stolen jewels. It was made of light,
of power, of magic, of promises.

If this wall was anything to go by, the torch and the crown were
amplifiers of some kind. I had taken my means for survival, for
protecting myself. Now was the time for me to use it.

A silent laugh escaped me as wetness spilled onto my cheeks.

For a heartbeat you had it, Annalise.

A heartbeat.

But you can't hide in the safety of your golden home on your hill forever.

I thought a single goodbye and started at a run down the hallway. Though the word didn't pass my lips, it felt like the most important thing in the world.

It felt final.

CHAPTER THIRTY-SIX

Zorya

Annalise had built a wall of blue flame in front of me? Annalise? The girl who'd vehemently stated she'd never be able to do *that*. And she'd used it to lock Hestia and me in this room. She'd covered the whole damn doorway in that blue stuff.

Cold wafted off the flames, and I watched as the blurred figure behind them disappeared from view. They were in stark contrast to the orb I could produce. Mine was dark like hers but etched in a deep maroon. A flame that had always reminded me of blood.

That sneaky bitch. I was both impressed by what she'd done and jealous it wasn't me who'd done it first.

I looked over to Ettie's still body. Her skin pale against the white sheets of the bed. Hestia had done her best to tuck her into the blankets. Still, she looked so cold.

What could I possibly do for her now? Every now and then a rogue heartbeat had sounded, and I was left wondering whether I'd heard it or imagined it. The thought that I'd failed her. That she was gone. It was too much.

Maybe I was just imagining it to make myself feel better.

In truth, Ettie had ceased to exist the second she'd been forced beyond the veil. She had passed the point of no return. There were no loved ones waiting for her down here. The dreams that might have once fuelled her were out of reach.

Maybe that bomb was a blessing. Maybe dying, truly dying, was better than living an eternity separated from those you loved. Never again feeling their embrace, or hearing their laughter, or growing old alongside them.

The weight of her stolen life crushed my chest. Not for the first time, I questioned whether I grieved for the girl's life, or for my own.

The Tuath Dé had stolen everything from me. My mother and father. My culture. My people. They had let me live in a prison. The bars built from lies and a false promise. It wasn't even a good promise. Their idea of a reward for my obedience, my devotion, was a life as their most prized hunting dog.

That shouldn't have been a life I ever wanted for myself. Yet here I was. They had built the bars of my prison, but I had wilfully ignored the open door.

My rebellion.

I looked back to those dark blue flames Annalise had created. The way she'd formed them in complete naivety, with no real knowledge of how to. That crown of light dancing above her head. She'd done what I hadn't allowed myself to dream of doing.

Demand more for myself.

Rebel.

Still, I knew that blue wall couldn't hold forever, and I was out the door at a sprint the second it faltered, Hestia on my heels.

If she was going to face this threat, for herself or for Dubnos, she wouldn't do it alone.

I was guessing my way out of the castle. The smooth stone walls curved and straightened; it was impossible to tell what direction I was heading. If the queen had gone out into the street like Hestia said she had, she'd have gone through the main entrance. Otherwise, she'd have passed me coming through the tunnel, which was well and truly blocked.

If only I could actually find the main entrance.

"This way," Hestia said once she realised I was lost. I followed as she backtracked a few paces to a hole in the wall. Down a staircase and round a sharp corner that led to the main hallway.

How the hell did Annalise figure out this maze of a castle so quickly?

We approached the heavy, wooden double doors of the castle entrance. They were closed, but large chunks were missing from one side of the door. Splinters folding outwards at the edges, their surface left blackened by cold flames that had since extinguished. The space was just big enough for us to fit through.

Hestia said something I didn't fully register and tugged at my arm, but I shrugged her off as I moved through the hole in the door. I needed to get to Annalise.

I saw what she was warning me against too late. An army of thirty or so guards in white stood ready in a protective circle of light. The first row sporting bows strung with arrows pointed directly at Annalise. And leading them, a silver-haired man in a dark green trench coat. Tierney.

My heart sank. How could I have let her even entertain the idea of coming out here? I should have stopped her. Maybe try to break that barrier of blue flames with my own orbs? We were completely and totally outnumbered.

Surrounding our standoff, rows of crumbling buildings followed the main road that extended away from the castle. Each building more broken than the last the farther I looked down the street.

Shouts and roars echoed throughout the city, bouncing off the cave ceiling and colliding with rubble. The sheer volume was more overwhelming and inescapable now than it had been while sneaking through the streets with Geira. I couldn't tell if that was because I was now in the thick of the chaos or the attack on the city had worsened.

Two smaller roads stretched off in my peripheries, each decorated with sluagh and their screaming underdweller prey. Some sluagh were held back by soldiers unlucky enough to be denied Tierney's protection. But with the city barrier down, their hold against those sluagh wouldn't last. They'd get tired and sloppy, and even if they managed to kill the sluagh in front of them, there'd be more coming through the tear at any moment.

I peered into the dome of white. Aed was missing.

Annalise was about as many steps from me as she was from Tierney. There was no way I'd let her face this monster alone. I knew what I needed to do. What Ettie had *shown* me I needed to do, even if she hadn't realised it.

Tierney noticed me and his lip curled. "My two favourite women!" The slime in his voice made me want to dry retch.

Annalise didn't look back. She was focused on something else. Her back moved rapidly like she was forcing air in and out of her lungs. *Was she—trying to sing?*

She still didn't have her voice. I quickened my pace, and in response, Tierney stepped outside his protective bubble. It was then I noticed a short, black blade in his hand.

One man with a blade wasn't the issue, especially since I'd be willing to bet Tierney had never set foot in a sparing ring in his life. I could easily pull a throwing knife from my belt and be done with it. He wouldn't get a chance to hurt Annalise if he had a sharp piece of metal embedded between his eyes.

The problem was the army of White Guards behind him. I was willing to bet their protective dome of light was not a two-way deal. They were protected against anything I threw at them and could send arrows flying my way at any moment.

I needed to close the gap between us, fast. What happened that day in the city, and again when we had talked out our issues. The things Ettie had seen within both of us. The pieces clicked into place. We were stronger together. We'd survive this together.

"I don't remember giving you permission to leave the dungeon, Zorya. But I suppose you could watch the slaughter before I return you to a cell. Or the servant quarters perhaps? I might feel generous when this is done." Tierney's tone was sticky, following its usual saccharine melody. I ignored him.

"Or maybe I'll give that position to your lover. *Her* name is—Geira? Yes?" Tierney knowing about my feelings for Geira didn't surprise me, but his words filled me with rage all the same. He was out of the protective circle; I could do it. I could plunge that knife between his eyes, but seeking satisfaction would only get me, Annalise and everyone else in this city killed.

I let my desire dissolve. The fact he was bringing Geira up at all meant he was clutching at straws. He was trying to distract me. I wasn't going to give in to his trickery.

Maybe he already knew what I had just figured out. What I hoped in this moment was true.

"Zorya!" Tierney's words were panicked now. Like the idea he could lose this fight had become apparent to him for the first time. It was the most terrifying thing in the world to him. I took his fear as confirmation I was on to something and leaped forward.

Nothing would stand in my way of getting to Annalise. This had to work. I held out my left hand.

Inches. I was inches away. My fingers collided with hers. Our hands turned cold and sucked together. A pulling, unbreakable force uniting us. Taking over. Breaking free—

CHAPTER THIRTY-SEVEN

Dariush

*K*ing was never something I wanted.

I had told myself that lie again and again, till who I was split in two. One part could reject glory and keep promises and not betray with every breath. For the longest time, I thought that part of me had died.

Really, it had fallen into a deep hibernation, and her song had awoken it. With the rising mist and straining colour of first light, her song had reached into me, pulled to the surface those broken things I'd long shoved away. I didn't like the feeling though. I didn't like that she'd placed my soul in front of me in the form of a thousand-piece puzzle.

It was unsettling. I'd felt off-kilter ever since.

A sickly scream sounded to my left, and as a talon of the beast before me sprang out towards a fire spriteling frozen in fear, the girl couldn't have been older than six, I struck downwards with my longsword and sliced the small shadowy sluagh in two. The barbed end of the talon disintegrated within an inch of the child's haunted face, and with it the rest of the beast's incorporeal form. Her bright amber eyes dimmed from shock before a taller figure swept her away towards the safety of the castle's tunnel.

Then there was the other part of me. The part that would never feel safe, or free, or complete without the horns of shadow on my head.

Except I didn't feel any of those things now.

Maybe the phrase I'd been trying to convince myself of all along sounded more like *I need to be king to be safe.*

A bright light swallowed my periphery. I turned my head towards its source, and in the distance, the light filled the shape of a person. It swirled with colour and fought against something, against someone. The light was sucked into a black knife, revealing Aed as the wielder and a sea of White Guards behind him.

My head split with the ringing of chimes as three will-o'-the-wisps dove from their great height among the stalactites above and danced around the orbed ring on my left hand. I dropped my sword and gripped my head, unable to push back against the barrage of sound.

My body fell to the hard stone street and my consciousness drifted upward. From my soaring height, I could see just how many sluagh infected the city, what districts had been hit the worst, where the White Guards were stationed. I tried to catalogue it all, contain it to memory, but a single sharp image sliced through my mind, and despite the world still moving around me, all I could see was a pocket in time. It was like someone had rewound the scene of bright enveloping light I had just witnessed, all to show me the few moments beforehand. Aed stood in front of the castle, greeting our mother.

Dubh only had a few more years left in her, but I was prepared to make the most of every second of them. I was prepared to make sure her legacy lasted beyond the span of her mortal life.

In a split second, that certainty had been ripped out from underneath me.

Aed shoved the black blade into her stomach. Her form shone with white light speckled with colour. Then she was gone.

I knew why she'd stepped outside the safety of her castle. Her last sacrifice to her people was to distract, to give us more time to close the wards and get the people to safety.

Had she known she would be killed on the spot? How could Aed have done this to her? And what was that blade? It looked like it had sucked her into it. Was her soul stuck in there? Still alive, unable to move on?

Two solas guards moved quickly beside Aed, stealing the blade from his fingers with ease. I watched him struggle under their arrest. Aed kicked and seemed to be yelling at Tierney, but his words died amidst the sounds of a warring city. Tierney didn't even glance Aed's way as he retrieved the blade from a solas guard.

Of course. Convince Aed to kill our mother, then steal the prize with clean hands. That cunning fuck.

A sick satisfaction rippled through me, and the shadows upon my head shifted at the thought of how Dubh had beaten Tierney to it. Their presence fuelled the shadows that remained close to me even with my physical body so far away. The shadows I'd been born with, and the ones bestowed upon me, talked to each other. Both amplified.

The will-o'-the-wisps closest to me gave me a wide berth, uncomfortable with my shadows' sudden stirring. I refocused my attention, cast a net of awareness out wide, and felt for the beasts that had crawled through the tear in the city's wards.

My city.

There were close to thirty swarming the streets now, and more were streaming through the broken ward. We were going to be overrun, swallowed whole by their shadowy mouths. Not even Tierney and his solas guard were going to survive this.

Dubh had died to give me time that I couldn't use.

I stretched my awareness, searching for those with hints of shadow in their souls. There was nothing I could do for Dubnos now, except help as many of its people as I could find.

Blue flame exploded from the large castle gates that had stood tall at Dubh's back and snuffed out instantly. Where the flames had extinguished was Annalise, colour dancing upon her head.

Dubh's deceit was revealed.

I could see my body. It was so close to her. I willed my two selves to come together, but picturing it in my mind was like wading through mud, my consciousness floated stubbornly above the disintegrating city.

You wispy fucks need to let me go, I thought to the will-o'-the-wisps, desperate for them to understand.

Screams from every corner of the city bellowed in my ears. They needed me. They needed my protection, but the white-haired woman stood small in the distance. The fiercest general of the only empire the fae had known, a larger-than-life enemy, before her.

Tierney spoke to her. She stood, not quite still. She was concentrating.

The will-o'-the-wisps answered my call, and I began to float downwards too slowly.

I silently begged her. Begged any powers above for her to not reveal anything else. Dubnos needed her true nature to be kept secret. As it's queen, the kingdom needed her safe.

I needed her.

Fuck. More than the air in my lungs, I needed her.

The city floor rose to meet me, quicker now.

Another figure stepped into view. Dark maroon swept towards Annalise. Their hands mere inches apart.

As the dual figure of death stood in their place, all secrets were torn open.

CHAPTER THIRTY-EIGHT

Bloodsong

B lackness. It covered our eyes, and for the first time, we could
see clearly. Moments in time entwined. Our minds fitting the
pieces together to form a truth so vibrant.

The man's rambling had itched our ears. Annoying, but now
that we were whole again, we would silence him.

"Such a pathetic excuse for fae. Keep dribbling your filthy lies,
it helps us know where you are." We spoke in unison. Our voices
crackled like flames licking at half-dried wood, sucking the air
from the crevices. We couldn't see the vermin, but his heartbeat
quickened with every second. His scent was palpable.

Obstinacy laced with a growing fear.

"You see our true form." A smile spread across our lips. We
sniffed the air, licked it. Someone had soiled themselves, but that
sour stench was coming from beyond our target.

No. Our target wasn't afraid enough. The idiot didn't know
how close to death he was. After a lifetime of conquering, of taking
and ruling, in this moment he thought he could control even that.
Pathetic.

"Truly terrifying, girls. Let go of this . . . facade and we'll talk
about your place in my grand new world." Words of a naive cow-
ard. His silhouette lit up with every nasally, pitched sound.

Metal whistled through air and embedded itself in our shoulder. Pain pulsed from the cut, but we didn't flinch, and the shallow ache was gone as fast as it had arrived. The arrow embedded there would be pushed out eventually. For now, it added to our image. Added to whatever personification of death these ants witnessed in front of them.

Flames at our sides. Our blood boiling with the need to release a very special song for this very unspecial man.

It vibrated from our throats, from our lips. Carried through the air and sank into our target's skin with far more precision than any arrow. Song connecting with blood.

That hot stream of life offered up its collection of stories. Both good and terrifying. It was the latter we sought out. As our song ebbed and flowed, we forced those most brutal of memories to his mind. What he had done and what had been done to him. The last wicked thoughts of a wicked man who lived a wicked life. His blood sped up with our song, feeding his last moments in hell.

"Ahh! NO! Sto— MAKE IT STOP!" He blubbered pathetic pleas. Maybe he'd choke on his tears before we'd have a chance to finish him off. The desperation was exhilarating.

Pity we couldn't savour this moment forever.

More whistling arrows and knives flew in our direction. Some missed completely, others were dissolved by our cold flames. We focused our listening beyond the dying man in front of us to the arrows' origins. Muffled, panicked murmurs and more of that sour stench. The army of cowards was behind a protective circle.

Casting our orbs forward, the flames smashed into the something solid. The protective circle cracked and dissolved. Screams filled our ears more clearly now, turning our deathly duet into a symphony of horror.

A few cowards scattered away, but some became stuck in our web. Warped scenes consumed their minds as our melody sped up once again.

Reaching a crescendo, our song softened and slowed. The vermin in front of us was the first to die. His dribbled words holding no meaning as he exhaled his final breath.

The army of cowards would follow him—

"Bloodsong! Release your prey!" a forceful voice bellowed behind us. Absent of fear. Absent of cowardice. Commanding.

"Who dares interrupt our duet?" We spoke to the figure behind us without turning. There was no need. We could see the figure clear as ever in our mind. Crown of shadow upon his head. More shadows in his palm.

These shadows called to the two within us. Forcing them to disobey us. They wrapped around our throats. Pulled at our fingers. Pulled at our bond.

CHAPTER THIRTY-NINE

Annalise

My hands flung to my throat as I desperately sucked air into my lungs, then again to my knees as I bent over and immediately coughed air back out.

A hand warmed my back in circles, and I felt the presence of someone by my side. The pattern of shallow gasps followed by coughing continued for a few moments longer before my breathing returned to somewhat even.

"I'm sorry. I had to." A pained voice sounded above me.

I straightened and gave Dariush a nod of understanding. I had watched, a spectator in my own body, as the Bloodsong stole Tierney's memories and used them against him. That thing inside me had tortured him to death.

Even as a spectator, I felt there was blood on my hands.

I looked to where a hand had brushed my fingers before the bond took over. Zorya stood tall and held her hands behind her head. Her eyes were closed, and her chest moved evenly in and out.

She had felt those shadows too, but clearly was better at recovering from them than me. *How was she always so practiced with . . . everything?*

My mind spun as I recalled the images, memories, of Zorya fitting the pieces together. The Nine Daughters had given me all the information I needed to figure out what I was. They had clearly spoken about the Bloodsong and Zorya's involvement, but she'd been the one to fit the pieces together, even without the prophecy.

Then there were other images. More personal, passionate. All this time I thought she hated me. Everything she had ever thrown at me, the constant avoidance of me, the dismissal of everything I said. Yes, it hurt. But it was all skin deep compared to the pain that ebbed within her soul. She'd given everything she had to the Tuath Dé Empire, and in return, they made her watch as they beheaded her family and denied her even the simplest of dreams after that.

Yes, her anger had been misplaced. But she knew that now, and at the final moment, she'd come through.

"You two are banned from touching each other," Dariush said, the crown of shadow still dancing above his head. I gave him a questioning look, one I'm sure Zorya reflected because he held the bridge of his nose and exhaled deeply with the realisation of how wrong his words sounded. "I mean . . . Don't hold hands. Don't hug. Just—a metre apart at all times, got it?"

A screech from beyond our battle scene pulled my gaze towards the destruction of the wider city. Tierney's corpse was mere steps from where the Bloodsong had stood, and three soldiers in white lay limply a few paces behind him. Their quiet sobs and quivering told me they, unlike Tierney, were not dead.

I tried to sew more pieces of information together in my mind.

Zorya's mind had collided with my own. The way I had perceived the world seemed clearer. Made of sound. The sounds of crashing buildings, screaming people and screeching beasts had etched out the shapes of the city within the blackness.

Only I wasn't just me. I was Zorya too. I felt everything she felt. About Ettie, about what she had to do to Hendrik to save her. About the bomb that had definitely killed the girl despite the tricks her mind played on her.

I looked to Tierney's contorted features splayed out on the ground and realised I felt little remorse for what the Bloodsong had done to him. Hazel eyes bugged out of his head, jaw dislodged sideways and locked in a silent scream. Maybe his death should have been less dramatic, but he had watched as Aed plunged that black knife into the queen. He'd put Ettie in danger. He'd destroyed countless human lives by smuggling them beyond the veil, imprisoning them here for eternity. And for what?

Tierney was a greedy man, and I couldn't help but feel that the world was better off without him in it.

My gaze moved beyond the soldiers in white to the source of the screeching. More buildings had collapsed under the weight of those shadowy beasts. Fara soldiers in both white and black moved against them, fighting alongside fomóire guards and a few courageous underdwellers. Some hid as best they could and scampered away whenever a beast neared.

I remembered what that thing inside me had thought of those who'd run. Cowards. Now, I couldn't say I shared her sentiments.

This was chaos. War without any real sides. And we were losing.

"The barrier," Dariush said. I followed his gaze to the end of the main street. Where a wall of white light should have closed it off as a dead end, there was blackness. And the shadowy wisps of a sluagh far larger in size than the ones that had intruded on the city before it.

Tierney had broken the barrier in full view of the castle. He'd done it to taunt. To gloat.

Tentacles of black mist wrapped around two buildings at the end of the street and reduced them to rubble. A horrid, low sound vibrated from a circular mouth adorned with eight rows of sharp black teeth. A woman and two men exited one of the crumbling buildings and ran screaming towards the safety of the castle. I looked to Zorya beside me, fear etched on her face. I was sure mine looked the same. Dariush sprang into action, sword and shadows in either hand. Zorya and I followed suit. A few figures in black joined us as we neared the beast.

I stumbled over small rocks and scattered bricks as I ran but managed to keep close to Zorya. Peering down the side streets as we moved, I noticed the other sluagh terrorising the city were far more interested in screaming citizens and the soldiers attacking them than each other or us.

Will-o'-the-wisps darted across the sky. The city turned dark behind us; all light focused on that space at the end of the street. They were forming a barrier to protect the city. The sluagh paused.

"They're closing the barrier," Zorya said what I was thinking, stopping for a moment. It was a breath too soon. Shadowy talons scratched against the wall of light. The will-o'-the-wisps darted out of the way like liquid.

Their line of defence was weak, and we needed something stronger than a few fara soldiers to push all these beasts back through.

I looked to the back of Dariush's shadow-adorned head and held out my hand to Zorya. Dariush was in full fight mode, his sword breaking and tearing at shadow. He was too busy to stop us, and truthfully—he needed us.

Without a word she reached for it.

"Don't—you dare—try it—" Hestia puffed out as her hands slapped against our wrists and held us away from each other.

CHAPTER FORTY

Zorya

The woman had a tighter grip than I thought her older frame was capable of, but she was an inexperienced fighter and out of breath from trying to catch up to us. It would only take me a second to push her away and close the distance between me and Annalise.

"I saw that thing completely take over both of you. You would have killed everyone if it wasn't for Dariush. What if it kills him and then lays waste to the rest of us? There's almost nothing left as it is." The fear in Hestia's eyes was real.

The woman wasn't completely right. Neither Annalise nor I knew how much control we had over the Bloodsong, but I was willing to bet we'd find a way to stop it before it got to that point.

The slight hesitation had brought to my mind another problem with our plan. I couldn't sense a heartbeat in this thing. Nor could I sense a heartbeat in any other sluagh I'd gotten close to. The Bloodsong called to blood. It sang to the memory within blood, just like my ability to witness memories when feeding.

The Bloodsong would be useless against the sluagh.

I looked at the small team of fara soldiers working with Dariush to push the giant sluagh back. *This* was useless.

"Fine. Just—I need to help." I pulled my wrist from Hestia's grasp. "Stay safe" was all I could give Annalise before a roar stole my attention, and I ran towards the beast, leaving the two of them to find somewhere else to be.

The will-o'-the-wisps dispersed again after failing at pushing back the sluagh. They focused themselves in little pockets around the sluagh, offering light to fighters who needed it.

I pulled my twin daggers free from their sheaths latched at my thighs and lunged into the fight. My daggers met a thin, shadowy tendril and sliced. What was left flailed around while it regrew itself. It was so hard to predict the way these creatures morphed and regenerated. At times a sliced leg grew back as a spear-like tentacle. Slice that, and it might grow back or not at all. And sometimes those spears came back as something completely new——wings or clawed legs.

We need to land more hits on the body.

Sidestepping the flailing tendril, I ran towards the belly. My dagger had barely kissed the smoky surface before another tendril hit my stomach and I was thrown to the edges of the fight.

It didn't like that. Good.

I tried again. This time employing a dance I'd learned for such an occasion. The aim was to always keep your daggers and feet moving while keeping your eyes on the target and never leaving your middle undefended.

I widened my stance and kept low, waiting for my best reentrance into the fight. A tendril sprang for a soldier to my left, leaving a clear line to the belly. Spotting my moment, I lifted a dagger swiftly above my head and brought it down upon the tendril. As quickly as it cut through smoke, that dagger moved to protect my middle and I spun. The other dagger hit true and fast farther down on the newly flailing tendril. Then the dance started again and repeated as daggers collided with shadow, and I forced my way towards the beast's protected belly.

There was nothing else except me and the beast. I sliced and spun and ducked, even landed a few kicks when more tendrils were thrown my way. My footwork quickened with them, and it seemed I'd reach my target in spite of the beast's attempts to protect itself.

Something cold gripped my right foot and stilled my momentum. My left arm was slow to replace my right one that had lifted from my middle to make the next slicing attack.

Solid shadow collided with my stomach to fling me to the edges of the fight again. Only my foot was held firmly in place, and instead, I smacked the firm ground beneath me. Air escaped my lungs in one quick movement, and blackness tinted the edges of my vision, keeping me pinned for a moment.

One moment.

That was all the sluagh needed to direct a spear-like talon towards my head. The tip of it lunged to the space between my eyes. It was too fast. I didn't have time to shield myself. I couldn't close my eyes.

The black, pin-like end dissipated to reveal a flash of gold above me. Cold rescinded from my ankle. A hand clasped against my upper arm, and I helped the figure pull me to my feet.

We spun together, that perfect heartbeat warming my back. I let it lead my steps. My daggers resumed their dance, my ears filled with the whistle of solid steel cutting through smoke.

She'd survived.

"I know—this is a really weird time—to ask—" Warmth and gravel, her voice sang even between grunts of effort. "But since the Tuath Dé—"

We moved and her axe caught a talon that had been aiming for my head.

"Probably won't take us back—after this—" Her axe hit more shadowy flesh between words. She was pivoting me away from the fight. I took a step backwards with my left foot and spun out from our back-to-back stance. My daggers caught a talon between the sharp blades and cut it like scissors.

"Did you want to go on a date sometime?" Geira grabbed my upper arm again, and in a second, I was facing her. A coy smile lifted her cheeks. My heart stopped. Then I kissed her deeply, promising more as our bodies pressed into each other.

The whistle of steel through smoke sounded again, and I spun away from Geira's grasp to see smoke dissolve around her axe. In the heat of our kiss, she'd somehow managed to stop a talon from embedding itself in the back of my head. I ducked, spun, and resumed my dance with more enthusiasm.

As we returned to our back-to-back stance, steel crashing into shadows, Geira's warm whisper filled my ears. "I'll take that as a yes then."

CHAPTER FORTY-ONE

Annalise

I looked behind me, suddenly aware of how far away the castle seemed.

"We need to get that ward closed." Hestia began to run towards the gaping break in the city's defences. The beast filled up that space, leaving no room for other sluagh to pass through but also showing no sign of being persuaded backward.

Hestia kept close to the broken buildings as she moved. I grabbed her by the shoulder before she could get too far ahead of me. When she turned to face me, I mouthed the word "*How?*" and offered up a doubtful look with a few frustrated hand movements so she'd get my point.

This was impossible.

There was no exaggerating that frustration. I was well and truly peeved that *this* was the way I communicated with the people around me now.

"No flipping clue." The woman ran farther down the street, and I followed. The closer we got to the beast, the more I realised how screwed we were. Many fara soldiers were out, scattered dead or unconscious throughout the street, and those who remained were hardly getting in any hits. It seemed they either hadn't been privy to Tierney's plans or they'd completely abandoned whatever orders they'd been given amid the chaos.

Geira and Nate had joined the fight. A nugget of joy welled up inside me that they were alive, but part of that feeling felt foreign. Like what I'd learned about Zorya's true feelings for Geira through the Bloodsong bond was having an effect on me. I watched for a moment longer as the two of them moved together, slashing, and ducking, and kicking. Then their mouths were on each other's, and in the blink of an eye they were back to fighting the beast again.

Nate kept to the edges of the fight with his bow. The beast flung a thin talon of smoke towards him, pointy side ready to skewer him in the middle. A scream of warning crept up in my throat, but before it could escape, a flash of silver sliced the smoke in two and the talon wriggled back inside the body of the beast. A pained growl emanated from the creature.

Dariush gave an inaudible order to Nate who latched his bow to his back and pulled two daggers that had been strapped to his thighs. They placed their backs to each other and began a pattern of footwork and slashes similar to Geira and Zorya.

Even with their teamwork, we would fail if we couldn't get the ward closed.

"Help me pull them out of the way," Hestia said.

We can bury the dead when we've won. What do we do now!? I wanted to scream at the woman. Had she lost her mind? There were talons of smoke skewering people. We had more important things to worry about.

I lifted the lifeless arm of a fara soldier that had fallen a step away from the sidewalk and let it drop to the floor with a soft thud.

Dead.

"Oh, have *you* checked for a pulse?" Hestia shot back.

Now *she* was the one to throw frustration my way, but my anger dissipated as I realised that was the only thing I could do.

Out of the corner of my eye I saw the four fighters move towards each other. Geira shouted something and Nate fell to one knee before her and propelled Geira into the air as she stepped into his cradled hands. The valkyrie, catapulted to the same height as the beast's mouth, steadied her axe and sliced into its jaw. Shadow split on her way down, and the beast shuddered and roared again. It was hurt, but far from defeated. Geira landed gracefully on her two feet only to dive out of the way of a rogue talon.

Hestia and I pulled the lifeless man into the threshold of the closest building. It was mostly rubble at this point, the half closest to the tear in the ward had been ripped open. We weren't exactly safe, but it would have to do.

I watched as Hestia checked for a pulse at his wrist and tutted after a few moments. She tried his neck after that, but I couldn't take my eyes of the glistening cuff around the man's wrist. There was so much more lustre in those white stones than in the ones on my wrist.

I waited for Hestia to confirm he was dead.

"If he has a pulse, it's too faint for me to register it. His neck doesn't feel right. There's—"

I grabbed his arm and placed it on the floor, completely repulsed by what I was about to do, but it needed to be done all the same.

Before Hestia could catch on or protest, I slammed my foot down on the man's hand, feeling bones crunch under my shoe. Hestia must have been in shock because she let me repeat the process twice before she pushed me away.

"What in the love of everything good are you doing?" she shrilled. It was the quietest shrill I had ever heard. Ignoring her, I kneeled down and checked the man's hand, too hopeful to be concerned with her pride.

The hand looked tortured, but blood wasn't spilling from any scrapes. *Yep, definitely dead.*

I placed my hands around the shimmering cuff and tried to ignore the places where my skin met cold flesh.

Oh, please let this work, I pleaded to nothing as I pulled at the cuff and squirmed internally. With a bit of effort, it came free.

I observed the stick of crystal locked in steel and held it against the crystal at my wrist. The cuffs looked almost identical, except the one I'd stolen had a shine to it. Like it had a purpose. There was more life in it.

It reminded me of the white stones under the castle. The ones Dariush had figured out the Tuath Dé had been stealing. The same ones that had been used to protect this city for decades.

Hestia paused for a moment, staring dumbly at the stone I held out before her.

Then it clicked.

"The ward—the ward is torn because of the stones. They're gone or broken, and these could be a replacement. Brilliant! This is brilliant!" excitement lit within her, until her eyes fell across the other dead soldiers. A large weight seemed to dip her shoulders.

"One cuff isn't going to be enough. is it?" Hestia said with a defeated huff. I shook my head and watched a million thoughts as to what she'd rather do float across her face. Then she set to work.

I moved my attention to the unbroken wrist of the soldier at my feet, while Hestia stepped over fara soldiers in black to get to one in white. At least she'd found a way to feel better about defiling the dead.

I gagged slightly once her back was turned but steeled myself for the next hand. The left hand was worse. Somehow it felt more wrong than the first time, and it kept rolling on its flat side as I stepped on it. I gave up after the fifth stomp and instead brought my torch down on the wrist like I was swinging a club.

A crunch sounded and the cuff slipped off the hand with the same amount of force as the other.

"How many of these do you think we need?" Hestia said, holding up two cuffs and a grotty red knife.

How did she—?

Two thumbs lay detached from the soldier whose dirty white uniform was now smudged with bits of red. I turned away but couldn't hide my dry retching, the burn of bile an empty threat in my throat.

"If we're going to mutilate the dead to save the city, we might as well be efficient about it." The woman was not wrong there.

A few deep breaths through my nose helped, but not by much. The street smelled strange, like dampness and body fluids and cold meat. None of it appealing.

"Now we get the crystals to the lamp. We can't get past that creature." Hestia's fear was showing in her eyes.

I watched the fight unfold before me. Only a handful of soldiers battled it out with the monster now. Geira had flipped into the air a few more times, causing the beast's mouth to look disfigured and of not much use. But those talons, there seemed to be more than before. Each one brandished a spiked tip ready to cut and slice and skewer everything in its path. It had no eyes, and I only hoped that meant I could sneak to the lamp undetected. Though I had no clue how it was hitting so many soldiers if it couldn't see.

As if in response to my thoughts, it wrapped a long talon around a soldier who had called out in pain after taking a hit to his shoulder. He screamed only a second longer as the talon squeezed hard and then dropped his lifeless body to the floor.

It responded to sound.

There was so much movement happening in front of it, I knew I could make it across the street and behind another pile of rubble where a building should have been. I could see the lamp from here, completely void of life. All I had to do was be calm and quiet enough to get to it.

I held out my torch to Hestia and laid my palm open after she took it.

"What are you going to do?" Fear crept into her voice, but she did as I requested and handed me the two cuffs.

I pressed a finger to my lips and glanced towards the lamp.

"I hope you know what you're doing," Hestia whispered, but I had started to move. I wasn't going to let her stop me.

With two cuffs in each hand, I crossed the rubble-scattered road.

The lamp was in closer view now, and I could see what we were working with. Next to it lay a partially formed wall, perfect for climbing to get to the lamp's top. The problem was the sea of brick and stone and glass that needed to be waded through to get there.

All I could do was push forward.

I placed my foot unevenly on a hill of rubble in front of me and pressed my weight on it. A rock slipped under me, and a small sound clattered out from the shift.

If not quietly, then quickly. Not letting myself catch a breath or change my mind, I pushed forward.

Each footstep caused a shift in the rubble more clatterous than the last. When my ankle caught in a pocket of brick, I fell into the wall with a loud smack. Pain shot through my face and forearms.

I didn't let myself think. I held on to the space above me and pulled. The cuffs clinked and scraped brick in the process.

A roar bellowed from the creature, and as something stabbed the rubble behind me, I felt the haunting woosh of a talon miss my back by mere centimetres.

I forced myself to look back. Beyond the shadowy spear, Dariush had frozen, his gaze fixed on me.

Fear had drenched his face white. I shook my head. *Do nothing.* He had to hear me. He had to trust that I had this.

Zorya went to move towards me, but he grabbed her arm. I couldn't tell if he too had unravelled what I had about the creature, maybe the mental chess board in his mind had played out this game to its end, and he'd realised what I was about to do was our last move.

Regardless, he had chosen this moment to trust me.

Before I closed my eyes, Zorya looked at Dariush incredulously and seemed to be about to yell at him. *Don't do it Zorya*, I begged, but I couldn't delay any longer or waste more time sending silent messages.

If I'd had my torch, what I was about to attempt might have been easier. I hoped my suspicions about the crown being an amplifier were right. Some help was better than none.

In my mind's eye I saw the beast. Its cold form blurred at the edges. Its shadowy state was in constant flow, but there was solid there too. There had to be. Otherwise, an axe or sword would slip right through it. A talon would be harmless against flesh and bone.

Others had been birdlike. This one was like a worm with legs, a monstrous excuse for a caterpillar, and part of it curved towards the opposite side of the street. It took up so much space.

Despite the distance from me and the target in my mind, I felt the flame open and crackle to life, a roar of pain followed it. The flame was small, barely bigger than the one I'd made the first time I used the torch, but it was enough. As I opened my eyes, I saw the beast recoil and move in the direction it thought it had been hit from—the other side of the street.

Dariush and Zorya got out of the way of the moving shadow, and the other soldiers became lost behind a sea of smoke and black.

This was my one and only chance.

I swung my leg to the nearest notch in the wall and levered myself up uneasily. From there it was a matter of finding my balance and reaching out to the lamp.

I could see part of the broken crystal, dull and lifeless, still sitting firmly in the lamp's iron claws. I didn't have time to pull it out. The four shimmering crystals would have to be enough to bring it back to life.

I placed the cuffs on the dead crystal and focused.

CHAPTER FORTY-TWO

Zorya

I t wasn't working.

Whatever Annalise's plan was, it wasn't working. She'd somehow set the sluagh's arse on fire without even having to see it. The thing had leaped away from us so fast, but it wasn't like it was gone.

Geira and Nate would make sure it couldn't get far, but I had run out of throwing knives, and it wasn't like any of us had the well of energy Annalise seemed to be able to pull from. Using our light to fight would drain us fast, and it seemed like the beast could keep holding on no matter how many times it was sliced open.

Dariush was reluctant to move even an inch away from Annalise now that he'd seen her in danger.

We needed those barriers up. We needed those crystals to do what they were supposed to do.

Annalise was perched on the wall. White had emanated and pulsed atop the lantern the moment Annalise's collection of cuffs had touched the lamp, but the barrier hadn't closed. *What was wrong?*

My hand flew to the hackberry brooch pinned just underneath my ponytail. I let the circle fall and stared intently at the bloodied, golden pin. It was perfectly straight. Leaves decorated one end in a sharp diamond shape and centred neatly between the leaves was a deep red stone.

Hendrik had used a stone just like this on Dylan and Cynthia. I thought of Hendrik flipping the needlelike pin between his fingers. Maybe this was one and the same. He'd used it to call their obedience through the cuffs at their wrists, but how did that work?

Pieces clicked together once more as a memory, not my own, formed in my mind. The red stone called to the white stones, and through that connection commanded those that wore it.

The white stone on Ettie's choker. I was sure Tierney, or his White Guard, had planted it on her to force her beyond the veil. It was probably what they'd used to make it look like she was bewitched by the will-o'-the-wisps.

Annalise took the stones out, moved them around into a different formation and placed them back upon the post. She repeated the process, tried to pull the crystals out of the cuffs. It didn't work. Nothing worked.

Her frustration grew with each moment, but she kept trying.

The stones thought they were merely cuffs. They were waiting to be told what to do. They needed to be commanded to work as part of the barrier.

Coldness whispered at the back of my neck and my heart sank. I didn't need to look to see what was there. The beast had heard the circular brooch piece clatter to the floor.

I was still. Perfectly still. Annalise looked my way, horror etched on her face. I needed to get the stone to her, but one step, a single flinch, and I would be torn between the beast's shadowy teeth.

I could twist and duck, try to drive the pin into the beast, but I couldn't tell how close I was to its weak points. I didn't truly understand where its weak points were. It wasn't like the beast had a sensitive temple that when pierced would deliver a fatal injury. It didn't even have a face, and without knowing what I was aiming for it was hopeless.

A colossal battle cry sounded behind me, and I felt the beast shift before the woosh of steel tearing through air filled my ears. The moment of relief was followed by a deafening roar.

And I looked back.

The blackness morphed and shrunk into something smaller. Geira had slashed the beast in the throat. It was badly wounded, but not enough that it couldn't send a talon to pierce Geira through the middle. Her mouth opened with a gasp. Her eyes settled on my face. She mouthed one word. *Go*.

It might have been my need to protect my breaking heart, but I did as she said. I turned as Nate fired an arrow into the space above the beast's mouth.

Tears streamed down my face as I stepped over rubble. Searching Annalise's eyes, hoping she knew what to do. Hoping she'd figured it out.

I stopped, stretched my arm back and flung the pin towards her. She caught it. Any other time I would have rolled my eyes at the near fumble, but right now all I cared about was that she had caught it.

It seemed she too had fit the pieces together. She placed the end of the pin with the red stone onto the collection of white crystals.

Her lips moved and for a moment I thought I heard a single word escape her lips.

Protect.

The barrier lit up.

CHAPTER FORTY-THREE

Annalise

I skidded down from the wall. Letting the bricks scrape my arms and bare legs. The small sharp slashes didn't bother me. Not when everything else in my body ached. Not when the city lay crumbled and torn before us.

I steadied myself on the pile of rocks before leaning backward, allowing their cascade to pull me from my height. Dariush helped me to my feet as I skidded to a halt near the edge of the rock pile.

The worst was over. The barrier was up. The sluagh that had overrun the city had all at once shrunk to slivers of black smoke and disappeared to some dark corner of the world.

But there was still so much destruction. So much noise echoed through the city cave. Only instead of screams of terror it was the wail of grief, despair. Loss.

Zorya and Nate were by Geira's side, blood pooled around them. Zorya kept yelling Geira's name. Hestia ran down the street, calling the attention of someone I didn't know.

"I can't make her stay here." Dariush's voice shook. I looked to his outstretched palm. Shadows danced, leaning in towards Geira as if they were searching for another shadow to dance with. A shadow that didn't exist within the valkyrie. "She's losing too much blood." His words were a whisper.

I took a step towards Zorya, knowing.

Dariush placed a strong hand on my shoulder as if to stop me but dropped it. He knew there'd only be one way to save her. Even if it risked us losing control. Maybe it said enough that as Dubnos's new rulers we were willing to risk the fragile safety of the city to save one valkyrie. But the beast within me had been freed once, and I'd felt its intensity, felt what drove it forward. It was all the monstrous parts of me. It knew my true desires, the pieces of me that I had ignored and shoved so deep within myself.

The Bloodsong's awakening had been my awakening. From that moment, I could see myself as a complete picture, and I wasn't afraid.

I had seen Geira and Zorya's love for each other grow—even if they'd done their best to hide it—and right now at least, it felt worth risking an entire kingdom for it. Even if it came to that, Dariush had severed the connection before. He could do it again.

Zorya felt me approach.

I saw the wetness of her face for only a second, before she stood, grabbed my outstretched hand and the world went dark.

I gave in to the darkness, knowing it wasn't the thing itself that brought chaos, destruction, death into the world. Only I had the power to do that. To choose that.

In that moment, I chose life.

CHAPTER FORTY-FOUR

Zorya

"**I** thought you were dead," I sobbed as I squeezed Geira's hand. The valkyrie gave me a smile as she lifted a hand to my cheek and wiped away my tears. I leaned into it and took in her face. She was tired.

Dark half circles lined the space between her cheekbones and her eyes. She had winced many times since she'd been placed in the castle's healing wing. Mostly when sitting up to take a sip of water or rolling onto her side when a healer came to check on her wound's healing progress.

The Bloodsong hadn't shoved me as deep within itself as it had when we faced Tierney. This time I was just as in control, and we, three within one, worked to keep Geira's blood contained within her body. We had sung, searching for memories that dripped in gold and warmth, and brought them to the front of the valkyrie's mind. Our song became a blanket to numb the pain and ward away shock.

We held the bond and kept singing as the healers stitched up arteries, veins, muscle, and skin on the city floor. Dariush had tried to break the bond after the most immediate work had been tended to, but the Bloodsong insisted we keep singing as they moved her to the hospital.

I tried to think of who had made that suggestion and came up short. It was like we were becoming more unified the longer we kept the bond up.

Dariush had broken the bond the minute Geira was in a hospital bed.

I'd sat by her side since then, watched as two royal Tuath Dé healers worked on her in tandem for hours on end. They'd gone over her surgical stitches with magical ones and wrapped her middle with gauze and tape.

Dariush, King Dariush, had been quick to call for the departure of Tuath Dé fae who'd travelled to Dubnos as part of their pilgrimage. Only Tuath Dé who had committed themselves to Dubnos and considered the kingdom their home were afforded the choice to stay. The same choice was given to all fara soldiers.

The healing wing of the castle had been opened to those significantly injured during the attack. Those with only minor or non-life-threatening injuries were redirected to the common hospital on the other side of the city.

As I watched the Tuath Dé healers move around the room, tending tirelessly to each patient, I wondered how many, if any, had wanted to return to the Glistening City. How many were here because they considered this place home, and how many were here because of their sacred duty to life and health?

"You should go to her," Geira croaked.

"What do you mean?" I felt my brows knit together, then squeezed her hand that was now by her side to let her know I wasn't going anywhere. Who was more important that I had to see them right this second? No one. Certainly not Annalise, even if she was a queen now.

"The girl. Ettie," Geira said simply.

I said nothing. Ettie was dead. I'd failed her. There was nothing I could do for her now.

"She has no one down here. Just you. Everyone deserves a proper send-off."

Geira's words hit a heavy place within me. She was right. Ettie had no family or loved ones here to give her a funeral.

"OK," I choked and wiped the remaining tears that clung to my cheeks. There were no more tears to follow them. It was like a purpose flowed through me again.

I leaned over Geira's bed and kissed her softly. I felt her lips move into a smile before she shooed me off again, letting me know she'd be fine.

I knew she'd be fine. The healers had paid special attention to her at the request of Dariush, and again by Annalise in the form of a handwritten note. From the way the healers kept shuffling patients in and out of the wing, I guessed that Geira was healed enough to be sent away in order to free up a bed for someone else.

I was too selfish to suggest Geira be moved to another bed in the castle. Just in case her stitches didn't hold.

Geira fell fast asleep the moment I stepped away from her bed, her perfect heartbeat tittering away strong as ever.

***

Moving through the castle was easier somehow. Images flooded my mind of curved walkways that veered off at funny edges, paintings, statues and decorative tables. Each image marked the path to a small room that looked over the castle's entrance. I couldn't place why, but they felt both mine and not mine. Like someone else had been inside my brain and left fingerprints, breadcrumbs, dirty footprints all over the place.

A whisper of them might have still been there. I shuddered.

The closer I got to my destination, the louder it became. A human heartbeat pumping slightly faster than normal thrummed in my ear.

My hopes jumped, then plummeted as the scraping of a broom on the stone floor pulled me back to reality. A human cleaner. Someone had found the mess I'd left Ettie in before me.

I turned the last corner.

"Hi," the man said, looking up from the neat pile of ash and splinters at his feet. There was a toolbox by the door and new slabs of timber leaning against the wall next to it.

"Er. Hi," I said sheepishly and slipped around him to move into the room.

"Is this your room? I'll still be a few hours with the door." His words barely registered in my ears.

I caught sight of the bed first. White sheets bunched towards the foot of the bed like someone had been in a rush to remove Ettie's body.

"Who—who did it?" I didn't know why but the words came out angry, and a hot rage spread through me. "Who took the girl's body?" I spun around and studied the very still man outside the door.

He was tall for a human with shaggy brown hair, younger than me. Maybe the same age Ettie had been, but time had sharpened his dark brown eyes. I wondered how long he'd been down here.

"There was a girl. She died in the explosion beneath the castle. I was keeping her body here. Who. Took. Her?" I pushed the last words through my teeth and stepped closer to the man.

"I-I don't know what—" He cut himself off with a nervous gulp as his pulse raced. It wasn't the racing pulse of fear. Well, it was. But something else drove that beat forward. Excitement? A buzz?

The guy was hiding something.

The thought to bite him and steal a glimpse at what he knew slid so neatly into my mind it scared me. Feeding just to get information out of someone was something I'd always been against, but I'd warped the use of my fangs so much over the past twenty-four hours, it didn't seem like this would make much of a difference.

I pushed down that desire to get what I wanted, and guilt filled me with clarity. Last time I fed off a human I had weakened her so severely, if the explosion that killed her had been a third as destructive, she'd probably still have ended up dead.

"What's your name?" I said instead, willing myself to sound nice.

"Uh. Michael," he said, the lying-induced buzz flattening off with his heart rate.

I nodded and slipped past him again as I exited the room, moving fast so he wouldn't ask me the same question. I heard a sharp inhale followed by a "Wha—" that died in his throat as I turned a corner the way I came.

Who the fuck would have taken a dead body? Who would have taken Ettie?

My thoughts danced through the possibilities. Kind castle employees who wanted to give her a proper burial. Unlikely, since they'd have at least searched for someone who knew her before moving her. *She was tucked into bed for fuck's sake.*

Another thought turned my stomach. *Who else knew she had second sight? What if they took her body to steal her eyes, do tests on her?* I didn't know who *they* were or what anyone would need a second sight's eyes for, but the thought darkened whatever joy I had left in me.

Ettie was dead. Her body was gone. And there was no one else to blame but me.

As I walked through the castle halls to find Dariush and Annalise, a shiver sent alarm through me. I stopped. There were no heartbeats near me that I could detect. I'd walked a fair way since bumping into Michael. So why did it feel like someone was following me? Stalking me?

I took note of my surroundings. Walls that curved on forever, a large painting of flowers with a golden frame and a chest beneath it. Nothing above me. Nothing around me.

I shrugged off the feeling. I was likely just wound up from so much fighting. I desperately needed to rest.

I found Dariush and Annalise and told them Ettie's body was missing before demanding a bed near the hospital wing, so I could be close to Geira and still get some sleep.

I needed a clear head for this. I would find her. I *had* to. But when my body hit the sheets, I still felt those imaginary stalking eyes press into me, and I couldn't shake them or the feeling that finding Ettie would do nothing to relieve me of my guilt.

CHAPTER FORTY-FIVE

Dariush

D ubh's pyre burned in the town square, the castle behind us a pale mourning mess amid the fragments of a city.

It had been three days since the death of the queen. The sluagh attack had purged the city of so many people. Underdwellers, both fae and human. Soldiers, both fara and fomóire. Even a handful of Tuath Dé who called the kingdom home had lost their lives in the attack. Those bodies would be burned and honoured tomorrow.

Tonight was for mourning the queen.

Thanks to Aed and his black knife, which I still knew absolutely nothing about, there had been no body to send off. No cremated remains to dust the dishevelled kingdom. Aed should hope the Tuath Dé had executed him already. If I ever found him, he wouldn't receive that kind of mercy from me.

I thought I'd have more time with Dubh to understand this role. Even as I watched the flames come to a flickering halt and will-o'-the-wisps surround the embers, taking over for the flames' dance, even then I could feel their eyes on me. Their king.

What a pathetic excuse for king they had received.

Reports had come through that fara soldiers guarded the three entrances on the surface. No doubt to rob the city of its access to resources.

One of the rings Dubh had bestowed upon me could open a mirror to communicate directly with the Glistening City. It had allowed her to keep in contact with the TDE without leaving her kingdom—something she was unable to do as the sole regent.

Someone in the Glistening City had angled the twin mirror to face a wall. The message was clear. The Tuath Dé refused to speak to the new king and queen of Dubnos, and thus, refused to acknowledge our rule.

Tierney was dead, and the wards were back in place, stronger than ever now that their weaknesses had been revealed, but none of that had been my doing. That was all Annalise.

The memory of her hanging from that wall by her fingertips, seconds from being speared by smoke, flashed through my mind. That moment had moved too fast and too slow at the same time. I knew I was right to trust her, but doing so had felt like my consciousness had been stolen by the will-o'-the-wisps all over again. I'd felt so far away. All I could do was watch.

My mouth was dry from standing near the heat and smoke for so long. Embers rose with the will-o'-the-wisps and snuffed out as they reached the smoke that swirled among stalactites; the only real sense of clouds that sky had seen for some time.

Despite my failure to protect Annalise, she'd risen to the task ahead of her. She'd been the one to save the city.

This pyre could have been hers.

I couldn't stop the shudder that rippled through my chest as that single terrifying image was branded on my brain. As if to say, *That thought is a lie*, long, frost-kissed fingers tangled themselves in my hand.

How could she stand to be near me now when all I'd done was keep her in the dark? I was still keeping things from her.

The Nine Daughters had only shown me in images, but I was the king of shadows. I'd known what slinked beneath her skin the second I'd called her body to stop in that forest. I knew the thing that had entwined itself with her soul.

How could I possibly tell her?

She leaned into my arm and rested her head on my shoulder. I wanted to keep my tears from falling. Kings shouldn't cry in public, but what was one more failure in front of these people?

Her other hand found its place over my heart, and as I breathed in, I tasted her bergamot and dried lavender scent on the air. She fit so well here, a space she'd carved out herself. I knew if she ever left, through death or desire, I would feel true cold.

***

Annalise

For the longest stretch of silence, it seemed like Dariush was simply going through the motions, treating his mother's funeral as another task to complete among a sea of tasks.

As the flames died down to embers and the will-o'-the-wisps surrounding his mother's pyre ascended, I saw his shoulders heave once. It might not have been the queenly thing to do. The entire city's eyes were on us, and queens were supposed to make their kings look strong, right? I slipped my hand into his anyway, leaned into his arm and rested my head on his shoulder. His tears came out in silent short bursts, and my tears for him and all he'd lost followed.

When the smoke thinned and the will-o'-the-wisps had found their place among the stalactites, the festivities began. It was strange to see the city celebrate throughout the night, if that was what you could call it. Cups of spiced wine and poitín, the harsh clear liquid I'd drunk on my first night in the city, were skulled and shared, and it wasn't long before a dancing crowd turned into a sea of stumbling, sobbing strangers. Each had a story, or a song, about some feat the queen had achieved all on her own.

I wondered how many of those stories conveniently excluded her Tuath Dé friend. Hestia had wanted to return to her bed after the last flame had snuffed out from the pyre. She'd barely eaten since Dubh's death. It was a miracle she'd left her room long enough for the funeral, but Dariush had demanded she stay for at least one drink. There was a new fire made, something much smaller than the pyre, and Dariush and Nate listened intently as Hestia shared stories of her own, downing a new drink with each one. Geira and Zorya spent most of their time observing the way the other's eyes sparkled in the firelight.

I tried to sit and listen, but I'd discovered over the past three days how frustrating sitting among a group of people had become. My thoughts came and, with no way to be heard, left unspoken. I made a habit to take a notepad and pen wherever I went, but firelight and darkness wasn't the best for reading, even for the most sober reader.

And the five sitting around the small fire were far from sober. They didn't notice when I stood and wove through the crowd.

Most underdwellers ignored me. A few stopped singing or drinking long enough to whisper to their friends and point at the crown of colour above my head. Those few gawked for only a moment before returning to their revelry.

I was alone.

Dariush had made every excuse to be by my side since the battle. The moment he'd seen what I needed to do and allowed me the space to get it done had been such a small, yet powerful gift. He'd trusted me in a way I was only just beginning to afford myself.

I knew now that he cared deeply for me, that truth was undeniable. The pull between us that had been there since the beginning, the one that sparked with each touch and left cold spots on our souls when we were apart, that pull made us desperate to see each other safe.

What I felt for Dariush was love. Soul-entangling, confirmed-by-fate love. I was certain he felt the same way, but love wasn't the same thing as lasting trust.

And it would take more than one moment to repair what he'd shattered.

Fragments of the person I used to be warred with the person I'd become, but those fragments were nothing more than ash. The girl who wanted to give in, to let someone else take control, to pretend like none of it mattered, and to fear herself for the rage that came so easily, was gone.

Dariush and I had jumped in to save the world. Committed ourselves to something more—through survival and a bit of spite on my part, yes—but now that it was safe, or safe enough, I needed him to see me as the person I had become.

I wouldn't go back to being the girl he met in the forest. Couldn't.

I had felt true power at my fingertips. Despite my lack of voice, I'd learned what it meant to be truly heard, tasted what it meant to truly be seen. There was no undoing that.

From now on, I would demand more. Not only of him as my love and my king, but of everyone.

I would demand more of myself.

A flash of white-blue in my periphery pulled me from my swirling thoughts. It had ducked through the crowd, down an alleyway. There wasn't anything special about a vibrant flash of colour in this city. Especially on a night like this. The will-o'-the-wisps were mostly keeping high among the stalactites, but I had witnessed plenty dive into the throng of fae and people, causing specks of colour to appear from seemingly nowhere. This flash of light felt different. It felt familiar in another way.

I moved towards the alleyway before I could think. I had left my torch in my new room in the castle. Bringing a weapon to the ceremony hadn't seemed appropriate, particularly when the last time I had publicly used the thing I'd looked like a beast far more dangerous than the ones that had destroyed the city.

As I stepped into darkness, I questioned whether I should have told someone where I was.

My back stiffened as an arm slid around my middle and the cold, familiar sting of steel met my throat.

"Finally alone are we, false queen?" Resh breathed in my ear. "You have something of mine."

Acknowledgements

To William, my husband (no, I'll never get over saying that!), thank you for kicking me out of bed at ungodly hours of the morning so I could get Annalise's story on the page. Double thank you for all those times you followed it up with coffee.

To my dear friends, Tina, Jayde, and Joy, thank you for cheering me on and being *Under City*'s first fans.

To Anna, my editor, your words of encouragement pushed me forward through these last hurdles. Thank you for being part of the process, for helping me grow as a writer, and for helping me make *Under City* the best version it could be.

And finally, I want to acknowledge the places that offered a sturdy and nourishing soil for the seeds of this story to grow roots.

Whilst many world myths have made their way into this book, none have had a greater impact on *Under City* than the mythology that is native to Ireland and the Celts. The Tuath Dé, the fomóire, the sluagh, and the Sacred Tree, which is based on both the Celtic tree zodiac and the pagan Wheel of the Year, are just some examples of this influence.

I can't recognize the impact of place without noting my homeland, Australia. I acknowledge the Traditional Custodians of the land on which this book was born and written, the Ngarigo, Wal-

galu, Ngunnawal and Bidawal Peoples, and I pay respects to Elders
past, present and emerging.

Yarrangobilly Caves, a place of great importance to the Walgalu
people, was a major inspiration for the way Dubnos City formed
in my head. If you ever have the pleasure of visiting this truly
beautiful place, I hope you see the underground city of Dubnos
caught between the cave's teeth of stalagmites and stalactites.

About the Author

Nicola, writing as N. Florence, spends an awful lot of time in rural places for someone so obsessed with urban fantasy romance.

When she's not writing in a sun-soaked corner of her house, Nicola is drinking coffee, daydreaming, and trying not to kill her plant babies - a monstera and two orchids.

Under City is Nicola's debut novel and brings to life her obsession with fae, dark myth, and a good romance with lgbtq+ rep.

To keep updated on all of Nicola's upcoming works, follow her on Instagram @nflorence_author or visit nflorenceauthor.com.

Playlist

Listen on Spotify
https://shorturl.at/jnsO6

Like – Alissic
Lilith – Halsey
Circle With Me – Spiritbox
Teeth – Mallrat
Freak Like Me – Transviolet
Siren – Kailee Morgue
go to hell. – luhx.
DARKSIDE – Neoni
Arcane Magic – HANA
MIDDLE OF THE NIGHT – Elley Duhé
I Choose Me – Amanati, Roniit
Sun Killer – Spiritbox
Zombie – triple j Like A Version – CXLOE
I am not a woman, I'm a god – Halsey
Wish On An Eyelash – Mallrat
Constance – Spiritbox